Critical Acclaim for Rebecca Rothenberg

The Bulrush Murders

"One of the year's best... spellbindin rich plot.... At the story's center, insightful portrait of a bright wc equality in an environment as prick wild grasses the author describes so well."

—Charles Champlin, *Los Angeles Times Book Review*

The Dandelion Murders

"Rothenberg is knowing and exact...and her tale is twistier than mile-high blacktop."

—*Kirkus Reviews*

The Shy Tulip Murders

"In the third of Rothenberg's sharp, engaging 'botanical mysteries'...Sharples is the mouthpiece for one of the freshest, most gracefully modulated new voices in crime fiction.... This is brainy, opinionated, enjoyable mystery writing, with one of the most believable heroines to show up in years."

—Richard Lipez, *Washington Post Book World*

...and for Taffy Cannon

Tangled Roots

"Cannon excels at capturing the flavor of her Southern California settings, as well as at creating complex, fascinating characters and intriguing stories, and those who hailed her debut will be equally delighted with [*Tangled Roots*]."

—Phyllis Brown, *Grounds for Murder*

The Tumbleweed Murders

ALSO BY REBECCA ROTHENBERG

The Claire Sharples Botanical Mystery Series
The Bulrush Murders
The Dandelion Murders
The Shy Tulip Murders

ALSO BY TAFFY CANNON

The Nan Robinson Mystery Series
A Pocketful of Karma
Tangled Roots
Class Reunions Are Murder

An Irish Eyes Travel Mystery
Guns and Roses

The Tumbleweed Murders

A Claire Sharples Botanical Mystery

Rebecca Rothenberg

completed by Taffy Cannon

PERSEVERANCE PRESS / JOHN DANIEL & COMPANY
SANTA BARBARA, CALIFORNIA · 2001

"Aromas," "Yesterday I Could Have Left You," "Mountain Time," and "Time Like
a River" copyright © Becky Rothenberg, and used by permision of the Rothenberg
Estate. "Miracle Worker" and "Old Fool" copyright © Becky Rothenberg and
Terry Fain, and used by permission of the Rothenberg Estate and Terry Fain.

A Perseverance Press Book
Published by John Daniel & Company
A division of Daniel & Daniel, Publishers, Inc.
Post Office Box 21922
Santa Barbara, California 93121
www.danielpublishing.com/perseverance

10 9 8 7 6 5 4 3 2 1

Book design by Studio E Books, Santa Barbara
Cover photograph © Phil Schermeister/CORBIS

LIBRARY OF CONGRESS CATALOGING-IN-PUBLICATION DATA
Rothenberg, Rebecca.
    The tumbleweed murders : a Claire Sharples botanical mystery / by Rebecca
Rothenberg ; completed by Taffy Cannon.
        p. cm.
    ISBN 1-880284-43-X (pbk. : alk. paper)
    1. Sharples, Claire (Fictitious character)—Fiction. 2. Women microbiologists—
Fiction. 3. Bakersfield (Calif.)—Fiction.   I. Cannon, Taffy. II. Title
    PS3568.O862 T86 2001
    813'.54—dc21
                        00-012622

For the Rothenberg Family

and for Becky

with love

I first met Rebecca Rothenberg when I called her in 1992 to ask about the medium-sized New York publisher that had just published her first mystery, *The Bulrush Murders*, and was about to publish mine. She had visited their editorial offices and likened the operation to WKRP. I knew instantly that this was someone I could love.

As I got to know her over the next few years, I learned that she was witty, wise, accomplished, self-deprecating, and possessed of an enviable gift for language. She had been a songwriter in Nashville and an epidemiologist in Los Angeles. What's more, she had seized the vast and arguably unlovable San Joaquin Valley for her Claire Sharples series and had invested the region with charm and appeal.

Becky and I did a lot of book signings together, often with a sheaf of bulrushes quietly crumbling in the back seat. Her series was botanical and one of my books took place in the flower-growing industry, so we also ended up on a lot of the same mystery discussion panels. We lived less than a hundred miles apart, but much of our time together was spent a continent away at the Malice Domestic convention in Washington, D.C. Becky's parents lived nearby and she attended as what she called a "day student."

In the fall of 1994, while Becky was staying with me during San Diego signings for *The Dandelion Murders*, my brother was diagnosed with a brain tumor. "I have a brain tumor," she told me matter-of-factly, adding that it had been diagnosed a full eight years earlier. This is a disease steeped in the rhetoric of hope, featuring dreadful treatments and appalling survival statistics— and she had survived eight years. With that astonishing revelation, she metamorphosed for me from a savvy and talented colleague into a shining beacon.

The beacon dimmed when that tumor finally caught up with her in 1998, and we lost her at the age of fifty.

Becky left an unfinished manuscript for *The Tumbleweed Murders*, the fourth Claire Sharples mystery. Being asked to complete that manuscript was a frightening challenge and an awesome responsibility. Many people participated in this process, and I am grateful to all of them. For all of us, this was a labor of love and sorrow.

Sandra Dijkstra, Becky's agent, set the entire process into motion and then graciously stepped aside to streamline the legal and contractual matters.

Meredith Phillips of Perseverance Press wanted to publish *The Tumbleweed Murders* and believed wholeheartedly in the project, and my role in it, from the beginning. John and Susan Daniel, of John Daniel & Company, Publishers, have been wonderfully supportive.

Jane Chelius, my agent, handled the necessary contracts and agreements, and did it without taking a commission. In one of those twists that define the family nature of the mystery community, it was Becky who first introduced me to Jane, back in 1993.

I would like to be able to thank all the people who helped Becky with the research she had completed on this book, but I don't know who you all are, so I can only offer a blanket, but heartfelt, appreciation. Heidi Asparturian and Liza Taylor offered me insights into this manuscript based on their relationships with Becky and her writing. David Alderete of Kern Delta–Weed Patch Cotton Ginning Company shared his knowledge of the San Joaquin cotton industry, including a terrific cotton gin tour. Wendy Owen of the *Bakersfield Californian* helped with agribusiness information and the *Californian's* excellent Oil Centennial issue was very helpful.

Sharan Newman provided the Latin, and Richard Barre shared his exhaustive Kern County connections.

One of those was musician Inez Savage, a veteran of the Bakersfield music community. When I sat down with Inez and began telling her the history of this project, a strange look came over her face. Several years earlier, she told me, Becky herself had talked to her as part of the research for this book.

Martha Rothenberg, Becky's sister and literary executor, has been helpful and patient and cooperative as liaison to the Rothenberg family. I am grateful to her, to her sister Tish King, and to her parents, Herbert and the late Marjorie Rothenberg.

When I finally met Martha and her husband, Vincent Griscavage, in person, she told me about a CD of Becky's original music that was produced by Terry Fain and engineered by Richard Haxton after her death. Since music is an important component of this book, I asked for a copy of that CD and was utterly charmed by it. Whenever song lyrics are used in *The Tumbleweed Murders*, they are from songs that Becky wrote.

I wish that Becky had finished this book herself, and I made every effort to complete it as I thought she would have wanted. To the extent that I have succeeded, it is tribute to the strength of her writing. For any shortcomings, the responsibility is entirely mine.

As I followed Becky's footprints and tire tracks around Kern County, I had a tumbleweed rolling around in the back seat for old times' sake. I sure do miss her.

Taffy Cannon

AROMAS

I remember a dusty road,
A house by a dry arroyo.
Blue sky and a blazing sun,
Eucalyptus and wild geranium.
And every night down in Aromas
Sitting on the porch and talking low,
Trying to get the Bakersfield station
On the radio.

I remember the golden hills,
The goats with their silver bells.
After supper if it got cold
We'd all sit around the Franklin stove.
And every night down in Aromas
The fog rolled in from Monterey
As I listened to the rock and roll station
From San Jose.

Now my life has led me on
And left so many roads behind,
But I can still recall them all
So clearly in my mind.

And I know right now in Aromas
Fog's rolling in from Monterey,
While the cars go by like thunder on the freeways
Of L.A.

Lyrics by Becky Rothenberg

The Tumbleweed Murders

1

IT WAS A SHRUNKEN HEAD that brought Claire to Jewell Scoggins's door.

The "head," actually a decaying peach in a Ziploc bag, had landed on Claire's desk at the Citrus Cove Agricultural Field Research Station with a bad case of what looked like leprosy, but wasn't. Claire had a bad case of what felt like San Joaquin Valley Summer Burnout, and was.

But here *she* was, chasing down the peach's origin in the hottest, bleakest pocket of the San Joaquin, generally a pretty hot, bleak trough that runs down the middle of California. In deference to the calendar, which read September 24, the thermometer had leveled off at a mere 93. In high summer down here in southern Kern County it would be 110 degrees, easy.

She turned west. Off to her left three mountain ranges converged—from the east, the Sierra; from the west, the Temblors;

along the south, the Tehachapis—cinching the bottom of the Central Valley like a drawstring. The land they contained was flat, hard, and white, dotted with saltbush and jimsonweed and tumbleweed when left alone, coaxed into a sullen, productive green when irrigated. A complicated system ran like intravenous lines from river to canals to ditches to furrows to the crops, which were, more often than not, squat cotton plants. An occasional vivid green field of alfalfa, a bit of corn now that the feed lots were moving in.

But no peach orchards.

A green road sign told Claire she was approaching Taft, which, she suspected, was not where she wanted to be. She looked at the scribbled directions that Ramón Covarrubias, the County Small Farm Adviser, had handed her along with the peach. She looked at her map.

She was lost.

Well, not exactly lost, not when the mountains flashed compass points at her from the horizon, but separated from her object. Which was the orchard of Mr. Erasmo Campos, who had produced the afflicted peach, variety Autumn Gem, diagnosis *Monilinia fructicola*, a.k.a. brown rot. Already she had overshot her target once, going too far west into scrubby hills where swarms of oil pumps rocked and sucked, a maze of pipes running busily among them, with bright silver ducting for steam injection taking periodic serpentine loops alongside the road.

Now, a quarter mile ahead a line of brush indicated, implausibly, flowing water. Ramón had said something about the north bank of the Kern River, so she turned onto a packed dirt road, nearly broke an axle in the first six feet, and rocked to a halt next to a sun-blistered sign. KERN WILLOWS TRAILER PARK, it said, and she started walking, figuring she'd ask someone where the hell she was, only more politely.

A moment later she heard it, a tune that Sam used to sing: "You Don't Have Very Far to Go." A gritty contralto, Kitty Wells or some old Nashville gal, she thought at first, but even though the voice itself was strong and sure, it was a cappella—no whiny pedal steel, no bored *boom-thwack* of bass drum and snare—and Claire realized it must be live. The first evidence of vertebrate life she had encountered in many miles, so she followed it.

She rounded a clump of mulefat, and suddenly there was this woman in the middle of the road—sixty-something, hard miles on her, skinny bird legs dangerously overbalanced by a shelf of a bust. She had her head thrown back and was just wailing. When Claire joined in with a fifth-above harmony, she never even opened her eyes.

But when the song ended she looked at Claire and grinned, showing big teeth like Chiclets.

"I always do hear that part in my head," she said, Okie twang making *haid* of "head." "Tune makes more sense with it. You know any more of Red's songs?"

Claire, who had learned this stuff entirely against her will, said, "I thought it was a Merle Haggard song." A Merle Haggard song that had once stopped her dead in her tracks in Harvard Square and then sent her back across a continent. To stay.

"Merle had the hit off it, but Red wrote it. Red Simpson. Suitcase Simpson, we all useter call him, 'cause he lugged around his songs in a suitcase. That was when I was in the band, you know. The Texas Tumbleweeds, Featuring Cherokee Rose, which was me. On account I got a little Injun on my ma's side."

"One thirty-second?" The Cherokee Rose nodded and Claire just managed not to smile. Every Dust Bowl migrant seemed to lay claim to one thirty-second part Cherokee, enough to be romantic but not inconvenient. "How about 'It's Not Love, But It's Not Bad,' " Claire said, and they launched into another duet, Claire trying out a high part on the verse that made her voice crack. I should do more singing, she thought, defaulting to unison. I should do more laughing. I should do more dancing, I should do more loving, I should decorate my house, I should eat at decent restaurants, I should get out of this place—

Whoops! The song was over. "You sound great," she told Jewell.

"Yep," Jewell said with satisfaction, "the looks give out, the legs is goin', and the ticker don't work like she useter, but I reckon God's done give me the voice for life. You do much singin'?" *Sangin'*.

"Just in the car." Suddenly Claire remembered what she *did* do. "Actually, I'm looking for a man named Erasmo Campos. He has a peach orchard around here. You know him?"

"He in the Court?"

Claire had a brief vision of Mr. Campos in judicial, or possibly royal, robes.

"'Cause I don't know nobody 'round here don't live in the Court," Jewell was saying. "I ain't lived out here but a year. Moved down from Oildale when Chet died. But maybe there's somebody else here can help you out."

She led Claire past the sign and into the Court, a dozen dilapidated trailers with a settled look to them, strung out along one dry strand of the braided Kern River. Among them were a few as-advertised willows, stunted and demoralized, trying to hang on until another wet year—an unlikely event, with the Lake Isabella dam upstream. Jewell stopped at the last trailer, double-wide and new. Too new for this dump.

Claire wondered why, of all the trailer parks in all the world, Jewell had wandered into this one.

"How did you find this place?" she blurted. At least she had managed "how" instead of "why," but Jewell looked at her as if she knew exactly what she was thinking.

"Most of the folks is here because they can't afford noplace else," she said, "but Chet left me pretty well fixed. I just always been partial to this part of the river." She pushed open the door and said, maybe ironically, "Home, sweet home."

Claire had learned from a few years in the field never to pass up a bathroom. She made inquiry, then walked purposefully down the hall, slowing as she passed a wallful of photographs. Jewell's family in conventional poses, one multi-generational portrait of matriarch (Jewell in a maroon dress) and patriarch (Chet, had she said?) at the center, and around them a whole... passel, a passel of kinfolk.

Claire would have to save "passel" for Ramón, who in a previous life had taught English to college freshmen, and liked words. ("'O peach, thou art sick,'" he had scrawled on the bag containing the peach, along with variety, date, and place of collection. Claire, who had the remnants of a good liberal arts education buried under the science, had managed to catch the scrambled reference and laugh.)

But beyond the photos, which could have been of anyone's family—well, not Claire's; too many children and not enough L.L. Bean—was a full-color promotional portrait of the Texas Tumbleweeds, taken in the early 1950s. The Weeds—three dark-haired guys in spectacular green and pink satin shirts—flanked the Rose, who wore a gold and pink shirt. Claire regarded the young Jewell. Big features: high (Cherokee?) cheekbones, wide mouth, sharp nose. Not classically beautiful, but vivid, like an Okie Sophia Loren. There were more pictures of the band: Jewell and a Weed waving gaily from a pastel car (*On the Road*, someone had written underneath); performing in a dark club with couples dancing in the foreground, leaning in toward each other, faces solemn, skirts twirling (*The Lucky Spot*); several head shots of Jewell herself (*The Cherokee Rose*); more nightclubs (*The Blackboard*; *The Four Queens*); and the band outdoors at night, with lanterns strung overhead (*Buttonwillow Barn Dance*).

What a lot of fun she must have had, thought Claire with vague envy, as she continued to the bathroom.

On the way back she lost herself, semi-deliberately, turning into the living room and then the bedroom...cramped, flimsy rooms into which a whole long life had been downloaded. On Jewell's nightstand was another photograph. It was clearly not a public picture, but nevertheless Claire moved to examine it, telling herself that as a photographer she had a professional interest, though in fact she was simply being nosy.

Two heads, close together as in a wedding picture, but the subjects wore casual clothes, and the black-and-white photo had the grainy look of a snapshot that had been enlarged. That was certainly a young Jewell in the halter top, showing smooth shoulders. But who was this dark young man with the strong nose and the faint smile and the startling eyes? A memorable, symmetrical face that could have been sketched in a few apt words or deft lines. Would that be Chet? Chet, whom life had somehow transmogrified into that elderly gent with the seamed face out in the hall?

Back in the kitchen Jewell had made instant iced tea for both of them, lit a Camel, and was fanning herself with a copy of the *Bakersfield Californian.*

"I was enjoying your photos," Claire said. "Of you and the band, I mean," she added guiltily.

"Oh, honey, I got a whole scrapbook of pitchers and clippings," Jewell said, rising eagerly. "And a whole memory full of stories."

Claire glanced at her watch. "Tell me one," she said. "Tell me about—" about the man by your bed, she wanted to say, but didn't. "About your costumes," she finished lamely.

Jewell laughed, a throaty smoker's rasp. "Them things," she said. "Them gaudy things. Got me into a deal of trouble. I remember my momma…"

***

"Momma, please, I cain't be late, tonight's our first gig at the Lucky Spot, I need my costume!" Jewell darted toward the "closet," a rope strung across a corner and hung with clothes. But big as her mother was, she could move fast when the mood was on her, and now she lurched to the right so that she was blocking Jewell's way like a buffalo in a muumuu.

"You look like a damn whore in them things," she roared, and then Jewell knew she was really drunk, because her momma had never used to cuss. Or drink, for that matter. Drinking and cussing had been her daddy's strong points, that and a quick right hand.

I never saw no whore in a fringed skirt and cowboy boots, Jewell started to say, but she'd tried that one before. "Momma, the band has got to look good tonight, we need this gig. We need the money, you and Alvin and me. With Daddy gone…" she trailed off cunningly, and watched her mother's angry red eyes dim with tears and her bulk slump under her dress like a circus tent deflating.

"Give his life for his country," Momma sniffled. "He were a good provider, your daddy...."

Jewell grabbed her stage clothes and ran, not waiting to hear the end of this.

Good provider. He'd drunk away whatever any of them made picking cotton, and when he got himself a better-paying job out at the oil fields, he'd still been too cheap to give his wife money for groceries. Cheap to the end, he'd only sprung for the minimum life insurance the army'd made him buy before they shipped him overseas. A few dollars more and they could have collected ten thousand; they could have moved out of their converted boxcar in Oildale into one of the new suburbs of Bakersfield that were rising up out of the cotton fields. One thousand had barely covered his debts.

Lefty's '42 Ford was pulled up to the curb and he looked like he'd been waiting a long time. He was already wearing the satin cowboy shirt Jewell had made for everybody in the band—theirs, green and pink; hers, pale gold, with pink roses appliquéd over the breast pockets. She'd had to send to L.A. for the fabric.

"You're late," he snarled as she scrambled into the car.

"Momma," she said breathlessly. "She laid into me over the clothes again."

"You're too old to have yer momma a-bossin' you," he said, and he was right. But her momma was about as much like other people's mommas as Hitler was like...like Lefty. "She's right, though," Lefty was saying. "Goddamn waste of money, these monkey suits." They swung out into traffic, heading south on Chester. "Hot as hell, too. I'm already sweatin' like a coon." The slick sleeves of his shirt fell away from his wrists, revealing long fine black hairs sprouting from the fish-belly white of his forearm. Jewell looked away in mild revulsion. "Fine as froghair," folks'd say, and "froghair" always made her think of Lefty.

"Lefty, let's not be draggin' through this again. People like a band to look sharp. Look what fancy clothes done for the Maddox Brothers and Rose—"

"You and yer highfalutin ideas—" he was saying at the same time, and she shut up because that was the problem, she knew. Not the clothes—the boys in the band liked the clothes—but the fact that they had been her idea. She picked the clothes, same as she picked the songs. Well, after all, she was the one singing the songs, but that was a sore point, too. When Lefty'd let her into the band, it had been as a favor. His idea was that she'd come out for a number or two, then fade back into the woodwork.

But Jewell had had her first highfalutin idea. Right then a few girls were starting to front for bands—Rose Maddox up in Modesto had been the first, now there was Rose Lee Maphis right here in Bakersfield—and Jewell'd figured, why not her, too? She was the one with the strong, pure voice people couldn't forget; she was the one people came to see. She was the Cherokee Rose.

"Just want to show off yer laigs," Lefty was mumbling as they passed the Coca-Cola sign at 18th Street. THIRST KNOWS NO SEASON, *it said, and then, above that, today's weather:* FAIR.

"…Always did seem to be 'fair;'" Jewell said, coughing and bringing Claire back to the present, to Jewell's grimy little kitchen. "Might be a hundred and ten, or winter tule fog thick as tapioca, and it would still be 'fair' on top of Kimball's Drugs. Maybe old man Kimball didn't like to climb up and change the sign. Or maybe Coca-Cola didn't allow no weather but 'fair.'"

Claire looked at her watch. "Oh, shi-oot—" managing to shift vowels in mid-word "—you've been too entertaining." She scrambled to her feet. "I've got to find this guy's orchard." She dug into her pocket for a card:

CLAIRE SHARPLES, PH.D.

PLANT PATHOLOGIST

UNIVERSITY OF CALIFORNIA

"That's me."

Jewell painstakingly wrote down her own name and phone number with arthritis-swollen fingers. "Come by again," she

said, handing Claire the scrap of paper. "I'm most always here."
"I will," she said, almost meaning it. What would it be like to
be always here, in this desolate outpost of rusting trailers? She
paused at the door. "I bet Chet was a looker as a young man."
"Chet?" Jewell repeated, startled. "He weren't never nothin'
to look at. Not *Chet*." She paused. "Good-hearted man, though.
A real good-hearted man."

2

CLAIRE STARTED TOWARD the truck, then stopped dead. A sharp pain had pierced her side—a familiar pain. Not appendicitis. Guilt. And for years guilt had meant her mother. I need to call her, she thought automatically, stopped, revised the thought, and brought on another, newer, pain.

But how had thoughts of her mother sought her out here in the middle of the wilderness? Jewell, she supposed. Jewell and Margaret Sharples would have shared a census category—white widowed female, sixty-something—if nothing else. But Jewell had revealed more of herself, her inner life, her sense of humor, in one fifteen-minute visit than Margaret had in Claire's whole adult life, as far as she could remember. In most respects, Margaret seemed to have died some twenty-five years ago, when her adored young husband, Claire's father, had succumbed to Hodgkin's Disease. Claire had spent a good part of her own life trying to compensate her mother for the loss and then had given up. Finally she'd even stopped calling regularly and now, of course, calling was no longer an option.

With a visit from her brother Charles due so soon, Claire had alternated in recent weeks between well-practiced guilt rituals, adhering like barnacles to her mother's memory, and a growing sense of dread. Charles was Claire's only remaining family unit, the last blood link to her past, and he could barely contain his contempt for the inexplicable jog her career path had taken when she settled in this godforsaken territory.

But it wasn't godforsaken to Jewell, Claire remembered suddenly, seeing the woman again, head thrust back and her golden music filling the hot, arid morning. Jewell had deliberately sought out this desolate and inhospitable stretch of dry river—as a widow, no less—not that leaving Oildale necessarily represented sacrifice.

By the time Claire reached the truck she had made two resolutions: She would stop worrying about Charles, and she'd visit Jewell again, to hear more stories. The pain lessened, the cramping in her side slithered slowly away.

Okay.

Next responsibility: Erasmo Campos. She leaned against her truck reading Ramón's directions, and it seemed to her that she should be standing right in the middle of the orchard. But all around her was Kern County scrub: packed earth, saltbush and tumbleweed that picked at her jeans, the line of brush that marked the poor old depleted Kern River a little way to the south, and in the far distance the ridge of the Temblors.

At that moment a phone rang.

Claire jumped and blinked as if the voice of Jehovah had just boomed at her from the nearest jimsonweed, then dove into the truck to retrieve the newest boon and bane of her life, a cellular phone. And there was a voice more welcome at the moment than Jehovah's: Ramón Covarrubias's.

"I'm running a little late," he said. "I just passed Tidwell Ginning." A little late, she thought with irritation; that cotton gin was miles north of Bakersfield. "Go ahead and talk to Erasmo without me," Ramón was saying. "His English is pretty—"

"I can't find Erasmo."

"Oh." A pause. "Where are you?" A brief exchange, then: "If you're at the trailer park, you're there. Look for the next dirt road and turn toward the river. You can't miss his place, it's pink."

Pink? she thought, proceeding with extreme skepticism, because this wasn't Ramón's beat either. Like her, he was based up in Kaweah County, as Small Farm Adviser. Ramón had heard about Campos and his blighted peaches through unofficial channels and had added him to his list of unofficial clients.

But wait—there was the dirt road, and there on the bank of the "river" was a small stucco farmhouse that looked to have been coated with Pepto-Bismol. When she pulled up, three or four motley puppies were running full-tilt in separate directions, while a human figure crouched in the middle of the yard, gesticulating at a cardboard box and shouting. She rocked to a halt. The figure, a slight young Latino man, stood and tipped over the box with his foot. Something squirted out and the dogs began to circle and yap. Claire saw a little bucktoothed rodent blinking stupidly at the barking puppies, and she deduced that Erasmo Campos was trying to teach his dogs to hunt gophers.

It didn't seem to be working. After their initial frenzy, the puppies' attention was captured by some other fascinating object—a fly, a turd, who knew—and they wandered away. Erasmo shook his head in disgust, picked up a shovel, and whacked the gopher. He had to swing three times before it stopped twitching.

Claire did her best to ignore this demonstration of farmer's pragmatism. She knew this young man with the thin, melancholy face of a medieval monk would have brained a big-eyed fuzzy puppy just as casually, had it threatened his livelihood. She stepped forward, hand out.

"*Buenos días, me llamo Claire—*" she began, but Erasmo cut her off.

"Where is Ramón?" he demanded, and she explained. His face

hardened—or rather relaxed, as if finding its natural expression—into stubborn, martyred lines, and he reluctantly led her toward his fruit trees, which ended a few hundred yards this side of the river. Both of them slipped into the deep shade of the sickle-leafed trees, where the Autumn Gems hung ruined from their branches. It was like a scene from *Apocalypse Now*. Late-ripening varieties were especially susceptible to fungus, and Campos had a textbook case. That's why Ramón had called her in.

"You're sort of an expert on brown rot," he had said.

Oh, great, she'd thought. She, whose college dreams had not excluded a Nobel, had now become the Brown Rot Queen. "Not really, I mean, I had kind of an unusual case a few years ago. But that turned out to be sabotage...."

Ramón had discounted the implicit question. "Nope. Can't see who'd have a grudge against Erasmo. Other way round, maybe. He rents that land; he'd like to buy it, but the owner won't sell. Erasmo managed to put together a good offer, too. Not like old man Tidwell to let a deal go by."

"Tidwell? C.C. Tidwell owns this land?"

"Yep."

"The developer of San Anselmo?"

"Yep."

So this orchard was history, Claire thought now, sighting down the neat avenues toward the river. Soon to be absorbed into a higher life form, i.e., the monstrous planned community of San Anselmo, which would fill to the brim the wide plain to the south, right at the base of the Tehachapis. No more cattle. No more grapes. No more vast fields of flowering spring lupine, like a shimmering mirage of blue water lapping at the base of the mountains, a memory of the great lake that the Great Valley had once contained. What, or if, the county planners had been thinking when they approved the project she did not know.

She frowned. There was something else nasty about Tidwell, which she no longer remembered, that someone had once told her. Sam, maybe, her ex-boyfriend? Ramón, her...her what? Her friend, her married friend?

Some scandal surrounding the land deal?

Well, it would come back to her or not, and in any case was not her concern. Her problem was *now*, here, this doomed crop in this doomed orchard, and together she and Erasmo walked the rows looking for clues to why he had twice the usual incidence of brown rot. Bad sanitation, maybe? Infected mummies left to overwinter and contaminate new fruit?

But Campos was a conscientious farmer. Too conscientious, maybe; the orchard was hospital-clean, the ground between the trees sprayed bare as a pool table. Claire liked to see cover crops in an orchard, fixing nitrogen, sheltering beneficial insects.

"Tell me about your trees," she said, and in quite serviceable, if grudging, English he gave her a medical history of the orchard: how it had fared last year, when he had noted symptoms this year, what he had sprayed and when. They were just coming to the topic of fertilizer when a rip of gravel and a spume of dust signified the arrival of another vehicle.

"Ramón!" they exclaimed, both relieved—Campos because he didn't quite trust this skinny *gringa*, or like the idea of her telling him what to do; Claire because she was always relieved, or comforted, or something, to see Ramón.

When they returned to the pink house he was alighting from his truck, which was identical to Claire's except that the ornate seal of the County of Kaweah on the door panel replaced that of the State of California. A big man with tea-colored skin and a bad back, he eased himself down with care. Beyond him the puppies were digging enthusiastically between the trees and the river.

"Your dogs are putting in a new row of trees for you," Claire remarked.

Erasmo blinked at her as if he had suddenly forgotten all his English in the presence of another Latino, especially a Latino male. Never mind that Ramón, who was third-generation, had had to learn Spanish in high school. He looked the part, and obligingly translated Claire's casual comment, which her own Spanish was certainly up to. Although, to be fair, she only caught about half of Erasmo's voluble reply. That was her problem: grammar tolerable, accent excellent, vocabulary limited but serviceable—in short, she could ask the questions, but she couldn't understand the answers. Much like her life, she thought ruefully. And unlike her science, where she might ask the wrong question, or a boring question, but at least the answer came back in the same terms in which the question had been posed. By definition.

"He says that's not his land," Ramón was telling her in his deep voice. "His ends at the last row of trees. His landlord—that would be Tidwell—won't let him put in anything between here and the river." He turned to Claire and nodded, the golden planes of his face impassive. "Oh, and hi, by the way. Sorry I'm late."

"Hi. We actually had a productive conversation. I was just about to ask him about fertilizer." She turned to Erasmo, determined to get him to answer her in one language or another, but he was making for his lease-breaking dogs, waving his arms and shouting. Suddenly he stopped dead. He squatted where they had been digging, rummaged in the dirt for a moment, then raised his face to Claire and Ramón.

"*¡Vengan acá!*" he called in a high voice. "*Hay algo aquí. Algo mal.*"

They walked toward the river, Claire bracing herself for something *really* bad. She'd seen more than her share of mayhem and carnage since moving out here from Boston, but so far no dismembered, rotting corpses. Only fresh ones.

But when they got to the excavation, there was no bloated, severed hand; no half-eaten face. Nothing. Just some glimpses of white, most likely a plastic milk jug. What was he talking about?

Ramón understood it before she did. He dropped to his knees, wincing at the impact, and started scratching around the "milk jug" with his fruit knife. Then she saw it, too, the smooth dome—once ivory, now stained and streaked—and gradually revealed, the hollow Halloween eye sockets.

3

~~~~~~

"*SE ANEGÓ,*" ERASMO SAID briefly, as he and Ramón continued to dig at the hard earth. Ramón nodded and Claire cursed inwardly; it was one of the words she didn't know.

"What?" she had to say.

"Drowned, probably," Ramón translated. "Poor sucker."

"In *this* river?" Claire asked incredulously, looking at the thin skin of green water several yards to the south.

"The Kern is notorious," he said. "Deadly."

"Deadly?" she repeated.

"Especially up in the canyon." He looked up briefly. "You don't believe me."

"I just think Californians are hysterical about water. Especially moving water. If it moves, you've got to do something to it. Stick a surfboard on it, or a white-water raft. Or put a dam in it, or a turbine. I mean, back east, we have lots of rivers. Big rivers."

He shook his head and turned to her again, and for a moment she thought he was going to smile. But he didn't. He kept digging.

"Yeah, high voltage, maybe, but low amperage. Don't forget, the Kern drops from twelve thousand feet to sea level. And before the dam, this water used to *move*, even way out here. I remember." The Lake Isabella dam had been completed in '54, and he glanced her way at this reminder of his age. But she hardly noticed, because they had now uncovered the whole skull.

There was nothing macabre or repellent about the skull. It was just poignant—a house where no one lived anymore—and more than a little awe-inspiring. "Wow," she breathed, and even Ramón failed to come up with an appropriate quote from Blake, or Marvell, or *Hamlet*. Erasmo crossed himself and Claire, lapsed Episcopalian, was tempted to do the same.

She settled for kneeling alongside the shallow excavation. "What's this?"

"*Raíz,*" Erasmo said. "Root."

"I don't think so." She unfolded her pocket knife without taking her eyes off the thin brown wire that curled out of the white earth. "It's definitely not a root. It's made of metal."

"Well, a spring, then," Ramón suggested.

"Nope. It goes straight back from the curve." The knife scraped against the chalky dirt. "It's rusty. I'm afraid I'm going to break something." Presently she said, "There's a little hinge here. And some...some shattered glass, I think. And...oh."

They all stared down at the empty, twisted wire-rim spectacles, protruding from the ash-colored earth. The spectacles stared back.

Claire used a Kleenex to gather up the fragments into a plastic bag. The two men kept digging. It was Claire who finally said, "You know, we should probably stop, and call the sheriff. We might disturb the evidence."

"What evidence?" asked Ramón. "The guy drowned."

"Well, maybe. Probably. But I still think we should leave

him—or her—" realizing that those wire-rimmed spectacles were unisex "—to the experts."

"Well, once I would have said, If it's experts you want, don't call the Kern County Sheriff," Ramón grumbled. He had grown up in Bakersfield and knew the town, but she suspected that, like her, he was reluctant to relinquish what had been a profound and personal experience, to watch it transformed into a rote exercise in forensics.

What Erasmo thought she did not know. He had disappeared at the mention of the word "sheriff."

"Can't be worse than J.T.," she said, alluding to the notoriously pea-brained sheriff of Kaweah County.

"No, and probably a good deal better. There's a new sheriff this year, supposed to be a clean new broom. Good guy, but whether he can actually sweep the dust bunnies of graft and corruption out of the corners of Kern County remains to be seen."

He stepped back, and she made the phone call. They moved to the shade of her truck then, where they could keep an eye on their excavation, which the dogs kept sniffing curiously.

Ramón groaned comically as he lowered himself to the ground. "If I'd known I was going to fall apart when I hit fifty, I would have stayed in academia."

So he's fifty, thought Claire, who was thirty-eight, glancing at his profile; I would have guessed younger. When he was going through puberty, I was learning to walk. When he was in college, I was skipping rope on the playground. When he was getting married—she shook herself back to the moment, like one of the puppies. This was not heading down a road Claire wished to travel just now.

Ramón's black hair was streaked with gray but still thick, and she had long admired his skin, which was fine-textured and burnished, like polished wood, and holding up better than her own under the Valley's merciless sun. She tried to see the hair, and the skin stretched taut over fat and muscle, as transient drapery, a sort of bathrobe, for the box of bone underneath. What would Ramón look like without a nose?

He turned to see her studying him. "What?"

"I was trying to imagine what your skull looks like."

"What a Renaissance thought." He considered. "Kind of flat, I'd imagine." He passed his hand down the back of his head. "Though not as flat as our friend's. His was almost concave."

"I didn't notice."

"Now yours..." He regarded her. "Kind of hard to tell with all that hair. But probably very nicely shaped," he ended gallantly.

"Thank you," she said, flushing under her transitory skin. "I saw it once. I mean, in a scan, after an auto accident. I couldn't identify with it—couldn't grasp that I look out through those eye sockets—but I did feel quite maternal toward it."

"Maternal!" he repeated, incredulous. "Well, I guess it's like those eggs that my daughter's tenth-grade class had to carry around last year, to teach them how fragile and demanding babies are. Only this is one egg we all hatch, eventually."

They thought about this for a while, Claire surreptitiously pressing her fingertips against her temples, her cheekbones, the knobs behind her ears. Then Ramón grinned.

She was always surprised when he did this. His face, broad at the jaw, a little stiff, a little asymmetrical—his nose had evidently been broken and had healed askew—seemed made for melancholy, and when it rearranged itself into a smile the effect was startling, like a monument taking a pratfall. It seemed impossible that the full, sculpted lips and wide jaw could lift, the sad eyes gather little smiles of skin under themselves.

But they did. Right now. In fact, he snickered. "Totally inappropriate thought," he said, "but I've always heard C.C. had skeletons in his closet. Just never expected to uncover one quite so literally."

"What skeletons?" she said eagerly. A line of dust to the north indicated the approach of a car.

"What?"

"C.C. Tidwell. What skeletons? I've been trying to remember all morning."

"Claire, that was a joke. This has nothing to do with Tidwell."

"I know, but I'm still curious." She had spent too much of her time out here feeling out of the loop of common knowledge, and had learned to soak up local gossip whenever she could.

"Oh. Well, you know, a rich man is going to accumulate enemies and rumors. Especially Tidwell, who's pissed off people in three areas: land, cotton, and oil."

Claire waited. Three years among tight-lipped men—of whom Ramón was not one—had taught her that if she just shut up occasionally, people would talk.

"But there's one specific, persistent story," he went on, rewarding her silence, "mostly promulgated by my cousin, as a matter of fact."

"Your cousin?"

"Yep. Cousin Yolanda... Poor old Yolie," he added after a pause, in that well-practiced tone people use when an adjective has been so often employed it becomes a sort of honorific. Poor old Yolie.

Claire cocked her head expectantly, but before Ramón could continue the sheriff's car pulled up, along with a coroner's van. And just as she'd feared, authority—in the persons of Deputy George Simmons and Coroner Bob Hansberger—expropriated the whole incident.

"Aw, man," Hansberger muttered disgustedly. The coroner, short and round, prodded the skull with his toe, looking to Claire as if he were going to kick it like a soccer ball.

"Sorry, Bob," Simmons said. He was a good-looking blond with aviator sunglasses and a reflexive swagger, even in the heat. "You know I can't do nothin' without you."

"Yeah, but. You know how many boxes of bones I got in storage? I farm 'em out to the colleges, but still. Oh, well. Let's see what we got." Hansberger folded over his belly and crouched by the bones. "Skull, clavicle, partial rib—looks like we got the whole enchilada here," he muttered, while Simmons obediently took notes. "Pelvis—okay, it's a male. A young male, I'd say—" Suddenly he looked up. "This ain't federal land, is it?"

Simmons shrugged, looked at Ramón, then at Claire, then back at Ramón. Claire imagined he was trying to decide who had more authority, a female or a Mexican.

Ramón shook his head. "Private. C.C. Tidwell."

"Okay, no NAGPRA, then," the coroner said mysteriously. "Anyway, he looks Caucasoid." Here he shot an appraising glance at Ramón, who, however much he sounded like an NPR announcer, looked like an *indio*. NAGPRA, Claire remembered, had something to do with Indian relics.

Simmons quizzed them about the details of discovery. Then he waved a dismissive hand. "You folks can go on home now. We'll take it from here."

"I'd just as soon stick around," Claire said.

"Suit yourself." He paused. "You can help us dig," he offered graciously.

"Yeah, but be real careful," the coroner interjected. "Looks like somebody's slipped with the shovel here." He was fingering the back of the skull.

"We didn't use a shovel!" Claire said indignantly, at which Simmons and Hansberger exchanged glances.

"Hit a river rock?" Simmons ventured.

Thereafter the two officials were every bit as unforthcoming as she had expected, wielding their proprietary knowledge and their silence like a truncheon. Hansberger took a few photographs and then resumed digging, using tools from his van. Eventually they'd amassed a pile of bones and a few strips of leather that looked like the tongue of a boot and maybe a belt.

Claire pressed ahead with what she knew were futile questions. How long had he been buried? How did he die? And most urgently, who was he?

After the third iteration of these questions, the coroner sighed and gave up. "Look. We probably won't know how long he's been buried. My guess would be, it was way too recent for carbon dating, so without a datable artifact like a coin—what?"

"The glasses!" Claire exclaimed, and brought forth the wire-rimmed spectacles in their plastic bag. "I forgot all about these," she apologized, handing them to Simmons. "We found these right by the skull," she added hesitantly.

"Right next to it?" Simmons hadn't spoken in a while, and his tone was sharp.

"Uh-huh. Sorry. I put them aside so they wouldn't get crushed. I just sort of forgot—"

But Simmons had turned away and was conferring inaudibly with the coroner.

"Can you tell anything about the date from them?" Claire asked.

"The date? Oh, I don't know." Hansberger shrugged. "Maybe the archaeologist at Cal State can, but I doubt it. So forget about identifying him. Bottom line—we'll know his age and his general health. And maybe what killed him. That's when I get around to an examination."

"*When?*" she repeated.

"You know how many of these old skeletons turn up every year? At the bottom of the California Aqueduct, for instance, when they drain it?"

Far too many, Claire thought, particularly since the aqueduct carried drinking water to Los Angeles. She recalled a missing Hollywood screenwriter who had disappeared while driving from New Mexico to Santa Barbara, amid rumors of UFOs and speculation about the CIA. A year later, the screenwriter *and* his SUV had been pulled from the murky aqueduct where it passed below the highway.

"A lot," Hansberger continued. "I've got quite a backlog. On top of my normal workload. Folks keep dyin', you know."

Another hour and only a few more bones had emerged. "They're going to be at this till dark," Claire muttered to Ramón, "and I still have other calls to make today."

Ramón looked at his watch. "Me, too. Gotta go up to Fresno,

but it's too late to do that today." He paused. "Think there's any chance we'll hear from the sheriff again?"

"Nope. They don't think we have any interest in the matter."

"How could we not have an interest? We found him!"

"Take it from me, that doesn't count," she said, from more experience than was really seemly for a plant pathologist. "Anyway, sounds like they're not even going to try to identify him."

"Yeah, but they might be able to date the bones. I'd like to know that, at least."

"I'd like to know whether that skull fracture happened before or after he went in the water," she said thoughtfully. "But I don't suppose they can tell that."

Ramón was looking at her oddly, and she wondered if he knew her peculiar history in Kaweah County. She sort of hoped he didn't. "I have a friend on the Riverdale Police," she said—if he did know her history, he would know why she had a friend who was a policeman—"and maybe he has enough leverage with Kern County to pry some information out of them."

"I have a little leverage in Bakersfield, too." They walked back to the trucks. "Well, so," he said, "it's been an interesting afternoon. You're not upset or anything?"

"Not particularly, no. I didn't know him, and whatever happened, it was all over and done with long ago. Anyway, I've seen worse things out here."

"That's right." He looked at her curiously. "Kind of a Typhoid Mary of homicide, aren't you?"

Ah, so he did know.

"Yep. Better keep your distance."

He hoisted himself carefully into the truck. "Oh, I'll take my chances," he told her, and headed home.

To his wife, Claire reminded herself, as she bumped back up to her next call back in Kaweah County, crossing the California Aqueduct with a mild shudder. She sliced through the desolate acreage, thinking that, like a third world country, Kern County's riches were in its land. Not fertile land, but tractable.

You could: (1) plant it if you added enough water, nitrogen, and herbicides; (2) suck things out of it; or if all else failed, you could (3) perch things on top of it and hope somebody bought them.

Only when she turned onto Highway 99 did she think, I never figured out what was wrong with Erasmo's peaches.

4

CLAIRE SAT ON her back deck.

She thought about Jewell, and whether she was lonely. She thought about this afternoon's discovery, wondering who he was, how old he had been, how long ago he had drowned. She thought about the Request for Proposals from the UC Davis Sustainable Agriculture Program, and what she could put together in the next few weeks.

But soon the roar of the river—not the once-mighty, now-crippled Kern, but Kaweah County's own more modest river—rose up the canyon beneath her, filling it with sound, filling her with sound from bottom to top, like a tumbler of water. When it rose to the level of her head it annihilated her thoughts and worries, as it did every night, until finally she was simply sitting.

Insofar as she was doing anything, she was waiting for autumn. A long wait, since as far as California was concerned—

even California at five thousand feet—September was still summer. But she could picture the fall, could remember it from last year, the first year she had spent up here on the western slope of the Sierra: how it had crept up the opposite flank of the river's steep canyon like a slow fire, lighting the oaks. Not blazing scarlet, like the maples of home—Massachusetts—but yellow, a nice, satisfying, buttery yellow against the stern black trunks.

Lower down the mountain the oaks weren't deciduous, and farther up the conifers started—green, green, green, until you hit the aspens on the eastern side of the range. So in fact she was at prime altitude for autumn, something she hadn't known when she'd bought this little A-frame cabin the previous summer. All she'd known was that she had to get out of the Valley. The Valley gave her spiritual asthma. It sat on her chest like a large unfriendly dog: the heat, the smog, the dreary winter fog, and most of all the suffocating presence of Sam Cooper, latest in her long history of romantic misadventures. No, not latest, just most serious. The latest had been a brief and spectacularly disastrous dalliance last summer.

She had acquired the house hastily and without much thought. And when she looked at the summer's two impulsive actions—the one, the cabin, a smashing success; the other, the rebound whatever-it-was, more like a two-car pileup—it strengthened her resolve to avoid any encounter requiring a consenting adult other than a loan officer. Because on the rolling deck of love she was clearly a loose cannon, a danger to herself and to her shipmates.

Claire had a theory about this. Having trained herself not to allow emotion to warp the pure rationality of her science, she had likewise ensured that no glimmer of rationality would ever illuminate the pure idiocy of her emotional life.

So, best not to have an emotional life.

This was a vow that she was having trouble remembering of late, and she kept searching for loopholes. Like: did that mean no sexual life, either? Probably. Last summer she'd tried to divorce the two—sex and feeling—and (a) it hadn't really worked, and (b) her judgment had been even worse than usual.

She walked back into the house to get herself a Dr Pepper, and stood at the kitchen counter for a moment picking at the 1970s do-no-harm-beige Formica, which the tile man was coming soon to replace with the blue-and-gold Mexican tile she had coveted for a year. Walking back toward the A-frame's south-facing wall of glass, which opened onto the deck, she saw for a moment both the nine thousand–foot peak of Slate Mountain through the window, and her own reflection superimposed against it.

Too bad that this was the period in her life during which she'd taken a vow of celibacy, she thought, because she was looking as good as she was ever likely to. Which wasn't spectacular, but tall and lean aged well, and since she'd never been particularly pretty, she didn't have to mourn the passing of her looks.

And she was right at her sexual peak, her estrogen waning and unmasking the testosterone underneath. At least, she *hoped* this was her sexual peak; Christ, she hoped it didn't get more urgent than this.

Because how long could she sublimate via new kitchen counters, and extra hours at the lab, and long hikes?

She settled back on the deck, pretended her cold soda can was hot chocolate and that the face of Slate Mountain, glowing pink with the sunset, was white with fresh snow. In Claire's home in western Massachusetts, you didn't have to go in search of the cold; it sought you out, probed with long fingers under the door and around the windowframe, unto the farthest corner of your cozy bedroom.

Like guilt. Once again she thought about calling her mother.

It was such a familiar thought that it had arrived, fully formed, before she remembered it was no longer appropriate.

Because her mother, her poor, unhappy mother, was dead.

Over the winter, swiftly, from a stroke. Died while Claire was over Kansas, flying to see her one last time. And still Claire retained the old habit of guilt, now overlaid with a dull pain like the throb of a phantom limb—a pain she had so far managed to keep at bay. A pain that Charles's imminent arrival was exacerbating.

She wiped the back of her hand across her eyes, then dug in her jeans and found the crumpled scrap of paper with Jewell's phone number. She could stop by tomorrow on her way once again to the orchard of Erasmo Campos, where she would finish today's truncated visit.

The phone in Jewell's trailer rang for a long time, and Jewell's voice was thick and breathless when she finally answered. Yes, Claire would be most welcome, but she "might should call first," because she, Jewell, had been feeling poorly today.

"What's wrong?" Claire said quickly.

"It ain't nothin'. Some days I just cain't seem to catch my breath, is all." There was an illustrative pause, as Jewell filled her lungs to say, wryly, "Don't you never get old, honey."

The alternatives are bad, Claire thought, but said, "Do you have somebody? Nearby, I mean, in case you need help." Surely some of that huge brood on the photo wall would come to their mother's aid; surely other offspring were not as neglectful as she had been.

"Oh, folks out here in the Court'd look in on me. But to tell you true, most of 'em is mighty decrepit themselves. My daughter Shelley'll come out from Bakersfield, iffen I need her. But shoot, honey, I ain't a-dyin' yet."

Claire had just hung up when the phone rang again. Expecting to hear Jewell with a change of plans, she was surprised by Ramón's voice, and noted with alarm the distinct bump of excitement, or pleasure, or something, in her solar plexus.

He was only calling to remind her of their class tomorrow evening, Thursday, over in San Luis Obispo, a class in soil science. Claire was guest lecturer tomorrow, speaking about an underground fungus crucial to soil fertility and structure. But of course what Ramón really wanted to talk about was something else under the ground.

"Quite an encounter this morning."

"Actually, it was my second interesting encounter today. I didn't tell you about the first," she said, wondering why that was, why in the entirely companionable time shared in the putative shade of her truck she had neglected to mention Jewell. Suddenly eager, she found herself telling him about Jewell, and the picture, and Jewell's costumes, and Lefty.

"I don't know why I had such a strong reaction to her," she finished.

There was a long pause. "Didn't your mother die last winter?" he asked.

Not an astonishingly perceptive response, but coming from a Kaweah County male it amounted to black magic, and Claire was startled into candor. "Uh, yes. But Jewell isn't much like my mother. More like the mother I wish I had had, maybe." Could this possibly be true, Claire wondered in a fresh flush of guilt, grateful that he couldn't see her discomfort.

"And with her you were more the daughter you wish you had been, maybe."

Where had he learned to talk like this? But suddenly she remembered where Ramón, that fraudulent Freud, got his bedside manner.

From his wife.

Miranda, a cool Connecticut blonde who had made Claire want to run out and get a two hundred–dollar haircut the one time she'd seen her, was some kind of therapist.

"I don't know," Claire said dismissively. "I think I just like her accent. Anyway, I've got to make some more calls, so I'll see you tomorrow afternoon, okay?"

"Oh. Sure. I'll come by the station." He rang off abruptly.

On Thursday morning, Claire headed south, to Jewell and Erasmo.

The air smelled like vinyl shower curtains. That was defoliant; the cotton harvest was beginning, and the little yellow airplanes swooped low over field and freeway, trailing clouds of toxic glory. At Tidwell Ginning the mound of cotton seed wrapped in gray lint, which would swell to a Matterhorn by November, was still a bunny hill, but mesh carts—lion cages of raw cotton—were lined up in the yard like a circus train.

The airplanes must have nudged her memory, because suddenly she remembered the story about Tidwell, the tale that yesterday she could have sworn she didn't know. It had happened before she arrived in Kaweah County, but Sam had told her: The developer who originally owned the San Anselmo property being developed near Taft had been killed in the crash of a light plane, and his heirs had sold the land to Tidwell. And then a rumor had begun to circulate that Tidwell had actually caused the crash, sabotaging the plane somehow. ("Sugar in the gas tank?" Sam had speculated).

And there was something else, something about a reporter who had written about the rumors being canned by the paper. Could that have been Ramón's "poor cousin Yolie"?

But she didn't want to think about Ramón, so she thought about cotton.

The first time she had passed a cotton gin, when she had just arrived, she'd been so fascinated by that fluffy white hill that she'd taken a tour with the Extension Expert for cotton, Jimmy Milpitas. The gin—not this one, but up in Kaweah County— had been low-tech but ingenious, sucking the raw bolls from their carts into the factory through huge pipes, heating it, and passing it on to the gins, Mr. Whitney's spinning rows of circular saws that straightened the fibers and removed the seeds. The seeds were then spewed onto that mound, and sold for feed, leaving snowy lint, which poured in a broad white cascade back into the system, to be blown on its way to the hydraulic baler.

But it was the fluffy gray mound of seeds in the yard that had drawn Claire that day.

"Kind of inviting, isn't it?" Jimmy had said.

"It looks so soft—like a big sheep."

"Yeah. When I was a kid my dad worked in a gin—he ran the baler—and I always wanted to run up that hill. He never would let me, of course. But one night my best friend and I snuck in and I headed straight for the pile."

"How was it?"

"Great for the first few steps. But I got about ten feet up the side and I started sinking. Real slow. It was weird—like you hear about quicksand, the more you struggle the worse fix you're in—that's how it was. I kept trying to climb and I kept sinking down. I was up to my neck when my buddy pulled me out."

She wondered if Jewell and her family had picked cotton when they came out, like so many of the Dust Bowlers. Nasty work, that…Claire had seen the old photographs, workers trailing long muslin sacks, inching like worms through the rows. The Central Valley Okies and Arkies picking cotton in the thirties and forties had employed the same methods as African slaves in the antebellum South. And cotton resisted picking, raged against the harvest. The soft fibers nestled in a deceptive cup of razor-sharp sepals, so that pickers' hands bled into the snow-white bolls.

Nowadays, of course, nobody picked cotton. After chemical defoliation, hump-shouldered machines buffaloed through the rows, vacuuming up the bolls and setting them bouncing like popcorn in a popper. Claire supposed that was progress; chopping cotton was rough work. But it *was* work. Now two men took the jobs of twenty.

At the trailer Jewell seemed revived, and dragged her photo album out of the kitchen drawer. Claire thumbed through it quickly. It contained more of what hung on the wall—barn dances, road trips, nightclubs, some pastoral scenes along the river—but there were fewer pictures than she'd expected. "When did the band break up?"

"Nineteen fifty-four, pretty much."

" 'Fifty-*four*?" Claire repeated in disbelief; from the photos it seemed the band had just gotten started in '53. "Why so soon?"

"The heart kinda went out of it for me."

Claire looked at her intently, but all she would say was, "It weren't no life for a grown woman."

"Did you always want to be a singer?" Claire figured that if Jewell wouldn't talk about the end, maybe she would talk about the beginning.

"Always did sing," Jewell admitted with a smile. "Out in the fields, with my family, a-pickin' cotton. Or on Sunday mornin', at church. Had me this big voice when I was just a bitty thing. But I never did think to sing perfessional-like. Just figured I'd git married, raise a family. I think," she said, settling back in her gray vinyl kitchen chair, "it was the quake done changed that, changed the way I saw things."

"The quake?"

"Nineteen fifty-two, summer. You ain't heard about the 'fifty-two earthquake? Lord, we had us a doozy...."

Jewell was standing at the kitchen window when the world cracked. A hard, sharp sound, as if somebody'd taken the house by its corner and snapped it out like an old towel. And then the floor began to move and she realized what was happening. There had been another one earlier that summer, but that had been a slow roller, like a nearby freight. This was a train wreck.

She started for the door, but the house was shaking too violently and she fell, just missing the corner of the old wooden kitchen table that had made the trip with them from Oklahoma. She rose and stumbled again, and then it was clear there was nothing she could do, so she just lay there, stretched out on the worn wood floor under the table, praying. Mostly out of habit, because she wasn't scared. Later, when everyone shared their terror (over and over and over again—if she had had to listen one more time to old Thelma Moss tell how but for God's grace and a touch of the trots she would have been in Lerner's when the wall caved in, she'd have whomped the old bat), what she remembered was the thrill of the earth shuddering under her, beyond her control.

The thrill of giving herself up to it.

The plates and glasses she had lived with all her life were smashing around her. Then, abruptly as it had begun, the movement stopped. But there would be more tremors—aftershocks, the radio called them. She remembered that from the first one. So she continued to lie, calm and slightly elated, staring up at the rough underside of the wooden table. She started to sing. "Farther along we-e-'ll know all about it; Farther along..." With no Momma there to hush her—"Stop that bellerin', honey, my haid's like to explode"—she let 'er rip, aiming her

*strong voice straight up at the table: "We-e-e'll understand wh-y-y…"
and hearing it come back at her, bigger than ever. And when the shaking started again she just sang louder, willing the earth to move and
the walls to crack, Joshua at the gates of Jericho.*

*So her mouth was wide open when Momma's soup tureen hit the
floor a foot from her head.*

"…I closed my eyes in time," Jewell said, "but you know, I felt
that grit on my tongue for weeks. And after that day, I reckon I
got a hankerin' to shake things up myself." She gave Claire one
of her girlish grins. Claire grinned back at her, then looked at
her watch and jumped up.

"Damn! You did it again!"

Jewell opened the kitchen drawer. "You find that place yesterday, all right?" she said, sliding her photo album back in.

"Yes. It was a pretty…unusual visit. We found a skeleton, buried next to the river. They figure it was an old drowning victim."

Jewell stood motionless at the counter. "They know who it
is?" she asked without turning around.

"No. They may never know. It's been there a while."

"How long? Forty-five years?"

"Maybe," Claire said, taken aback by the specificity. "Maybe
they can tell that, from some kind of tests. And from the eyeglasses."

"Eyeglasses!" Jewell finally turned to look at Claire. Her face
had lost all its color. "What kind of eyeglasses?"

"Wire-rimmed." Claire was now really curious.

"Oh, Lordy," Jewell said on an intake of breath, then sat back
down, hard. After a moment she offered weakly, "Reckon a lot of
folks wear them—those, spectacles."

"True. People wore them in the thirties, and then again in the
sixties. And they're wearing them again, come to think of it."

"Yep," Jewell mumbled to herself as she fished in her purse
for a cigarette. She was still so pale that Claire was ready to suggest she put her head between her knees. "Could be any pore
feller went in the river."

"Did you know somebody, Jewell?" Claire blurted. "Who drowned and whose body wasn't recovered?"

Jewell had found a crumpled pack of Camels. She lit one and took a long, grateful draw. Oddly, it seemed to return the color to her cheeks. "Honey, when I was growing up I knowed two or three kids drownded in that ol' river. Had some bad moments myself. It was wild, that river. We knowed it was dangerous, but when it's hot as blazes you cain't keep a child out of water." Her voice had gradually lost its tension, as if to ease Claire out the door. "You better git on to your appointment."

Claire dutifully stood to leave, then stopped suddenly by the door. "You know, he might not have drowned."

"And why's that?"

"Well, the eyeglasses, for one thing. They were right by the bones; you'd think they would have been swept away by the water. And there's some damage to the skull...."

Jewell blinked at this, several times, and her color went bad again. But all she said was, "Hit his haid on some big ol' river rock, most like. Pore soul. You go on now, honey."

Scooting Claire out the door.

When Claire had gone, Jewell sat smoking and staring vacantly at the kitchen clock. After a while she forgot about the cigarette, and jerked when it burned down to her fingers. Her hand flew up convulsively and sent the cigarette flying onto the hall rug, where it started to smolder. "Hell's bells," she grumbled, and groaned as she bent to retrieve the burning butt, scratching at the smudged spot in the carpet. Her daughter Shelley always said the things were gonna kill her, one way or the other. She knew she ought to quit but they were about the only thing left she enjoyed, and there didn't seem to be much point to it.

Especially now.

Lordy, she was tired. Maybe she would take a little nap before dinner. Maybe she would take a nap *instead* of dinner. Why not? She wandered into her bedroom, slipped off her clothes, and pulled on a nightgown, automatically fingering her scar. Then she shrugged into her grimy old dressing gown. Shelley always scolded her about her clothes being dirty, but she couldn't see 'em too good herself, not unless she hunted up her glasses. Couldn't see herself in the mirror, either. That was one of the blessings of old age: the less you wanted to see, the less you could see. Her momma would've said, That's the Lord's mercy. Jewell would've said, If He's so all-fired merciful, why make people get old at all? Just snip 'em off, peaceful-like, when they've had their three score and ten.

But not young. Not when they're twenty-one, and just starting to find the shape of their life. Where was the mercy in that?

She perched on the edge of her bed and lifted the picture from her bedside table. Didn't need her glasses for this. Didn't need to see it, because she remembered it like yesterday. Better than yesterday, because yesterday nothing had happened worth remembering, nor the day before it, nor the day before that. But those early years, seemed like every moment had been full as a drop of water: all she had to do was brush it with her memory and it all flowed out.

〰〰〰〰〰〰

It was in April of '54, when the Texas Tumbleweeds, Featuring Cherokee Rose were playing the Four Queens in Taft, that Jewell noticed him sitting in the front of the bar. A real good-looking, dark-haired fellow, dressed in a sharp two-tone charcoal shirt. But what caught her eye was how quiet he was. It was all oil over by Taft, roustabouts and roughnecks for Texaco and some small outfits like Western Oil and Gold Star, and they were a noisy crew. They worked hard, and when they got off they were ready for a good time. She had to watch her back in Taft; if she walked through the bar her behind would be black-and-blue.

But this fellow was just nursing a beer, listening to the band, watching. Watching her. And he was sitting by himself; that made him different, too. If the guys weren't dancing, they were all tangled up in one wiggly mass, like puppies.

So during the break she sat down with him, which she almost never did. But she was drawn to the quiet.

"You have a nice voice," he said. "You almost make me like this kind of music."

He *had a nice voice—soft, educated—and Jewell figured him for one of the college men, the geologists, on the crew. "You sure know how to knock a gal off her feet with compliments," she offered lightly.*

He smiled. Just a little smile, as if he knew something she didn't, or was hiding something. His mouth, maybe: she knew a fellow once who was missing a front tooth, and smiled like that.

"I have to admit this isn't my favorite type of music," this fellow said now.

"No? What type of music you like?"

"Oh, jazz, swing. They call this hillbilly music where I come from—sorry. That wasn't very polite." Another smile.

"And whur's that?" she said.

"Where's what?"

"Whur's…where's, that place you come from?" The sounds that her mouth was producing suddenly seemed wrong, crude and ignorant.

"New York City."

Well! If he'd said Heaven's Pearly Gates she couldn't have been more surprised. She thought of New York as a made-up place, a place in the movies.

But then he looked like he could have stepped out of the movies.

Because as they sat awhile, she began to take note of just how handsome he was. Especially when he took off those little glasses, to reveal really beautiful eyes. Green, set deep under his brows, caught by the light every now and then, like a trout flashing in the sun on the Kern River.

And he was so dark. Now, all the fellows who worked in the oil fields were dark—a mix of sunburn and dirt. Seemed like they were dyed bone-deep in oil.

But this fellow looked like he'd been born dark. He could have been Mexican, even, except she'd never seen a Mexican with green eyes. And there wasn't anything wrong with his teeth, either.

She stood. "Time for my last set. You gonna stick around?"

No, he said; he had to get back to the camp. "Are you playing here tomorrow?"

"*Naw. Tomorrow we play Bakersfield,*" *she told him.* "*The Lucky Spot.*" *She was bragging, because the Lucky Spot was a big club. But then she saw he had never heard of it.*

"*Maybe I can get a ride in,*" *he said slowly.*

"*Thought you didn't care for no hillbilly music.*"

"*I wouldn't be coming for the music,*" *he said, giving her a look from those extraordinary eyes.*

"*What's yer name?*" *she had called as he turned to leave.*

Oh, she was bold in those days! she thought, smiling and settling back for sleep. Then the animation drained away, leaving her stern-faced. Not yet. Plenty of time to sleep later, but not yet. If God couldn't be counted on for mercy, He sure as hell couldn't be counted on for justice.

She picked up the phone by her bed and made a call.

Then she leaned back against the pillow, closing her eyes and letting the picture settle against her missing breast.

Claire was worried enough about Jewell that she almost turned around halfway to Campos's orchard. Jewell had been thinking about a specific person, she was certain. Someone who had died forty-five years ago. Who? And why was she so secretive?

And what, for Christ's sake, had possessed Claire to blurt out the inspiration that the victim might not have drowned after all? She was only thinking out loud, of course, but it was bound to have upset Jewell.

She was too distracted and guilty to do more than a cursory job at Erasmo's—gather some fruit samples (healthy and not), jot down more notes without taking in the information. *Benomyl, applied as a dormant spray in the fall and again in February. Nitrogen, 250 pounds per acre, applied in fall.* The puppies began to dig, and Campos ran at them with a stick.

"You want dogs?" he asked seriously when he returned.

Ordinarily she would have laughed, but today she just answered absently, "No, thanks."

She was halfway back to Citrus Cove in Kaweah County

when she finally gave in to worry and thumbed Jewell's number into her cell phone. There was no answer. Without giving it any real thought, she veered off at the next exit and reversed direction. Twice again on the way back she hit REDIAL, twice again she heard the hollow unanswered rings. On the off chance that she'd entered the numbers wrong the first time, she did it again, starting from scratch. More rings. No message machine; no need. Jewell hardly ever left, she'd said.

She took the turnoff to Kern Willows hell-for-leather, slowing at the bend where she'd seen Jewell that first day, on the off chance that she was just out singing. No sign or sound of her, and Claire rocked along the rutted road to the Court. She rang the bell, and slapped the screen door.

No answer.

Napping, probably. Nevertheless Claire felt her stomach tighten. She tried the door, remembering that Jewell hadn't used a key the other day, and it swung open. "Jewell?" she called, walking through the kitchen, where the smell of stale cigarette lingered in the air.

"Jewell? It's Claire." She passed down the hall, looked in the bathroom, poked her head in the bedroom, and was just deciding to look around outside again when two things caught her eye— an absence and a presence. The picture beside the bed was gone. And on the floor, just beyond the end of the high, old-fashioned bed, was the edge of a crumpled pink blanket.

There was no reason there *shouldn't* have been a pile of bedclothes on the floor—such a thing had been known to appear in Claire's own room, for example—but the bedroom seemed unnaturally still, as if the oxygen had been recently sucked out of it. She approached slowly.

It wasn't a blanket. It was the hem of a bathrobe, pink terry cloth.

And the bathrobe was wrapped around Jewell.

5

JEWELL WAS WEDGED so tightly into the narrow space between the bed frame and the closet that Claire had to clamber across the high bed to see her. And then she wished she hadn't. Jewell was staring unseeing at the ceiling, but when Claire reached down to touch her face it was still warm. Did people pass out with their eyes open?

"Jewell!" Claire said fiercely, and tried to shake her by the shoulder, but she could barely reach her, so she scrambled backward and tugged at the heavy farmhouse bed until she'd made enough space to crawl up to Jewell's head. No pulse, no breathing that she could detect. She raced to the kitchen and called 911, then raced back.

There was a little card in Claire's wallet that certified she'd taken a course in CPR the previous spring. But even at the time, as she'd pummeled the rubber dummy, she'd known that she would never remember the routine, and now she felt genuine panic. How many chest presses, how many breaths, how many counts in between? And anyway, there still wasn't enough room for her beside Jewell, so "Don't move the victim!" appeared to conflict with "Administer CPR!" But assuming that this was a heart attack, not a head or neck injury, she grabbed Jewell's ankles and tugged.

Jewell was surprisingly light and moved easily out into the bedroom. But at the same time her robe and nightgown hitched up around her hips. Claire fumbled to pull the material back down, and when she brought her hand away from the robe, saw a long streak of red. Like menstrual blood, she thought, confused—and then felt the sting in her own left hand, and noticed the deep slash in her palm.

Shrugging, she straddled Jewell's legs and began the percussive thrust of CPR, leaving a neat bloody handprint on her chest. Seven…eight…that seemed like a good number, and anyway the paramedics would be here any moment, with defibrillators and injections and other death-reversing remedies that would surely bring Jewell back to consciousness. She grabbed the sash of the robe to wrap around her bleeding palm, and the nightgown fell away from Jewell's right shoulder, revealing a long seam and a flap of skin where a breast should have been.

Claire stared for a moment in incomprehension, remembering yesterday's profile when Jewell was singing on the road, the large breasts thrust forward. A prosthesis, of course, she realized, feeling guilty at uncovering this sad secret, pulling the gown back around Jewell's narrow shoulder. She crawled up to Jewell's head, and bent toward her mouth to begin artificial respiration—no, what had they called it? "Rescue breathing."

Unlike the rubber dummy, this victim tasted of her life, of cigarettes and lipstick and something else, something sour and spent, and the rescuer recoiled for a moment. Then adrenaline carried her along, just as it had made her unconscious of the pain in her hand.

She continued her version of CPR for what seemed like

forever, but was really about ten minutes, before she heard a banging at the kitchen door.

"In here!" she shouted between breaths, and in strolled a sheriff's deputy.

"Do you know how to do this?" she gasped, simultaneously realizing it was Deputy George Simmons, the foxy-faced blond from yesterday. Either he was very cool or he didn't recognize her. "Because I don't really know what I'm doing, and anyway I'm beat."

"Yeah, sure," he said, hesitating a moment. "Stroke? Heart attack?" And then he saw the blood on Jewell's chest.

"That's mine," Claire said. "I sliced my hand up somehow."

He squinted at this, and then his eyes widened again as he finally placed her. "Weren't you—"

"Yes. Look, could you jump in here? You could do the chest compressions and I'll do the breathing."

"How long you been at this? She's prob'ly gone. She looks gone."

"Well, she's not. And where the hell are the paramedics? I called a long time ago!"

"Fifteen minutes, the call come through, and it's a big county." But he knelt at Jewell's feet. "Shit!" he exploded, jumping up again and holding his knee where a red stain had blossomed on his chino trousers. "What the fuck?" He held up a long triangular shard of glass and glared at Claire as if she had booby-trapped the floor.

"I guess that's how I hurt my hand. Look," she snapped, "either help with CPR or get out of the way so I can do it."

"Lady, this ol' gal ain't gonna make it—"

And at that moment two paramedics from the Taft Volunteer Fire Department arrived. They looked at each other as they moved Jewell onto a stretcher.

"You a relative?" one, a Latino kid, asked Claire.

"Yes, I mean no. Just a friend."

"She got a history of heart disease?"

Claire nodded.

"Well, we'll take her back to the emergency room in Taft, but I'm afraid she's gone."

The deputy shot Claire a triumphant glance as she shouted, "That's impossible! I just saw her a couple of hours ago, and she was fine!"

"It don't take long to die."

The words ricocheted around Claire's mind as she followed the ambulance to the hospital, where Jewell was pronounced dead.

Claire didn't drive straight home. Instead she took the turnoff once again to Kern Willows, holding the wheel gingerly with the fingertips of her bandaged left hand. The deputy's car was gone—he had filled out his paperwork at the hospital, where the ER doctor had persuaded him that Jewell had indeed died of a massive coronary, not foul play—and the neighbors had drifted back inside to brood about their own looming final rides.

Claire tried the front door, but the deputy had done his job and it was locked. She hoped he hadn't done too good a job, but that was academic if she couldn't get back inside the trailer. She rattled the door futilely; so flimsy, yet so impassable.

"Honey?"

Jewell's voice. Claire whirled, heart bumping. Not Jewell, of course; a wizened elderly neighbor with frizzy hair and that same indelible Okie accent. The woman wore shorts and a sleeveless blouse in a vivid shade of tangerine, and her deeply tanned arms had the toughened texture of cured snakeskin, souvenir of decades of unrelenting ultraviolet exposure. "I saw you leave with Jewell before. How is she gettin' on?"

"I'm afraid she, um—" What was the right phrase here? *She's gone*, the deputy and the paramedics had said. "She passed on. I'm sorry." She uttered the phrase mechanically. So far she wasn't sorry, she was just angry—angry at the whole sorry Kern County emergency system: What had taken the fucking paramedics so long? Why hadn't they treated Jewell as soon as they arrived, instead of writing her off? Angry at the deputy, who'd dithered over the CPR, more preoccupied by his harebrained suspicions—

And angry at herself, most of all. For upsetting Jewell.

"You leave something behind?" Jewell's neighbor was asking.

"What? Oh. Yes. Yes, we left in such a hurry—"

"Jewell, she leaves—used to leave—a key under the mat. Mostly we don't lock our places." She shrugged her bony shoulders. "Don't have nothin' nobody'd steal."

Claire's fingers had already found the cold key under the rubber mat. "Thanks. Thank you very much." And then she was on her knees in the bedroom, feeling gingerly under the bed...yes! Still there!

A long triangle of glass; that was what had stabbed her and the deputy. Another shard, sharp as a razor, and another, and another. She stretched her arm farther, as far as it would reach, searching for a wooden rim and feeling nothing. Finally she got down on all fours, peering into the darkness under the bed. Then she searched the closet floor, pushing aside Jewell's dingy old clothes.

Nothing.

It wasn't there.

Could she be wrong?

She had seen it so clearly: Jewell, after her visitor had left, feeling shaky, walking slowly into the bedroom and picking up the photo, thinking about old times and sweet flesh, and maybe bones by the river—and then, as the spasm hit her, losing control of the photo, sending it flying against the wall.... Claire gathered all the glass fragments into a pile. Pieced together they would fill an eight-by-ten frame.

But it wasn't there.

The photo, the photo of Jewell and her mystery man, was gone.

Shit! The goddamn deputy, Mister Tight-Ass Simmons, must have taken it with him in an excess of investigative zeal.

She used Jewell's phone to call the Kern County Sheriff's office and explain the situation. Deputy Simmons was still out; he would return her call when he got off duty at midnight.

Right, thought Claire, slamming down the phone. Fat fucking chance.

She would call him at 12:02. And at 12:03, and 12:04, and tomorrow at dawn, until she got that photo.

At the front steps she suddenly stopped, turned around, and
walked back into the kitchen, where she opened a drawer and
lifted out Jewell's photo album. At least he hadn't gotten that.

Ramón's truck was parked in the field station lot, and Claire
looked at her watch. Oh, God, she was supposed to lecture
about...what? Fungi, mycorrhizal fungi, in two hours. Could she
really do it?

Of course she could. She was a professional. And anyway,
work was an anodyne. Work was where you went when life hurt.

In her lab Ramón was leafing through a journal. "I was just
about to leave," he said, without looking up. "Thought maybe
you decided to drive straight over—what's wrong?" he blurted
when he finally saw her.

She held up her hand, which the nice doctor had bandaged
right after declaring Jewell dead. "Oh, I just sliced my palm.
Nothing ser—"

"I meant your face!"

"My face?" She touched her cheek. "Is there blood on it? I
didn't even—"

"No, there's no blood *in* it at all, it's gray! Did something happen?"

She leaned wearily on a lab bench. The anger had drained out
of her somewhere north of Bakersfield and nothing had yet
flowed in to take its place. Beyond her window the dry foothills
of the Sierra stretched out in voluptuous curves, like big yellow
cats lazing in the late sun.

"Something hap-happened," she said. How interesting: her
voice was quivering. Fascinated to see what it would do next, she
went on, "S-s-somebody d-d-died."

"Claire!" He was on his feet. "Not your brother?"

Her brother; why would he think that? Of course. She had

mentioned Charles's impending visit, had noted the dwindling of the Sharples clan. "No. This was s-somebody I hardly knew." Ah, her voice was back. "That woman I was telling you about. Jewell." "The Cherokee Rose? Oh, no!" He put an arm around her shoulders, and at the slightest invitation would have enfolded her in a real hug. The temptation was strong, but she stood stiffly, arms at her sides, looking past him at the lab's experimental plots out the window, refusing solace. She didn't want to be comforted now. She wanted to focus on tonight's lecture.

And she didn't want a generic good-buddy hug from Ramón. After a moment he backed away. "I'm sorry," he said formally. "I was looking forward to meeting her. What happened?"

"Heart attack," she said briefly. "Excuse me." She went to the lab's deep sink and rinsed her mouth for maybe the fifth time in the last hour; she couldn't seem to get rid of the taste of Jewell's mouth.

"We should call and ask somebody to put up a sign canceling class," he was saying.

"Why? Don't you want to go?"

"No, I just assumed you..." He trailed off, looking at her helplessly.

"I hardly knew her. Let me get my slides; then we'd better get started or we'll be late."

"Yeah, sure."

In the parking lot she said hesitantly, "Ramón?"

"Yes?"

"Would you mind driving?"

He gave her a shrewd look; Claire always wanted to drive. "Sure."

It was a long, silent ride to San Luis Obispo. Claire kept looking at her watch.

"...two main types of mycorrhizal fungi," she explained, writing it phonetically—*mike-oh-RYE-zal*—on the board. She switched on the projector and a slide of the fungus's hyphae, a network of fine fibers, appeared. Someone coughed restlessly in the darkened room, and she couldn't blame them; she was having trouble holding her own attention. She could feel the pressure of other thoughts trying to burst up from the underground into the plain air of consciousness, like the arm thrusting from the grave in *Carrie*.

And even under the best of circumstances, when other matters weren't competing for her brain, "soil science" still seemed like an oxymoron to her. It was only under the influence of Ramón, whose enthusiasm for the subject was apparently boundless, that she'd become so very aware of soil.

So for forty minutes (forty minutes—that meant she had another three hours and twenty minutes before she could call) she had tried to convince a darkened room full of strangers to revere their soil—its structure, the processes of decomposition that created it, and especially tonight's subject, the mycorrhizae—"tiny roots"—that knit it together. That an alien organism that sent its underground tentacles deep into their crops might be a *good* thing was a hard sell.

She kept talking. "It's, um, a symbiotic relationship," she said for the third time. "Both partners benefit. The fungus gets its carbon and energy from the plant, and keeps the plant supplied with inorganic minerals, especially phosphorus and zinc. And increases water uptake, and improves soil structure. So almost all plants need a rich mycorrhizal network. Except for a few invasive aliens, like tumbleweed, that seem to be non-mycotrophic. They don't need mycorrhizae, and it may actually kill them."

"Kill tumbleweed?" someone repeated, in a deep voice resonant with skepticism. Alive and prickly or dead and "tumbling," *Salsola kali*, or Russian thistle, was a pain in the ass for growers and motorists alike.

"Maybe," she said, picking up on the first indication of interest she'd received. "That's one reason you're likely to see it in disturbed ground—areas that have been disked, or burned."

"Good presentation," Ramón said later in the truck. "I learned something."

"Really?" Claire checked her watch. It was 9:32; two and a half hours to go. "I tried to keep it pretty simple," she said. "And I left out a whole section, about truffles being the fruiting bodies of certain types of mycorrhizae. Somehow this didn't seem like a truffle-eating crowd."

"No. Even I, sophisticated dude that I am, have never to my knowledge consumed a truffle. Anyway, I didn't know about tumbleweed."

"No. I just learned about that. Actually, I'm doing a little work on it right now," Claire said.

"And I found the whole presentation, I don't know, moving...."

"Moving? Soil fungus is moving?"

"Yes. It's such a powerful metaphor—"

"For the subconscious," Claire finished. "I know, I've been thinking about that myself lately. About how what's under the soil's surface—" She stopped.

"What's under the soil...?" he prompted.

Bodies. Secrets. "Oh, you know," she continued with effort, "roots as hidden mirror-image of tree, as essential but unknown..."

"Interesting," Ramón remarked. "Actually, I was going to say it's a metaphor for love."

"For love!"

"You know, the symbiosis. Each supplying what the other needs, making one another stronger, making a whole new organism out of two. It's astonishing."

He paused, giving Claire time to reflect that this certainly did not characterize any relationship to which she had been a party. Did it describe his own marriage? He and Miranda had separated for a while last year, but now were back together in—in perfect symbiosis, she presumed, of one sort or another.

She checked her watch.

"...the Donne poem," Ramón was saying, "'The Extasy.' You know it? Where the lovers lie all day on the riverbank, rapturously commingled? That's what it's like."

Lovers on riverbanks; Claire gave an involuntary exclamation. Now that the lecture was over, there was no way to suppress thoughts of Jewell.

"What?" he said again.

"You know that..." You know that skeleton we found; I think I've seen him with his skin on, she started to say, but the speciousness of her own reasoning stopped her. Just because Jewell *might* have thought she knew the identity of the victim didn't mean she was right, or even that she thought it was her handsome lover. She might have thought it was an old pal, or anyone else who went missing near that treacherous river.

But she had died with a picture of the dark mysterious man in her arms.

Maybe.

"Nothing," Claire said. "I guess I'm all for rapturous commingling, but I want to take my own DNA with me at the end of the day."

He laughed. "Yeah," he said, "at this point I'd settle for some straight commingling, myself," an extremely provocative remark that she was too distracted to take in at the time.

She gnawed on her own thoughts for twenty minutes. The headlights picked out trees along the highway; a grove of powdery-leaved olives lit up like silver as they passed. Got to finish that paper on Olive Leaf Spot, she thought briefly. She looked at her watch three times.

The third time Ramón said, "How did you hurt your hand?"

"What?"

"Your left hand," he repeated slowly and patiently, "on which you wear your watch. How did you cut it?"

"On a picture. Or the glass from a picture."

"What picture?"

"Just a photo."

Oncoming headlights lit his face for a moment; his luxuriantly curled upper lip was stretched into a line. "Okay. You're not going to talk about it."

"About what?"

He clicked his tongue in exasperation. "About Jewell dying!"
They were pulling into the station parking lot. "Oh. Well..."
She had half opened the door, but paused. "No, actually, I would
like to talk about it. It concerns you, in a way."

She considered how to begin. "Jewell had this photo," she
said, "but now it's gone. I guess the deputy took it, though I don't
know why. Of herself as a young woman, with a very good-looking young man, a boyfriend. The love of her life, I guess. At
least, he wasn't her husband, and she kept the picture next to her
bed." She knew how disjointed she was being; the lecture
seemed to have depleted her organizational abilities. "Anyway,"
she said with effort, "I think...I *think* he might be who we dug up
yesterday."

"*What?*"

Claire explained.

"So Jewell seemed to know someone who had also drowned
in the river—" Ramón recapitulated slowly.

"Not drowned," she said. "Not this one, anyway."

"*Not* drowned? Oh, because of the damage to the skull? That
could have happened afterward. In the river."

Claire didn't answer.

"You think somebody bashed this fellow on the head, don't
you?" he said. "Has it ever occured to you that you might have
just a teeny-weeny little preoccupation with murder?"

"Yes, it has, actually. But in this case what makes me suspicious is not the dent in the skull but the presence of the glasses.
They should have been torn off by the water."

"Maybe he had a what-do-you-call-it, an elastic strap." He
paused. "But let's leave that aside for a moment. This guy, this
true love of Jewell's. Was he wearing glasses in the photo?"

"No. You're pretty good at this cross-examination stuff."

"I went to a Jesuit college. Anyway, what's the connection?
Just because Jewell seemed upset when you talked about it—"

"Upset? She had a fatal heart attack! And she was holding the
photo just before she died! And she once said she had a fondness
for that part of the riv—"

"Wait a minute. If the photo was gone, how do you know she was holding it?"

"That's where the glass must have come from," Claire said impatiently. "It was all around the bed. I cut my hand when I was doing CPR—"

"CP—you mean, *you* found Jewell?"

Sudden silence.

"Well, yes, I found her," Claire said. "I told you she died."

"Yes, but not that you were the one to find her! And you proceeded to give a comprehensive lecture on mycorrhizae?" His tone was incredulous, and she thought, disapproving.

Okay, he thinks I'm a frozen bitch. And maybe I am. "I had to."

"We could have canceled…oh. I see." After a minute he said, "Close the door."

"What?"

"Close the door."

For some reason she complied. Without the truck's dome light it was suddenly very dark; the one sodium light at the corner of the lot had burned out months ago. "What are we doing?"

"We're going to sit here," he said, "and you're going to talk. About Jewell. Or this photo, if that's what interests you. Although I think that's just a diversion."

Ah, not a Jesuitical inquisition at all, but a Freudian one. Ramón was playing Miranda, she thought. But she must have said it out loud, because he exclaimed, "Miranda? What the hell has she got to do with this?"

"Nothing. Only you're not my goddamned therapist."

"Christ, I don't want to be your therapist! I want—" He stopped abruptly, and the silence swelled to fill the truck cab. Eventually he said, "I want to talk about Jewell. And who this guy might have been."

The hint of ambiguity, the possibility that he had gone into a mid-sentence skid and made a desperate ninety-degree turn, made her relax. She would not talk to an absolutely composed

Ramón, not when she herself was so…so decomposed. But she might talk to a disconcerted one.

"Even though," he continued, "I think your reasoning is pretty shaky. About the guy, I mean."

"I realize it's shaky. It's not exactly reasoning. A feeling."

He made a skeptical noise in the back of his throat that seemed to mean, In your case, they're probably the same thing. "Anyway," he was saying, "even if you were right, how would you know? You'll never be sure what Jewell was thinking. And you heard the coroner. They might be able to date the remains, but they'll never identify them. And you may never know who the man in the photo was, and you don't even have the photo! It's hopeless." He paused, then said cryptically, "You could have picked a better puzzle to distract yourself with."

"I'm going to get the photo back," she responded quickly, focusing on the one part of the problem that was soluble. "I have to call Deputy Simmons as soon as he goes off duty. And then, there's a daughter in Bakersfield. I don't know her name, but Simmons would have had to notify her. I'll show her the picture; maybe she'll know who it is."

"Okay," he conceded, "that would be something." After a moment he added, "Let me know if I can help. This isn't exactly my line of work, but I do still have some connections in Bakersfield."

He's humoring me, she thought, but the idea didn't bother her. She nodded, realized he couldn't see her, and said, "Yes, okay. Thanks."

She meant it as good-bye, but made no move to leave. Her eyes had adjusted to the night, which was not after all absolutely black: the ambient haze of the Valley diffracted moonlight into a watery fluorescence that spread over the foothills. The hills, as always, were like reclining bodies—but not feline, tonight; tonight they made her think of Jewell. The sparse pubic hair like dried grasses, the missing breast like a bulldozed hillside—a classic "disturbed" landscape, as the biologists said.

"Could I have some water?" she asked abruptly. Everyone

carried water in this climate. Ramón fished behind the seat and handed her a plastic thermos; she rinsed her mouth and spit out the window, apologizing. "I keep t-tasting it, cigarettes and lipstick. From the CPR, you know."

A heavy, warm arm settled around her shoulder. She didn't shrug it off this time, platonic or not. She was in no position to quibble about degree and kind of affection. "I was p-planning to borrow a record," she said, "of her, s-s-singing, as a g-girl...." Funny, her voice was wandering off on its own again.

His arm tightened a little, and she relaxed into it, but jumped when she felt his mouth on hers. Lightly at first, like an exhalation, a rescue breath. But she responded—which seemed to surprise him a lot, and her a little—and suddenly their mouths behaved like willful little animals and locked in a wet, fervent kiss that was hard to end.

Claire broke away first, and fumbled for the door handle. "Shit," Ramón muttered, looking straight ahead, "what made me think I could pull that off?" He turned back to Claire, who was already out the door and making for her car as if her life depended on it. "I'm sorry," he called across the parking lot. "I only meant to give you beer and pizza instead of lipstick and cigarettes."

When she drove up the mountain she tasted it all: beer, pizza, lipstick, cigarettes, one big casserole of lust and death.

6

CLAIRE COASTED DOWN her driveway and took in a big lungful of night air, sweet and cool, with a skunk chaser. Not a good star night; there was too much moon, and anyway her brain was zizzing like a Van de Graaff generator, making showers of shooting stars just beyond her field of vision wherever she looked.

Halfway up the hill she had turned on the radio and miraculously managed to pull in a signal that had bounced up the canyon from Cal Poly at San Luis Obispo, that had followed her clear across the Valley from tonight's lecture room. Sinead O'Connor was singing that she did not want what she hadn't got. A young woman's conceit; what else would you bother to want? Not to want what you *cannot* have, that was more like it. Something to strive for, anyway. Not to want Jewell to still be alive; not to want Ramón to...

To what?

What was that tonight—blip, or trend? Impulse, or truth revealed? Would they recover and revert to a comfortable, collegial friendship? Or proceed to a messy, furtive, ill-advised affair, ending in acrimony?

No contest, when posed like that. Her history showed an uncanny knack for selecting the stupid and self-destructive option, every time.

Luckily it wasn't up to her, but to Ramón, good old solid married Ramón, who could be counted on to exercise a little judgment.

Sinead had given way to a tune she hadn't heard before, yet another song of star-crossed lovers. As she went into the house, the chorus kept running through her mind:

> *Yesterday, I could have left you,*
> *Yesterday, I could have let you go.*
> *Yesterday, I could have left you,*
> *This morning, I don't know.*

Reduced to a song lyric, she grimaced, striding through the narrow hall and into the living room. She laid Jewell's photo album on the carpet and knelt before it.

It was an old-fashioned thing, its speckled green covers laced together with tasseled satin cord, its pages made of heavy black paper. As she lifted it a handful of black confetti sifted onto the carpet—the little triangles that had held the corners of photographs.

The first few pages she had seen: the Texas Tumbleweeds playing up and down the Valley, barn dance to county fair to nightclub, all labeled underneath in white ink with jokey captions. *We keep on tumblin'—Hanford, August, 1953. Cutting a rug—Buttonwillow, December, 1953.* Here was Jewell, holding hands with one of the band members, an undernourished young man with a pinched, Appalachian face. The shoulders of his fancy jacket poked stiffly above his own, while its cuffs stopped several inches short of his wrists. This must be Lefty, she thought, even before she saw the caption: *Jewell and Lefty—Modesto, June 1953.*

She turned another page—and caught her breath.

It was the photo. Or rather, the snapshot from which the photo had been enlarged. Jewell and what's-his-name—call him Harry, that was a neutral, old-fashioned name—shoulder to shoulder. Here you could see, even in black-and-white, that they were sitting under lush foliage by a river. Fifty yards behind them turbulent water splashed up against the far shore: the Kern presumably, pre-dam, untrammeled, in all its deadly glory. Jewell in halter top and capri pants, hands laced around her shins, and "Harry" in white T-shirt and jeans, leaning on one hand, looked absolutely contemporary, although the sun had set on that hot Valley day some forty-odd years ago.

But underneath this photo there was no neat white-ink label. Instead, a thick smear of white had a caption scratched into it in ballpoint: *Kern River, August 15, 1954.*

Claire read it in disbelief. Jewell, how could you! Identifying Lefty and not this man? In frustration she slipped the photo out of its corners to flip it over; the corners came loose and fluttered like moths to the floor. The back of the photo was blank.

With her botanist's hand lens she studied the photo for several minutes, traversing by centimeters the landscape of people and river, scanning the tiny faces for clues. Clues to love, to a kind of love about which she knew nothing, the kind that persisted through a lifetime of marriage to someone else, of kids and grandkids, so that you keeled over when reminded of your lover's death—

Reminded? Or informed?

Had Jewell not known that "Harry" was dead?

Maybe not, Claire realized suddenly. Maybe not until she, Claire, had delivered the news in her ham-handed fashion. Probably "Harry" had just been missing, presumed drowned, for... forty-five years? That was the number Jewell had mentioned, and that was when the "heart had gone out" of the music for her.

Maybe Jewell had even imagined that he might come back to her—a comforting fantasy of lonely old age.

Until Claire, with the best intentions in the world, had blundered into her kitchen this afternoon, telling Jewell that they had unearthed what were probably the remains of "Harry"—*and* hinting at a violent end. Not that drowning was peaceful; no, it left no marks, but it was a terrible, desperate death all the same.

Back to the picture. Along about the third minute of scrutiny she discovered something new: in the grass, beside the man's hand, a curve that might have been the wire rim of a pair of eyeglasses.

Eyeglasses! "Harry" must have removed them to have his picture taken, maybe to reveal his astonishing eyes! Claire kept imagining his eyes the color of seawater, the color of her father's eyes, she'd been told—she couldn't remember—and the color of her own. But she had the smoking spectacles, didn't she? They clinched it, didn't they? The man in the photo—Harry—was the skeleton by the river! It had to be.

She looked excitedly at the phone...and looked away. Bad idea, calling Ramón. Best to see how things shook out the next time they met. Probably neither of them would say anything; they would just resume their old relationship, a little bumpily at first—a car with a rough idle—then settle back into their smooth groove. Besides, it was too late to call Ramón; it was past midnight....

Past midnight. Damn! What with one compelling subject after another, she had forgotten Deputy Simmons.

She called, but she had missed that brief window during which he passed through the station on his way to bed, or a bar, or wherever Kern County deputy sheriffs headed when they got off at midnight. And now that she had the original of the photo, the call felt less urgent, and she was tired, and tomorrow was a work day. She would try again tomorrow, from the office.

On her way to her own bed, she flipped over one more page of the album—and blinked.

Because there it was again: the greenery, the river, the ridge,

everything but the leading lady and leading man. *Kern River,*
October 28, 1954, this one said. Claire stared at it, at the bump of
ridge in the background, at the crooked sycamore. She flipped
backward, then forward. It was exactly the same place, she was
sure.

But why take another photo of an undistinguished spot along
the river, two months after one that was nearly identical but far
more interesting?

There was something else about the photos. She studied the
second one again. Imagine it bare of greenery, with the river
reduced to a trickle. That distant humpbacked ridgeline would
remain unchanged. A teasingly familiar view...

Ah, she had it. It was the view from the orchard of Erasmo
Campos.

In the morning Claire headed west down the mountain, the
sheer granite road cut zipping by on her right, the river crashing
along far below her. The previous summer she had learned the
hard way about driving this road too fast—an abrupt, heart-stop-
ping lesson that had taken her a whole year to unlearn. Now she
was back to her former tire-smoking speed.

But at the small settlement of Riverdale, where the river split
and the road flattened and straightened like yarn unsnarling,
she scrupulously braked, because last month Tom Martelli, the
local police chief and an old friend, had himself popped her for
speeding.

"Don't you ever learn?" he had scolded her.

"Can't you make a living without running a speed trap?" she'd
countered. So he wrote her a ticket, and she was so furious that
she made no attempt at pleasantry, didn't even ask about his wife,
Marie, who had been deeply involved with Claire in the previous
summer's anti-logging efforts. Nor did she inquire about his
New Testament quartet of children: Matthew, Mark, Luke, and
Brittany, the lost apostle. She missed seeing Marie, who had returned to the insularity of her wifely and maternal chores.

This morning she looked for Tom's car as she poked along

past the cinderblock structure that housed his office and the vol-unteer fire department. Maybe he could shed some light on why a policeman might pocket a photograph from the scene of an accidental death.

But Tom's Blazer wasn't on the street. She'd have to stew over it herself.

She followed the river past the dam and the lake—no river plunged out of the Sierras without a dam and a lake—turning south before Parkerville and paralleling the foothills, through citrus and olives and vineyards. Finally she turned east again, and half a mile later pulled up behind the low brick building that was the Citrus Cove Agricultural Field Research Station.

The parking lot looked far less romantic under the coppery morning sun than it had by moonlight. But that dark spot prob-ably marked where they had sat last night. Like a semen stain on a sheet. Ramón's truck must leak. Suddenly she felt quite happy. She laughed at herself and the absurdity of it all, but she still felt happy. For some a shady riverbank, for others a grease spot on a parking lot. She began to sing without even thinking, that she'd be seeing him in all the old familiar places, startling the recep-tionist and taking the steps down to the lab two at a time—

Halfway down she stopped dead. Suddenly she had the an-swer to last night's question, and it sent an altogether unseasonal shiver along her spine.

Why take an identical photo of a spot along the river two months later?

In memoriam.

Sometime between August and October of 1954, "Harry" had disappeared, and Jewell had gone back to document the place they'd been happy.

Now if she could only find out who Harry was.

The phone rang just as she was fishing out Simmons's num-ber, and she felt a mixture of surprise, alarm, and pleasure at Ramón's voice.

"Thought I'd stop by late today, if that's all right."

"Sure." Her voice had more warmth than she intended; she

controlled it and added, "I'll probably be out in back with my marigolds," then hung up before she could say anything else stupid. Then she dialed Simmons, who sounded neither cordial nor casual, and became downright testy when she asked if he'd taken the photo.

"Why would I take a goddamn photo from some old broad?"

"I thought maybe…as evidence…"

"Evidence of what? You and the doc ganged up to tell me the old lady died of natural causes, remember?"

"Okay, okay," she said soothingly. "Maybe her daughter took it. Do you have her number, by any chance? What was her name?"

"Shelley somethin'. Yeah, I got it. Had to notify her after the old lady was pronounced dead."

"Do you suppose I could have it?"

There was a pause, while Simmons appeared to be trying to think of some reason other than pure spite why he shouldn't oblige Claire. "I guess," he agreed finally, and gave her a number for a Shelley Bonebrake Devine, Bonebrake evidently having been Jewell's married name.

Claire's moment of triumph at having coaxed that information out of Simmons faded to dismay when she realized that she still hadn't solved the mystery of the missing picture. In fact, she had deepened it, because if Simmons hadn't taken it, who on earth had? And when, and why?

"When" was easy. It had to have been while Claire was at the hospital with Jewell, because before that—before she died— Jewell must have been grasping it. While Claire was administering CPR and cutting herself on the glass, the photo itself must have been in Jewell's room—under the bed, in a corner, wherever it had landed. And it must have landed with some violence for the glass to shatter like that. Claire's mind skittered away from a dying thrash and spasm. Jewell had looked so peaceful, as if she had simply died in her sleep. Except that she *had* fallen off the bed.

But Shelley couldn't have come by while Claire and Jewell

were at the hospital. Simmons hadn't even notified her until after Jewell was officially pronounced dead.

Could a neighbor have taken the opportunity to rob the place? They knew where the key was....

To steal a photograph of two strangers? That didn't make sense.

Nothing about the photo's disappearance made sense. So she called Shelley Devine and left a message on the machine asking if she could stop by after dinner to return a photo album that Jewell had lent her, then let the problem run in the background while she turned her conscious mind to other, easier conundrums. Erasmo's peaches, for example.

She looked over her sketchy notes, and was immediately struck by a number that would have caught her attention yesterday if she hadn't been so distracted by Jewell. Nitrogen, 250 pounds per acre. Was that *right*? It was awfully high; normal applications were more in the 100–150 range. If correct, all that nitrogen would account for the trees' exceptionally luxuriant foliage, which could maybe add to the moisture content of the orchard, which could maybe increase the incidence of fungus.

...But what if the picture had broken and disappeared *before* Jewell died? What if someone had visited her after Claire? If someone else had spoken with her before her death, then maybe...

Maybe Claire hadn't killed her.

Ramón would say it was crazy to think—no, not think, feel— that she had killed Jewell, and he would be right. Ramón...oh, hell. She returned to Erasmo in a hurry.

Somewhere recently she'd seen an article about the effect of surplus nitrogen on the thickness of the fruit's skin, the cuticle. After thirty minutes of a futile cruise on the Internet, where she did learn a certain amount about nitrogen dioxide in smog, nitrogen poisoning in scuba divers, and manicure technique, she riffled randomly through her journals based on her memory of what the cover had looked like, and found it.

...Maybe the photo had disappeared earlier, and the glass

was from something else entirely. But how likely was that? The simplest, most parsimonious explanation was that the frame that had sat by Jewell's bed, the frame that was now missing, was what had ended up on the floor. But, not for the first time, the simplest initial explanation seemed to spawn the most complications....

The authors suggested that excess nitrogen created thicker fruit cuticle, which in turn created higher susceptibility to brown rot. That was the point.

She worked for a couple of hours with only occasional stray thoughts about Jewell, and Ramón, bought a sandwich from the vending machines, ate lunch at her desk, sat through a staff meeting, and around five o'clock wandered out the back to the field station's experimental plots and orchards, which nestled up against the yellow foothills of the Sierras. Her own little patch of sun-bright, lollipop-headed marigolds, which she had been growing as part of a field trial on nematocides and now was using for something else, seemed to generate their own heat, and she was reluctant to kneel among them.

But kneel she must.

She was pulling marigolds to purée when she heard Ramón's greeting behind her.

"Oh, hi. Listen," she said rapidly, "I think I may have figured out what's happening with Erasmo Campos's peaches."

"Great."

"It's a matter of too much nitrogen. He's applying over two hundred pounds an acre, and it's making his fruit more susceptible to fungus in a couple of ways."

"Mmmm."

"So we need to talk to him about cutting back next year."

"Right."

"And as long as you're here, do you want to help me set up an experiment to see if mycorrhizae are pathogenic to tumbleweed? I just got my boxes made—"

"Actually," he said, "I wanted to talk to you about something else entirely."

"Oh?" For the first time she really looked at him, and had to squint and look away again. His face radiated light, which meant that either his burnished skin was reflecting the bank of vibrant marigolds—or that she was in bigger trouble than she had thought. "What was that?"

He bent to squat next to her, and instantly clutched his back. "*¡Ay!*" he cried, in pain, sounding like *un mexicano auténtico* for the first time since Claire had known him. Without thinking she reached for his shoulder. "I'm okay," he muttered through clenched teeth, lowering himself cautiously to the ground. "I just have to remember to move slowly." A pause. "I think I may have aggravated it last night in the truck," he added deliberately. "That was an awkward position."

"Very awkward," she agreed gravely, after a yelp of surprised laughter. "In fact, I assumed that we were both going to forget about it. Or at least not mention it."

"Well, I won't mention it if that's what you want. But I certainly am not going to forget it. As a matter of fact I've been thinking about it with a great deal of pleasure for—" he checked his watch "—eighteen hours."

"Huh. I didn't detect such childlike pleasure at the time," she said. "As I remember, your comment was, 'Shit!'"

His turn to laugh. "Yes, well, it caught me off-guard."

"Off-guard? *You* kissed *me!*" Her voice rose, and they both swiveled their heads, reflexively scanning the immediate horizon. No one was visible, but you never knew who might be lurking among the orange and peach trees.

"Yes, I did," he conceded, "though it sort of got away from me. What I mean is, the reaction caught me off-guard—mine, and yours. Especially now. Are you angry?"

"What else can I be? You opened—could have opened, a can of—" What? Not worms; worms were a good thing here at the Ag Station. "Of rattlesnakes," she finished lamely, "given the circumstances."

"Circumstances?"

"Ramón, don't be a dope!" She ticked off on her fingers:

"One, we work together. Two—a big number two, like a log scale —you're married!"

"Yes. That's true."

She waited for some qualifying or clarifying clause to follow, but none came. All he said was, "Look—can we go into your office?"

The trip downstairs to her lab was silent and interminable, Ramón leading, Claire tasting sour disappointment the whole way. A familiar taste, one that she had been willing to live a life of total emotional isolation to avoid, and one that she had not been expecting now. One lousy little kiss had gotten to her more than she'd realized.

And it had just been a kiss, after all. No big deal.

Only it had felt like a big deal, and not just to her, she was pretty sure. Ramón had behaved like a hungry man, not like someone who was happy with the fare at home.

Ah, but maybe he was simply greedy. She watched him as he walked. A big, sleek guy, thickening a little around the middle, he didn't look like someone who denied himself much of anything. A large capacity for pleasure, she would have said—

She immediately banished *that* thought.

Finally he pushed open the door to her lab, which looked out on the scene they had just left: rows of trees—bright peaches and dark-leaved oranges—and beyond, the hills, bleached and wrinkled like old towels dropped in heaps at the foot of the mountains.

Like Jewell's bathrobe.

"You said I could have opened a can of rattlesnakes," he said as soon as the door closed behind them. "Did I? Open something, I mean."

She perched on a stool next to the lab bench, in front of the six "ant farms"—transparent plastic boxes, open at the top—the clever guys in the shop had delivered to her that afternoon. "How could you, given the circ—"

"Forget about the circumstances for a moment, and just tell me what you felt."

Oh, sure, make myself completely vulnerable. Mutely she began writing four-digit numbers on labels and sticking one onto each of the ant farms. But he was watching her closely, and pretty soon she said reluctantly, "Nothing I can't close again."

His full mouth and melancholy eyes began to lift into one of those unexpected smiles. "So you—"

The phone rang.

She grabbed it out of relief and uncontrollable reflex, and was glad she had. It was a woman's voice, almost inaudible. It turned out to be Shelley Devine: Claire was welcome to bring the album down after supper.

"Thanks. You didn't by any chance take a…a photo out of your mother's bedroom yesterday? What?" Claire concentrated hard on the whisper at the other end. Was Shelley fearful of being overheard? By whom? "No, I didn't think so. Okay, I'll see you tonight, then."

"Jewell's daughter?" asked Ramón.

"Yes. The sheriff's deputy says he didn't take the picture. And neither did she."

"Strange." He paused a moment. "Is it the picture itself that interests you? Or the fact that it disappeared?"

"Both," Claire told him. "But mostly the puzzle of its disappearance. Because I found the original of the photo."

"The puzzle." Ramón nodded, as if confirming an idea. "Can we return to the previous subject?"

"No," she said flatly, having recovered her equanimity during the interlude. Thank you, whispering daughter. She began filling the plastic boxes with a planting mix. It seemed that good old solid Ramón couldn't be counted on to behave sensibly after all. But no matter what he had to say—whether "I realize this was all a mistake," or, less likely, "I realize I love you and can't live without you"—it would ruin their friendship. "Sometimes things are better left unspoken, in my antediluvian opinion," she said.

"So the words are the snakes that have to stay in the can."

She nodded, filling the last plastic box, and poured a little more water into two petri dishes. The dishes held folds of damp paper toweling; she lifted a corner and peeked at the white root-tips beginning to sprout from the seeds. Good. They could wait one more day.

"Antediluvian is right," Ramón was saying. "Straight out of Genesis, in fact. And a dangerous way to live."

"Letting them out is just as dangerous. Look at Jewell."

"*What?*" he asked. She had just spit it out, but it distracted him. "What does that mean?"

"If I hadn't blathered on about the bones we found, she might still be alive."

"Claire, for Christ's sake! She was an old woman with a bad heart! You told me so yourself. Anyway," he added, "how do you know someone else didn't talk to her after your visit? And upset her?"

"And take the picture? I was thinking about that." She looked up from the lab book. "It's possible…. No. I just realized. That won't work."

"Why?"

"Because only the photo was gone. The glass was still there. If someone visited her and took the photo, it had to have been *after* it broke, that is, after Jewell's death." She stopped. "Or during it."

"During it?"

"Yes. A struggle of some sort—I've wondered why she was on the floor."

He clicked his tongue in exasperation. "You have a slightly wacky preoccupation with homicide, Claire. And you're grasping at straws with this whole missing picture–bones–Jewell's lover story, so you won't have to deal with your feelings. Of various sorts."

"Okay, maybe I am preoccupied by homicide," she answered defiantly, "with a certain amount of reason, given my history. And incidentally, I don't believe that all the snakes ever get out of the can. Also with a certain amount of reason. You only think they do, and live with a false sense of security—until the one that was hiding bites you on the ass." She checked her watch. "I have to drive down to Bakersfield to see Shelley Devine." She hesitated. "Friends?"

There was an unsettling pause before he nodded. "Friends. Of course. But remember—you can't keep a good snake down." He snickered at the sexual innuendo, and she grinned, too, but pushed open the door.

"Oh, Ramón," she added casually, "by the way. That original snapshot I found, of Jewell and her boyfriend? There's a pair of wire-rimmed glasses in it."

She had the satisfaction of seeing his startled look as she turned to walk down the hall.

7

CLAIRE DROVE PAST Tidwell Ginning and its mound of lint, growing like the great white whale himself breaching from the soil, then past the Bakersfield exits.

Ramón. Now there was an unexpected turn of events. He seemed to be telling her that he was available for...something, an affair at least.

Unless he merely wanted to hear her say that *she* was interested.

Or maybe he just wanted to talk. Like phone sex, but without the phone. That would figure. She'd finally found somebody who was good at talking, and that was *all* he wanted to do.

Well, that didn't interest Claire at all; either do it, or don't talk about it, was her feeling. She turned west toward Jewell's trailer park. Parking just before the axle-breaker, she walked into an apparently deserted court and faced Jewell's trailer.

Right or left? She approached the battered aluminum door of the trailer to the left of Jewell's, where a hand-lettered index card said M. KNAPP, and rang the bell. In a moment the frizzy-haired neighbor with the snakeskin arms appeared dimly behind the screen door.

Claire reintroduced herself—"friend of Jewell's"—and persuaded the woman to open the door to her.

"I wanted to ask you about yesterday afternoon," Claire said. "You didn't...borrow anything from her trailer, did you? I know you were good friends," she added hastily, trying to take the sting out of the implied accusation.

Myrtle—her name was Myrtle—took no offense. "No, honey, I didn't take nothin'. Jewell would have let me have anything, anyway. She were a good soul." Pink scalp gleamed through her sparse silver hair.

"Did you see anyone stop by after the deputy and I went with Jewell to the hospital?"

"Nope, not that I recollect."

Claire turned away in disappointment, though not surprise.

But Myrtle was still talking. "Seems as if I did see somebody earlier, though. Before you and the deputy come by."

"Before?"

"Yep, I b'lieve so. A car drove in here. That don't happen every day, so I took notice. And Jeanette and me—she's over in the next trailer, the yeller one—we remarked on it. Last night. Talkin' over Jewell and all."

"What kind of car?"

"Oh, it were a big thing, with big ol' wheels...not a truck, but kind of a Jeep, like. A four-by-four, that's what. My great-nephew Webb has one. This one was dark red. Mow-roon, I guess you'd call it—or is that Webster's? Anyway, a four-by-four."

"Did you see the driver?" Claire was fairly certain there was a limit to the number of questions she could ask before Myrtle rebelled, but evidently she hadn't yet hit it. And probably the irritation bar was quite high for someone whose life was as uneventful as Myrtle's.

"Nope. Jewell done let him in before I got to the window."

"Him," Claire repeated.

"Or her. Like I said, I never seed him."

"And he was here *after* I came the first time." Obviously, this chronology was crucial. Because if someone came between Claire's first and second visit, *that* was when the photo could have disappeared.

And that was also when Jewell died.

But how reliable was Myrtle's memory likely to be?

"Yep," Myrtle was saying. "I remember. Because not too many strangers come and go here in the Court, but yesterday you come, right in the middle of 'General Hospital,' and left before 'Oprah.' I remember her phone ringing in there somewhere, and then this Jeep thing came."

"How long was it here?"

"Oh, maybe a half hour. Oprah, she had just finished talkin' about a book by some colored gal. Then this Jeep left. And then you come back, and then the deputy, and then the ambulance, and then you come back again." She grinned, proud of her memory.

"Did you—" Claire began, but she had bumped up against the bar.

"That's all I saw," Myrtle said.

When Claire drove back toward Bakersfield, she saw, or imagined, a red sport utility vehicle on her tail.

The big houses on the bluff in northeastern Bakersfield looked down on the green coils of the Kern, tamed and sedate here in the city, and beyond that to the busy grasshopper oil pumps of the Kern River Field, whence had come the wherewithal for the big houses in the first place. A mile east of the bluff was another, smaller rise, where the houses were spacious but more modest, and looked down on the lowlands in between— East Bakersfield, largely a neighborhood of peeling California bungalows whose residents looked down on nothing, except possibly their neighbors.

Shelley Devine lived in this valley.

She grudgingly opened a barred security door—which would stand long after the fabric of the house had thinned and splintered—until she could see the photo album that Claire proffered. Then she let the door swing wide and welcomed Claire into a small living room littered with kids' toys. A TV chattered from another room, offering the unmistakable sound of cartoon explosions.

"Sorry," Shelley said. "Thought you was sellin' something." Only what Claire heard was "hot...ooo...ell...um." She had misinterpreted the furtive sound of the phone call. The situation was much simpler: Shelley couldn't, or didn't, speak above a whisper.

"Sounds like you're getting over a touch of something," Claire said sympathetically—then realized Shelley might have cried her voice out.

"Me? No, I'm fine."

"Oh. Well..." Holding out the album, Claire embarked on a short speech. "I was really sorry about your mother. I only met her recently, sort of by accident...." She trailed off when it became clear Shelley wasn't listening. Her small face wore an abstracted look, as if concentrating on a sound only she could hear. Listening for her husband to come home, maybe?

Claire had figured there was no Mr. Devine. Funny, she automatically assumed this when she met the mothers of young children. Men seemed to be so unevenly distributed through life, clumping here and there—like on the front page, and at work— but notably absent elsewhere. In the trailer parks of the elderly, for example, and in families with children.

Excepting Ramón, of course.

Claire cut to the chase and opened the album to the important snapshot. "This picture—" she began.

"She kept this album in her kitchen drawer," Shelley interrupted, if you could use such an aggressive word for her whispered utterances. Claire managed to interpret by watching her small mouth, a sort of half-assed version of lipreading. Small face, small mouth, fine features, hair frosted to that color that was no-color, Shelley Devine made almost no impression at all, except through the amount of effort the listener had to expend to hear her. Claire looked down at the picture of Jewell, and back at Jewell's daughter.

It was like matter and antimatter.

"Do you know who the man in the photo is?" Claire asked softly, involuntarily coming down to Shelley's volume, then repeated the question in a normal voice.

Finally Shelley paid attention, lifting the album out of Claire's arms and scanning the photo. "Isn't that the picture that used to sit by Mama's bed in the trailer?"

"Yes. Do you by any chance know who the man is?" Claire had a whole elaborate story ready, should Shelley ask why the hell she wanted to know, but there seemed to be a total lack of curiosity on the part of the other woman.

"Old boyfriend, I reckon. At least—" here she smiled "—Ma never dragged out the picture till Daddy died. Billy, turn that trash off," she continued in the same whisper. Claire looked around wildly, for a moment thinking the woman was talking to imaginary children, then realized the warning was directed toward the other room. Was this what passed in this house for yelling at the kids? "Good-lookin' fellow," Shelley said. "Maybe it was somebody from the band." With a shrug she handed the album back to Claire.

"You never actually asked her," Claire said.

"No. There's a lot I never asked her." She hesitated. "Kinda wish I had, now. But to tell you the truth, I was sorta embarrassed about her singin' and all. Seemed so tacky."

Tacky! Claire thought for a minute that her own mother would have approved of Shelley's neat hair and prim figure, and that Shelley might have taken comfort in Margaret Sharples's blameless facade.

But probably they would have found something else to dislike about each other.

"If you wanted to," the other woman was saying, "you could

maybe ask Johnny Treadle about it. He was the drummer in Ma's band and he used to be around a fair amount. Worked as a mechanic, mostly, but I remember Ma tellin' me a couple years ago he'd opened a store over on Edison Highway, by the rail yard. 'Treadle's Treasures.' Used records and such. Antiques, it says, but it's really just junk."

"Thanks. I'll try that. Do you suppose I could hang onto that photo, then? Just for a few days?" And the other photo, she thought, the later photo of the riverbank. She wanted that one, too.

"You can keep the whole album," Shelley said, or rather, mouthed. "At least for a while. I haven't figured out when I'm gonna get over to Ma's and clean out that junk, and where I'm gonna put it." She looked ruefully around her little room, which was already stuffed with stuff. "Maybe I'll sell some to Johnny."

Her attention had wandered, and once again she seemed to be listening for something. Her own voice? Claire wondered. Or her mother's?

On her way back to Parkerville, Claire detoured to cruise Edison Highway, a forgotten road out of town that paralleled railroad tracks headed for, inevitably, Edison. The highways out of Bakersfield all bore utilitarian, informational names, signaling both route and destination in a homely economy of language: Rosedale Highway, Stockdale Highway, Edison Highway.

She drove past Treadle's Treasures without recognizing it, then backtracked when she realized she must have gone too far. Yes, there it was, on the south side of the highway, a few doors down from the boarded-up remains of the Lucky Spot, identifiable from faded script outlining a neon skeleton. Jewell had reminisced about the Lucky Spot, had made a big deal out of having played here. Well, forty-five years could do a lot of damage to anything, and in the case of the Lucky Spot, that damage appeared to be fatal.

Treadle's Treasures, however, looked mildly interesting: lots of garish old record jackets in the window—maybe even the Texas Tumbleweeds. Definitely worth a visit, on Saturday, perhaps. Maybe she'd ask Ramón if he wanted to go along.

Oh, right.

Call Ramón? At *home*? What if his wife answered?

Her eyes flicked to the rearview mirror, where there was another sport utility vehicle. Red.

Well, of *course* there was a sport utility vehicle; they were only the most popular vehicle in the Valley, in California, probably in the country. And what if she *did* get Ramón's wife? Ramón had a wife. *Ramón had a wife.* Claire had better train herself right now to deal with that fact.

On the plus side, his wife might not be home.

So after Claire got home, and after she drank a glass of wine, and after she once again reviewed the particulars of her brother's California itinerary—after, in short, she had stalled in every conceivable way that didn't actually require work—she did call Ramón.

And got his wife. Miranda's voice—the fact of Miranda—made Claire flush a little, but she managed a normal request to speak with Ramón. Hell, she thought as she waited, I might just as well have spent the night rolling with the guy if I'm going to feel like this. What a waste of guilt. Not that it wasn't a renewable resource.

It was Ramón who lowered his voice when he heard hers. This is what it would be like, she thought. Hushed voices, terse conversations: where, when, with what excuse? I'd be terrible at it. I can't keep a secret.

"Want to go to a junk store in Bakersfield?" she inquired brightly.

"What?"

She explained.

"Sure, why not?" he said finally. "Though I feel like I'm encouraging an unhealthy fixation."

"Don't worry, I'd go anyway. Your conscience is clear."

"Hardly," he answered, and hung up.

8

~~~~~~

JOHNNY TREADLE WAS PALE and lumpy, like some unpalatable root crop from a northern clime—a really large root crop, a State Fair winner. He was a big man, maybe six-foot-three, and 250–plus pounds, with a few strands of what had probably been sandy-colored hair scraped across his scalp. He goggled with surprise at Claire. Probably can't believe he's got a customer, she thought. He was in his early sixties, but his size made him formidable still.

He turned out to be a cream puff, however, all but collapsing when Claire told him why she was there.

"Jewell's *dead*?" he repeated, holding onto the glass display case full of guitar-shaped objects: ashtrays, saltshakers, chip-and-dip sets. How anyone could make a living with these places remained one of life's profound mysteries.

"Honey," he yelled, "Jewell *died!* Jewell Scoggins! I mean Jewell...what was her married name?"

"Bonebrake." A woman appeared suddenly beside Claire, seeming to materialize from behind a floor-to-ceiling display of record album covers in no particular order: Buck Owens, Elvis, the Mormon Tabernacle Choir, Donny and Marie, Black Sabbath. The woman was trim, pretty, with a bouffant flip and careful makeup, wearing a coordinated slacks-and-pullover ensemble in beige and lime. Her thin lips were carefully colored a bright perky red, but they didn't seem to move when she spoke. "Married Chet Bonebrake, from up in Oildale."

"She was fine," he said plaintively. "When I saw her—"

"—about three years ago," his wife finished swiftly. Claire assumed she was his wife, anyway. She had the proprietary air. "That was the last time we saw her." She spoke in the first-person plural, also a definitive clue. She evaluated and dismissed Ramón in a single glance: another Mexican. "And she was looking bad. Pretty much of an old wreck." She touched her pert hair with a certain satisfaction. "She had a bad heart, I heard."

"It was her heart," Claire acknowledged, fighting an urge to push her fist into the smug, perfectly powdered face.

"It don't seem possible," Johnny said, still sounding dazed. "I was just...she was so...when we were young, she was more alive than anyone I've ever known." His wife's mouth set in a hard line and she faded back into the aisles, behind a player piano that was painted a high-gloss purple.

Claire let Johnny recover from his initial shock, then launched into a story about doing a little research on Jewell, maybe putting together a memorial. Ramón drifted off to her right and began leafing through a bin of 33-rpm records. "So," Claire went on, hauling out the photo album and spreading it open on the counter, "I was wondering if you recognized this man. I thought he might have been a fellow band member."

Johnny looked at the photo for a long time. When he lifted his face he had the blank, desperate expression of someone trying to remember something—*anything*. It was a kind of panic Claire had seen on the face of a friend's father with Alzheimer's.

But then his face relaxed. "Oh, sure, I know this boy," he said. "Only he wasn't in the band. What was his name? Something goofy. Hubert? Rupert?"

"Elliot," came a female voice from behind the player piano.

Claire gave an involuntary start.

"Elliot!" his wife called again.

"Elliot, that was it!" Johnny agreed. "That there's Elliot! He was a college boy from back east somewheres. Worked summers for some little independent outfit—Gold Star? No, no, Western, I think—as a petroleum engineer." There didn't seem to be anything wrong with Johnny's long-term memory, Claire thought, but then that was how it was with her friend's father. His childhood memories were evidently stored in a different part of his brain than last year, or yesterday, or ten minutes ago. "Oh, yeah, Jewell was crazy about him. I remember the night they met, out at the Four Queens in Taft. She was going out with Lefty Tatum in the band," Johnny continued, "but then this other feller showed up. Yep, after that first night he come to every set when we wasn't on the road. Of course, Elliot was a Jew."

Ramón made an inarticulate sound. *Of course?* But from the corner of her eye, Claire could see that he never broke rhythm as he flipped through the albums. *Thuck, thuck, thuck.*

Johnny cocked his head. "Oh, I got nothin' against Jews, never did. Tell you the truth, prob'ly never met one, at least to know it, before this feller. But back in those days, things was a little different. Wasn't too many of 'em out in the oil fields, for one thing. And I remember hearing Jewell tell one time how her friend was tired of washin' yellow paint off his gear."

"Yellow paint?" Claire repeated blankly.

"Yep. I said, what did they paint? Stars, she said. Maybe it was the boys from Gold Star playin' pranks, I said, but she said, no, they wasn't that kind of star. And there was swastikas, too.

"Anyway, we was all just waitin' fer Jewell to dump Lefty. Waitin' for the explosion, you know, 'cause Lefty, he had a temper on him. But I guess Jewell wasn't sure how things was going to work out with this feller. She was nuts about him, near as I could tell, but she wasn't so sure about him. But then one night... Well, look, c'mon outside for a minute."

The three of them stepped out onto the sidewalk and faced east, toward the rail yard, and beyond, the smog-dimmed Tehachapis where they curved southwest from the bottom of the Sierran spine.

"Wouldn't think, to see it now," Johnny said as a lone car cruised by, "but back then this street was hoppin'. And right down there—" pointing to the left "—was the Lucky Spot. It's boarded up now, but man, it was *the* place back in the fifties. And the Tumbleweeds was the house band for years, when we wasn't on the road.

"So like I was sayin', one night—would have been 'fifty-three or 'fifty-four—we had just come off the road...."

The band had been on the road for a month—just locally, up and down the Valley, caravanning in Lefty's Ford and Johnny's Chevy convertible. Jewell wrote Elliot postcards telling him where they'd be, but he only showed up twice, when they were in Buttonwillow out near Taft. She knew how hard it was for him not to have a car, but she still scanned the crowd, sick with nervousness and anticipation, in every town, and when the band finished touring and came back to Bakersfield to resume their weekly gig at the Lucky Spot, she was a little angry.

After their last set she sat at a front table, drinking a Coke and waiting to see if he'd show up. A few feet in front of her the couples were dancing to the jukebox, leaning into each other so their rumps stuck out—"like baboons," her mother would sniff. The hem of someone's twirling skirt brushed her leg.

"Mind if I join you?"

She looked up hopefully, but it was only Lefty.

"It's a free country," she said, making her voice indifferent despite the cold spreading through her belly. He'd been drinking all through tonight's gig, and now he was swaying a little on his feet and itching for a fight.

"Maybe a little too free," he said loudly, wasting no time. "Maybe this country's a little too free, with kikes goin' out with white women, and—"

Here Johnny faltered. "I can't repeat what he said. Filthy language." Claire's mind supplied the words as it had the other unspoken details. Prick. Cunt. Fuck.

"You're drunk as a ol' weasel, Lefty. Go sleep it off," Jewell said. She kept her voice calm, but she felt like he'd slapped her—which he had done, a few times.

"No, I wanna know. Does it feel differnt to a white man's? Bein' as how it's kinda pruned an' all."

How would I know, she wanted to say; all I ever done is feel your ol' wad through your pants, back when you begged me to. And Elliot and me, we never. But just then Johnny came up.

"Lefty, what in hell you up to, usin' that language?" he said. "C'mon, ol' son, let's take a walk." He clamped Lefty's upper arm and pulled.

"No, lis'n, Johnny," Lefty said, shaking him off. "I wanna know. Does it feel differnt to a white man's?" Johnny was tugging at him, but Lefty was planted. "Maybe all us white boys...maybe that feller Hitler...all us white Amer'cans who risked our lives to save them Hebes, maybe we shoulda just waited. Till he finished the job." He was starting to crumple. "You know, Johnny? All us...us..."

"Us white boys, yeah, Lefty, I got it. C'mon, brother, let's just step outside for a minute. Sorry, Jewell," Johnny called, as the two of them steered toward the back door. "He's just a little drunk, is all."

Jewell finished her Coke and asked Velma to bring her a beer, something she rarely did, but she was shaky. Those words. What did they have to do with what she felt for Elliot? What had Lefty meant, "pruned"? Not that she was likely to find out, she thought, grinning as the beer hit her; Elliot hardly touched her. Maybe she disgusted him, with her hillbilly ways and her crude speech—and him hardly trying to see her in the whole month she was gone.

That wasn't fair, she knew; he had to depend on his friend for a ride...but then, why was that? Why didn't he buy a car? He claimed he had to save all his money to return to college, but still, a car. You had to have a car.

"Hi." Elliot himself, sliding in across from her. He squeezed her hand.

"Hey." She stayed cool, proud of herself at appearing so unconcerned. She'd actually worked herself up into kind of a state by now, feeling none too good toward him. Why didn't he declare himself? Were they going out, or weren't they? How was she supposed to deal with Lefty if she didn't even know where they stood?

"Since when do you drink beer?"

"Since I growed up." She knew it was "grew," but let it be.

Silence. He released her. "Let's go outside," he said. "It's starting to cool off."

Side by side, not touching, they walked out into the soft night. Jewell was light-headed from the beer and stumbled on the threshold; he caught her by the elbow, then let her go. Johnny saw them leave, then stepped outside and watched.

Here Johnny said, "I wasn't spyin' or nothin', just sort of keepin' an eye on Jewell. I used to worry about her. A woman alone in some of the places we played..." Claire nodded and thought, He was in love with her.

Their side of the street was bright with neon: the Lucky Spot behind them, up the street the Sad Sack with its usual group of sniggering boys on the sidewalk, egging each other on; down the street, Pete and Annette's Café. Two feet in front of them the cars flashed by on Edison Highway. But just beyond the headlights was the dark rail yard, the boxcars silhouetted against an iridescent night sky, and way off in the distance were the black mountains.

"That's where we come through," Jewell said, pointing. "That's the Ridge Route."

Elliot stood behind her and sighted along her arm. "So that's where the Joads stopped and looked down into the promised land."

"The Joads? They out at Taft?"

"No, silly," he teased, and she flushed. "The Joads. From The Grapes of Wrath. *The book."*

"Ain't never—haven't never, read it."

"Ah, you should. It's about your people."

"My people?" she flashed, stung by the condescension. "You mean the Okies? Then whyn't you say so?" From the north a train was coming; she could hear it rolling toward them like a quake.

"I didn't—"

"Whyn't you jes' call me Okie and I'll call you—" she paused for a second, then pronounced it defiantly "—kike, and we'll stand even?"

"Sweetheart—" His face twisted, the word torn out of him.

"I ain't your sweetheart!" By now she had to shout above the train, which was roaring into the yard. And then the engineer hit the air brakes—a horrible shrill squeal, like a hundred pigs being slaughtered, that made her want to clap her hands over her ears. But for some reason she clapped them over Elliot's instead, and in an instant he had pressed his hands over her ears.

They stood that way, hands cupped around each other's faces, long after the train had passed through and rumbled off to the south.

<hr>

"So then I knew," Johnny said simply, bringing them back to the present: to the quiet rail yard, where a train hardly ever passed; to the deserted storefronts and empty street—and along the horizon, the same ridgeline Jewell had pointed to. Behind Claire, Ramón expelled his breath in a long sigh. Incorrigible romantic, she thought, then realized she'd been holding her breath, too.

"So what happened to them?" Ramón asked.

Johnny shrugged, and looked troubled again, as if something else had eluded him. "I figured they were gonna git married," he said slowly. "But one day...one day this Elliot character just stopped showing up. I don't know if they had a fight, or what.

Jewell wouldn't talk about him, at least to me, so maybe they did. But—say, let's go back in, it's a mite cooler inside."

A very small mite, it turned out to be, with the ancient fans clattering from the corners. The purple paint on the player piano was so shiny that it seemed almost to bear a sheen of sweat. Where had it come from and how had it made its way here?

"If you want to know the real inside story," Johnny continued, pulling out the bench, settling his bulk deliberately in its center, "you oughta talk to Diana Dare. She and Jewell, they were pals."

"Who?"

"Diana Dare. You ain't never heard of Diana Dare, the Singing Cowgirl?" he said to Claire's blank face. "She starred in about thirty movies with the Laredo Kid. You ain't never heard of the Laredo Kid?"

"He sounds familiar," she lied.

"I remember him," Ramón broke in. "Probably before your time."

"Where would we find this…singing cowgirl?" Claire asked.

"Honey," he called, "where does Diana Dare work?"

"Goldschmidt's," came the voice from the back of the store— what did she *do* back there? And where exactly was she, anyway? "Perfume counter."

"There you go." Johnny shook his head fondly and offered a bit of a smile, exposing seed-corn teeth. "Peg knows everything. Me, I can't remember my own name."

"You remember 1954 pretty well," Claire noted slyly.

"Oh, yeah. I remember them years, no problem."

"You still play some music?" What was the path that led a person to this conglomeration of unwanted, discarded, unnecessary junk? Did it parallel the path that led Jewell to her trailer park on the Kern, or had the lines meandered a bit, occasionally intersected? Still, Jewell had been singing up to the day she died, singing with lust and fervor, and it was difficult—no, impossible—to imagine this mass of protoplasm drumming. Or even seated at a drum set.

"Naw. I ain't played in years. I was a mechanic till a few years ago, then—" He stopped abruptly. "The work got too hard for me," he continued, "and I opened up this place. Always had collected this memorabilia and I figured, hey, why not make a hobby into a business." He gestured toward some shelves loaded with bric-a-brac. "One thing led to another. And now that Buck's opened his Crystal Palace, I reckon the Bakersfield Sound's gonna be back on the map. Say, y'all ever hear a record of the Tumbleweeds?"

"No!" Claire said eagerly. "Do you have any?"

"Got 'em all," he answered, pride in his tone. "We only made six sides. Three forty-fives. Paid for with our own money. I believe we would of got an offer from somebody, maybe even Capitol, but Jewell stopped singin' too soon. We weren't nowhere without her. No, they ain't in the rack," he said, as Ramón started off toward a section of bins holding 45s. "I got my own private stash in the back. Hang on."

He got to his feet with effort and disappeared—in a different direction, Claire noted, from the way his wife had gone. The place was large and badly lit, and followed no discernable sense of order the farther you got from *axis mundi*, the glass case of guitarabilia. In a moment he came back clutching three little jackets. He spread them across the glass counter with a sweep of his giant palm. "Take your pick."

"Which is the best?" Ramón asked.

"Prob'ly this one. Jewell was in real good voice on that session, and the rest of us even got through 'Tumbling Tumbleweeds' on the B side without embarrassing ourselves too bad." He shook his head. "It was our signature tune, I guess you'd say. But it's a hard number, 'cause of the harmony. No matter how many times we rehearsed, and Jewell went over our parts with us, it always took us about a verse to sort ourselves out. Lefty, he was always completely sure of himself, but he had a tin ear. There was no tellin' where he'd come in. Don, our bass player, had him a voice like a bullfrog. And me—well, I kinda sung in a whisper. Jewell always said I was 'true but shy'—"

He halted suddenly, and stooped to fiddle with an old hi-fi in a Danish modern cabinet behind the register.

"So Jewell always wanted us to drop the song," he continued in a muffled voice. "I remember her and Lefty arguing about it. 'It's the theme song for the Texas Tumbleweeds!' he'd say, and she'd say 'Yeah, and it's a real purty song, when the Sons of the Pioneers sing it,' meaning, we wasn't no Sons of the Pioneers, and we couldn't hit the parts. 'But it's slow and kinda old-fashioned,' she'd say. 'People wanna hear somethin' they can dance to. Somethin' with that new shuffle rhythm.'

"'You tryin' to turn this band upside down, Jewell!' Lefty'd say, and that would be the end of it. Funny, he'd take her talkin' back when it was about music, 'cause we all knew she was the best. She was the *best*," he repeated, slipping a licorice-black platter out of its sleeve and bending to fit it onto a fat spindle like a toilet paper roll.

Claire and Ramón examined a yellowed color photograph of the Tumbleweeds that Johnny had taped to the underside of the glass counter. Jewell, bright red lipstick outlining her five hundred-watt smile, gold satin shirt gleaming; the boys in *their* satin shirts, leaning in toward her; Johnny just a kid—rawboned and sandy-haired—but towering over the others.

"She made those shirts," Claire said. "She told me—" And then she stopped, because there was Jewell's clear contralto.

Oh, there's no fool like an old fool,
None so blind as those who will not see.
I know that we should part, but inside me beats the heart
Of an old fool.

Even through the scratchy recording and the tinny speakers, Jewell's voice rang out like a bell. Impassioned but youthful, she was like a sweeter, lighter Patsy Cline. The notes floated effortlessly on the breath, shaped with a delicate vibrato. It was artless, yet absolutely in control.

Claire was speechless.

"Wow," Ramón said. "I'm not crazy about country, but even I can tell that's a voice in a million."

"Yep," Johnny said. "We thought she was gonna make us a million, too. And I do believe she would of, if she'd stuck with it. But after this Elliot character left her, she just up and quit."

"'The heart went out of it,'" murmured Claire.

"Reckon so," Johnny said. He looked around at his racks of records. Well, she thought, he probably *has* sold thousands of records—just not the way he planned.

Johnny flipped the 45 over and played the B side—"Tumbling Tumbleweeds." He was right, the band was mediocre. The Weeds would definitely have been relegated to forgettable backup band status pretty quickly, Claire thought. What had Janis Joplin's band been called? She couldn't remember.

"Do you have any of these for sale?" she asked.

"I've got one or two I could part with. Hang on." He disappeared into the back of the store and returned with two 45s. "That's okay," he said, as she pulled out her wallet, "you just let me know when that memorial is gonna be, hear?" He turned to a befuddled-looking customer who seemed to have wandered in by mistake.

"I guess you're going to have to organize a memorial," Ramón said over the top of Claire's Toyota. They had opened its doors and were now waiting for the interior to cool down, or at least air out, a little.

"I'm sure her daughter—" She stopped. Actually, Shelley had seemed so distracted, by shock or by disposition, that she might not be planning *anything*. She'd regret that later. Claire and her brother Charles had been so clueless as to what to do when Margaret died that they'd defaulted to the generic minimum—cremation and a drive-thru Unitarian service—telling themselves it was what Margaret would have wanted. And maybe it was, but it had turned out not to be what Claire had wanted. It had left her feeling empty and guilty.

She reached inside the car for her telephone, called

Goldschmidt's Department Store, and, miraculously, was connected with Diana Dare herself, who had an hour for "lunch" at five, and would be happy to meet Claire for dinner and talk about the old days. Diana said she'd stop by her house on the way and pick up some old photos.

Five o'clock was almost two hours away. "I was thinking," Ramón said. "I should really visit my cousin Yolie. I've been worried about her, and I'm one of the few people she'll see. Maybe you could take me over there, and drop me off while you meet the Singing Cowgirl. Yolie might be willing to meet you, too."

"Might be willing?" Not a phrase commonly used for family introductions in these parts.

"Well, she's a little paranoid," Ramón explained carefully. "With some reason, maybe."

Cousin Yolie...oh, yes, the skeletons in C.C. Tidwell's closet. "Is Yolie—*ouch!*" She had forgotten to cover her steering wheel from the heat, and it seared her sore palm, which kept bleeding anyway, like a stigmata. "Is Yolie by any chance the reporter who was fired for writing about Tidwell?"

"Oh, you knew about that. Yeah, that was Yolie. Yolanda Covarrubias, the family favorite—up until then."

"It happened right before I got out here," Claire remembered, "and people were still talking about it. But I would have thought with three graduate degrees, *you'd* be the family favorite."

He slid in beside her. "Two and a half, actually. I left business school before I actually got my M.B.A., and then I was like a ball rolling down a flight of stairs, as far as the family was concerned. Comparative lit, *whump*—"

"No points for Yale?" She'd have to tell Charles that. Or maybe not. Charles was not one to poke fun at his sacred cows, and he considered Yale, which had conferred his graduate degrees, the holiest of holies.

"Maybe, but a big *whump* for uselessness," he said. "Coming back here, *whump*. Studying agronomy, *whump*, *whump*. Working for Kaweah County, *whump* at the bottom of the landing.

Miranda—" He stopped and looked at Claire, but went on with the thought. "Miranda thought she'd landed in the cellar, too. She thought she was marrying a respectable East Coast academic, not a grubby San Joaquin Valley farm adviser."

Well, I'm glad he can talk naturally about his wife in front of me, Claire thought. I guess we're back to colleagues. "Which way to Yolie?"

"Can I use your phone? I'd better call first."

Evidently he got an answering machine. "Yolie," he said sternly, "pick up the phone! It's Ray. I know you're there. Yo—oh. Hi. I wish you'd answer your goddamned—yeah, I know, I know." There was a brief exchange. "All right," he said to Claire. "She says it's okay. Make a U-turn."

"I don't know for a fact that Yolie was fired, you know," he said as they drove. "The paper said they were just restructuring. It's Yolie's interpretation that she was fired for writing nasty things about Tidwell, which God knows is the kind of craven thing they'd do, but she's also a little paranoid—a little!" He interrupted himself. "No, she's nuts! Wait till you see her house. She's really become like one of those JFK assassination buffs, absolutely obsessed with this case, and convinced that her own life is in danger."

"Maybe it is."

"What? *Et tu?*"

"Well, I don't know what I think about JFK or MLK—*or* C.C., for that matter—but I don't dismiss the suspicions out of hand," Claire told him. "And as for Yolie, it's not unheard of for a reporter to be murdered."

"In Latin America, maybe—"

"In the Yew Ess of Ay," she said, feeling a distinct empathy for Yolie, whom Ramón was probably labeling a hysterical female.

Ramón shook his head, but all he said was, "You two should really hit it off, then." They drove the streets of Bakersfield for almost twenty minutes before he said, "This is it."

"*Here?*" Claire gaped in disbelief. "It looks like a crack house!"

On a quiet street of neat, modest homes with tended yards and gardens, Yolie's house was a bizarre eyesore: a Spanish-style house that had been converted into a fortress. A high, spiked, wrought-iron fence topped with razor wire circled the whole—compound, there was no other word for it. I should have known, she thought, that Ramón wouldn't call someone crazy lightly.

They stopped by the front gate, where Ramón pressed the button on the intercom. "Yolie? It's Ray. And my friend, Claire."

Claire saw a curtain move behind an iron window-grate, and then the buzzer sounded and they pushed open the gate and started up the walk. Claire looked around at the dry, bare yard and thought, Everything about this house is bolted, even the weeds.

"No pit bulls?" she wondered, too late.

"Oh, there's a dog." Ramón rubbed his elbow reminiscently. "Sometimes more than one. She must have put them inside, because she knew we were coming."

Opening the door—or rather, doors, there seemed to be several—was a production. They heard three locks being unlatched, and then one by one the layers swung open, to reveal...a perfectly normal-looking young Latina wearing jeans and a man's shirt, with long hair brushed back into a neat French braid. Not for the first time, Claire thought that homeless women had an edge over homeless men, in grooming only, because they didn't grow beards. If Ted Kaczynski had been female, he would have looked far less like a caricature of a mad anarchist.

Not that Yolie was either homeless or Ted Kaczynski, of course.

She admitted Claire to the sanctum, and Ramón enveloped her in a big, comforting hug. She clung to him for more than a minute. Claire could certainly imagine wanting to cling to Ramón, but she realized suddenly that this might be Yolie's first social interaction—and certainly her first physical contact—in a long time, maybe since Ramón's last visit.

A dog—it sounded like only one, albeit a whopper—was

roaring from a distant corner of the house, and every now and then there was a loud thump, as it hurled itself against a door. Yolie had boarded up her windows from the inside, very neatly, with plywood cut to the various window sizes and painted the same creamy white as the walls. Evidently only the window by the door, where the curtain had twitched, could still admit light, and that was barred with heavy iron. Towers of paper—newspapers, magazines, Internet printouts, and just plain paper, reams and reams of it—leaned against every wall. The towers were neat, however, and had a sense of purpose about them. Yolie was clearly not simply squirreling away at random. There was a decided method to whatever her form of madness.

"Let me look at you." Ramón held his cousin at arm's length. "You're thin," he told her, scowling. It was a formidable scowl, and Claire cringed in empathy. "Are you eating?"

Yolie shrugged. "I've got my garden out back, and I get groceries every now and then." Her voice was gruff from disuse. "I was having them delivered, but then I decided it was too easy to slip something into the bag. *Tick-tick-tick,*" she added for clarification. "Though sometimes I think it would be worth it for a pizza with the works, hold the anchovies. And the *plastique.* Pleased to meet you," she said in Claire's general direction. "You a government agent like Ray?"

Claire started, but then saw Yolie's mouth twitch. "I guess so," she replied. "Cooperative farm extension agent, anyway."

"University of California," Yolie said. "A major arm of the corporate fascists."

"I couldn't agree with you more." Claire grinned, and Yolie nodded, as if Claire had passed the humor—as opposed to humor*ing*—test.

"So what's new?" asked Ramón.

"I've been looking at Tidwell's early career," Yolie said. "Some pretty interesting stuff. C'mon into the office." They followed her down a hall.

Big Brother, Claire thought suddenly. That was Janis Joplin's band. Big Brother and the Holding Company.

The office, once again, was packed but organized. Fax, photocopier, crosscut shredder, and an array of fancy computer equipment on the desk. Thank God for technology, Claire thought, recalling the printouts in—what would you call it? certainly not a living room. Yolie could probably do a lot of her research online if she didn't want to go outside, like to the library.

She bent to open one of the file cabinets lining the wall, and her long glossy braid flopped over one shoulder. "I got some pretty interesting personnel records from his first employer after he came out from Oklahoma in the early fifties. He was a roustabout for a little wildcat outfit over near Lost Hills. Western Oil. They sold out to Texaco, and I finally tracked down the old records—what?"

Claire had made a muffled exclamation, and Yolie turned to her.

"Nothing. We just heard about somebody else who worked for Western Oil in the fifties, that's all. Coincidence."

"Huh," said Yolie. "C.C.'s life is full of coincidences. And they all break his way. Like the coincidence that brought Doug Collins's Piper Cub plunging down into the Tehachapis just after he refused to sell C.C. half of Kern County. And the coincidence that the newspaper was downsizing just as I began my series. See, here," showing Ramón a photocopy, "this is Tidwell's record. Hired in 'fifty-three, quit in late 'fifty-four. And—"

"Ramón, Yolie," Claire interrupted, "sorry, but I should probably be heading over to meet Diana Dare."

Yolie walked her to the door and peered through the window before she began the rigamarole with the locks. "He's not there," she said. "He seems to have taken the day off. He usually parks across the street." Maybe "he" lives there, Claire started to say, whoever he was, but Yolie was still talking. "He'll sit and watch the house for hours. And follow me, if I go to the store, or the library. But he never threatens me or anything—just watches. So far. So you should be okay."

"See you in—what? An hour and a half?" Ramón said.

"Sounds right." She had the feeling he didn't want to hang

out with Yolie for too long. "She only has an hour break. But if it's going to be longer, I'll call, okay?"

Yolie gave her a business card with no business mentioned. Well, what would she put? Conspiracy theorist? "I screen my calls, so if you get the machine, keep talking."

Ramón, whose protective instincts were now in overdrive, caught Claire by the elbow for a moment. "Well…be careful," he told her gruffly, and gave her a brotherly peck on the cheek.

9

CLAIRE WASN'T EXACTLY expecting buckskin and six-shooters, but she wasn't expecting haute couture, either. The Singing Cowgirl, who met her at the Red Lion Motel in slinky dress, chunky jewelry, bottle-blond hair, and long red nails, was extremely chic and well maintained, and looked a good twenty years younger than Jewell, whose contemporary she must have been.

She also smelled.

That is, she was heavily doused in this month's fragrance. Claire sneezed violently as they were seated in the faux-Tudor restaurant, and twice more as molecules of "White Linen" or "Pink Lady" or whatever quickly bonded with all the oxygen in the immediate vicinity.

"Summer cold?" Diana asked sympathetically.

"Allergy," Claire croaked, as she rummaged in her bag, fairly certain she had no tissues, wondering how she could avoid blowing her nose on the linen napkin.

Diana handed her a little packet of Kleenex, also scented. "Always carry it this time of year. I have problems when they start spraying the cotton." The Oklahoma in her voice had been as ruthlessly suppressed as her original hair color, but in both cases the roots showed a little. "So you'd like to hear about the old days," she said. "I get historians and journalists from time to time—they're all going to write books, but they never do." She set a photo album she'd been carrying on the table. Claire eyed it greedily.

"I'm not writing a book," Claire explained. "I'm just trying to put together a memorial service for Jewell Scoggins. Sorry," she said hastily, remembering Johnny's reaction. "You may not have heard. Jewell died a few days ago."

But Diana remained perfectly composed. "Didn't know she was still alive, to tell you the truth. Haven't thought about her in years. We were great friends back in the old days, but once she stopped singing and got married, well, my career was just beginning to take off, and we drifted apart."

Diana talked for a bit about the thirty-odd movies she'd made with the Laredo Kid, and showed Claire movie stills and gauzy head shots from her fifteen minutes of Hollywood fame. "But that's not what you came to talk about," she said abruptly.

"No, but it's fascinating. Maybe *you* should write the book." Claire pulled out her album and laid it on the table, well away from the ranch dressing and water glasses. She opened it to the photo. "Mostly I was hoping you could tell me something about Jewell and this man."

Diana pulled up the ornate reading glasses from around her neck and propped them on her powdered nose. "Well, well," she said slowly, "if it isn't Elliot Klein." She paused. "My, he *was* a looker, wasn't he? I should have learned my lesson right there. Handsome men will break your heart," she said with a certain authority.

"Is that what happened? To Jewell, I mean?"

"Oh, yes. He just ran out on her. After he'd talked her into marrying him, too, and against her better judgment. She was going to go back east with him. She'd've had to stop singing, of course—no country music in New York City. Elliot said she was smart, maybe she could go to nursing school. Nursing school!" Diana practically spat. "Jewell, with a voice like an angel! She could have made a name for herself! And oh, she loved to sing. But she loved Elliot more, poor kid. I tried to warn her, but that was like telling a flash flood to stop dead in its tracks."

She took a mouthful of salad and chewed carefully before she spoke again. "And then I guess *his* better judgment finally caught up with him. He probably went back to New York, finished college, and married a nice Jewish girl."

"Probably? You don't know?"

"Oh, no. He left without a word, the drip. Left her at the altar, practically, only in this case he just left her coolin' her heels by the river. And she stopped singin' anyway. What a waste!" Oklahoma was resurfacing in Diana's voice along with the past.

"What exactly happened when he disappeared?"

If Diana thought this line of questioning strange, she didn't let on. "Well, he was supposed to meet her at Taft Beach, like always. That's what we called it, Taft Beach, though it was just a little ol' wide spot on the Kern. I remember Elliot was pretty snooty about it. Of course, now that I've been down to Santa Monica and Malibu, I can see his point. But he never did respect that river, never paid any mind when Jewell warned him about it. Anyway, our crowd used to hang out there—drive over from Bakersfield and Oildale—and Elliot would meet Jewell. He'd get a ride with his buddy…what was his name?"

"Buddy?" Claire asked absently, trying to square this slightly superior cad with the romantic, sympathetic lover Johnny had seen, admittedly through the lens of hopeless love.

"Yeah, he was always with this other fellow, seems like," Diana said. "Little ol' pumpkin-headed thing. What *was* his name?" She shook her head and offered a pouty little smile. "I ought to be able to remember somebody I actually went out with, though of course there wasn't anything to it. Just a convenience in a way for Jewell, 'cause Elliot didn't have a car. He had to depend on his runty little buddy to bring him to see Jewell sing. Goofy name he had—Clyde! That was it. He tried to call me Bonnie, for them bank robbers in Texas. Clyde." She sat back, pleased with herself.

"Clyde was a friend of Elliot's?" Johnny Treadle hadn't mentioned anybody, but perhaps that wasn't surprising. Days, months, entire years, seemed to have slipped into neural crevasses in Johnny's memory.

Diana frowned prettily. "Well, I guess they were friends. Clyde stuck to Elliot, that's for sure. We were pretty innocent in those days. Today I might say that those two were, you know— well, not Elliot, maybe. From what Jewell told me he was always trying to get her off in the bushes. Though maybe he went both ways. Down in Hollywood you meet people like that," she said knowingly. "And he was almost too good-looking, if you know what I mean. Clyde seemed real fond of him. Wonder what happened to him. Clyde, I mean. After I went down to Hollywood I pretty much lost track of that whole crowd."

Diana's psychosexual observations were interesting, but not quite what Claire was after. "They were suppposed to meet by the river?" she prompted.

"Oh. Right. Clyde was bringing Elliot over, like always. Only that day he was late, and finally it was *real* late—starting to get dark—and they still hadn't shown, and we were all ready to go. But Jewell wouldn't leave. 'He'll be here,' she kept saying. So finally we all had to leave her there. But I was worried about her, and later, say around ten, I borrowed a car from a feller and drove back to look for her. Well, I found her, walking by the side of the road, shoes in her hand. She was going to walk back to Bakersfield! She got in the car, never said a word. And she never *did* say a word. Never talked about him again."

"Not a hint about what happened?"

"I *know* what happened. He got cold feet. Bastard. Probably

only told her he'd marry her to get her to sleep with him.
Because up until then she hadn't."

Claire was silent as the shreds of her last romantic illusion
about Great Love floated away on the cold breeze of Diana's
cynicism. If Diana was right. Maybe Elliot hadn't shown up for a whole
different reason.

"She did say one thing that night," Diana continued, "right
after she got into the car. 'I thought I heard him.' Isn't that pathetic?"

"Maybe she did hear something."

"Naw. Men are weasels," Diana said.

There was a brief pause as each reviewed examples of this
profound truth from her own life. Then Claire cleared her
throat. Even if Diana was correct and Elliot Klein had been a
bastard, he may not have made it any closer to New York than
the bank of the Kern. "You have pictures," she reminded.

"Right." Diana flipped through the heavy pages of her book,
muttering, "Family...family...here we go. Here's the four of us,
at the Lucky Spot." Claire had to restrain herself from grabbing
the album. Yes, there was Jewell in full Cherokee Rose regalia,
managing to look radiant instead of ridiculous. And there
was Elliot. This time he hadn't had a chance to snatch off the
wire-rims for the camera, but if anything they made him better-
looking, because more contemporary. He looked like a cute
grad student.

Oh, and there were two other people at the table. Diana, a
perfectly attractive brunette with a ponytail, and Clyde. He
wouldn't have been that odd-looking if he weren't next to Elliot,
whose perfectly proportioned features called attention to Clyde's
slightly oversized head and caved-in chest.

"I always ended up with Clyde," Diana was saying, "like I was
his date. As if I'd want anything to do with that runty ol' thing.
And, like I said, he wasn't interested in anybody but Elliot, near
as I could tell. Sure didn't seem interested in Jewell, and the men

just swarmed around her back in those days. She wasn't even that pretty. It was like she was giving off some special scent that only men could smell. I'll tell you what, if I could sell *that* from behind my counter, I'd make quite a commission."

Claire was reading the caption. "'August 20, 1954. Celebration.' What were you celebrating?"

"Huh. Must have been somebody's birthday. Let me see." She leaned over the picture. "Hell, that's no birthday. We're drinking champagne! Ooh, I remember that night. Elliot and Clyde were really jazzed—they kept laughing for no reason, and talking about how they'd proved something, and how pretty soon we'd be drinkin' champagne *every* night. And I remember Elliot said, 'Dorothy'—that was my name back then, Dorothy Dobbins, the studio changed it—'Dorothy, how'd you like a pair of silk stockings for every day of the week? And a mink coat?' What I'd do with a mink coat in this heat I don't know. Had me one in Hollywood, though. The nights get kind of cool down there. Anyway, I wasn't surprised at all when Jewell told me—now this would have been a few days later—that Elliot was about to come into some money, and he'd asked her to marry him. Didn't have the money yet, though—he just gave her any old ring, said he'd replace it with ten carats in a month."

"And that was before you had to go out and pick her up by the river."

"Oh, yeah. Not long before, though—maybe a week or so, is all." She looked at her watch. "Oh my gosh, I've got to get back. Listen, why don't you keep the album for a few days? Maybe you'll find some pictures you can use. For the memorial."

Oh, right. The memorial.

Diana was dabbing at her lipstick, looking in a compact mirror. "Tell me," she said, standing and smoothing her dress, "how was Jewell doing there at the end?"

"Not too well," Claire said. "She had a bad heart, and was short of breath. Though she could still sing. It was amazing."

"But did she…how did she look?"

"How did she look?" Claire repeated, bewildered. "Old and sick. She still had that big smile, but her teeth were bad."

Diana nodded, and touched her own hair with the same gesture Johnny's wife had used. Satisfaction? Or reassurance? "Thanks for dinner," she said, leaving Claire slowly simmering as she gathered up both albums and headed for her own car. Why this gloating about Jewell, as if having become old and sick were some kind of payback?

But in the car on the way back to Yolie's she realized uncomfortably that she could feel smug, too, at the fact that she was holding up well under the combined drag of time and gravity, and that part of her own dismay at the signs of age in her own body was because they reminded her of her mother. Somehow she had managed to believe that growing old was some kind of moral failure of her mother, one that she, Claire, could avoid through clean living and right thinking.

But there was, after all, only one way not to get old. Maybe Elliot Klein had found it.

It was an unpleasant thought, and she banished it immediately. Instead she imagined one of those long, late-summer afternoons on the river, at "Taft Beach," where Jewell and Elliot would have had a chance to get to know each other in sunlight, somewhere other than the neon-lit nightclubs where Jewell sang.

The day after the mysterious celebration in Diana's photo, say.

⸺⸺⸺⸺

Jewell would be sitting in the long grass in her halter top and shorts, and Elliot would be showing off, maybe, grabbing a branch, swinging out over the river with a Tarzan yodel, and dropping off into the middle, right where the current was strongest.

"Elliot, honey, be careful," Jewell would say, but under her breath, where she had once prayed, knowing it wasn't any use to tell him out loud. He wouldn't take her any more seriously than he took Taft Beach.

"Beach?" he had hooted the first time she'd taken him there. "Where's the sand? Where's the hot dogs? Where's the ocean?" Then he'd told her about someplace called Jones Beach: miles of white sand,

breakers rolling in from the Atlantic. He'd been a lifeguard there in the summer.

Maybe Taft Beach was just a wide place along the Kern, and maybe the Kern wasn't the ocean or even the Hudson, wherever that was— but she'd bet a new Buick it was meaner. It dropped down from the high country and by the time it hit Bakersfield it was moving. Even way out here it was moving, and you couldn't always tell; it would come up from underneath and grab you and shove you under a rock or a tangle of weeds and hold you there, and they'd find what was left of you five miles and five months later. The new dam was supposed to take the ginger out of it, but that wasn't finished yet.

But Elliot would just laugh when she told him all this, like she hadn't lost three, no, four friends to the river, one this summer; like she hadn't nearly drowned herself, as a kid. He'd act like she'd said something cute. Sometimes she thought—

But then there he was, walking toward her and waving, and the hardness inside her melted. Lord, he was handsome. Stripped to the waist, he looked better than any movie Tarzan. And so smart, with such a fine future, and so gentle, never raising his voice or his hand to her. She knew how lucky she was. It must be a mistake, she thought sometimes, and he would realize it sooner or later.

Only there wouldn't be a "later." He'd be going back east, to college—less than a month away now. She didn't want to think about it.

Anyway, he was here now, dropping down beside her and throwing an arm around her shoulders.

"Ow!" she said, "you're cold!" She squirmed away from him.

"You'll just have to warm me up, then." He pulled her closer and whispered, "Let's go down the river."

She knew what he meant. "Naw, Elliot, I don't feel like it right now. I got to sing tonight."

"Come on, sweetheart," he coaxed, and slapped his bare chest. "Or I'll die of love and hypothermia," he warned in a doleful voice.

She laughed. Even when she didn't know what he was talking about, he had such a comical way about him that he could always make her laugh. "Okay. But just for a little while."

He hauled her to her feet and they started walking west, past the other folks—a few families, a few couples, but mostly single young fellows from the Taft oil fields who stared at them sullenly. If they hadn't already disliked Elliot for being a Jew, they disliked him more for being a Jew with a girlfriend. A white girlfriend.

Only Clyde, who was fishing from the bridge, lifted his hand in greeting as they passed.

"I guess he ain't such a bad ol' boy," she said. "Wonder if he'll ever get hisself a gal."

"Well, he rents one every now and then." They pushed into the tall greenery along the river.

"Where's he get the money for that?"

"Clyde always seems to have a little money. Of course, I'm going to have some money one of these days, too."

"You mean, when you get out of college."

"Oh, maybe sooner than that," he said, as they stooped low under the vines and cottonwoods. "Maybe a lot sooner than that."

"Like you and Clyde was talking about last night."

The four of them—Jewell and Elliot and Clyde and her friend Dorothy—had had a little celebration last night. "Our ship's a-gonna dock!" Clyde had crowed over and over again, and Elliot wouldn't explain what he meant. And now he just gave her one of his secret smiles. "Here we are," he said.

They had found this little clearing a few weeks ago—a bed of soft grass underneath two crooked sycamores, curtained by trailing vines. "An elegant boudoir," Elliot said now.

"Boudoir?"

"Bedroom."

"Now, Elliot, I done told you—"

"I just want a private place. To talk to you. I've got something important to say." They settled into the grass and he began to stroke her shoulders. She shivered. "The semester starts in four weeks," he said.

"You think I don't know that? You think I don't wake up thinking about it every day—about what it's going to be like to have you gone?"

"*Shh,*" *he said soothingly.* "*That's what I wanted to talk to you about.*" *He paused for a moment, as if wondering how to proceed.* "*How would you like to go with me?*" *he asked finally.*

"*Go with you? Like, to visit you? I can't afford to do that—*"

"*No, silly. I meant, as my wife!*" *By now he was kneeling in front of her, pressing her hands between his in a gesture of prayer.* "*Marry me,*" *he said.*

They were words she had been fantasizing about for months, but actually hearing them didn't bring the wave of pure ecstasy of her imaginings. Instead she felt fear. Marry him. What would that really mean? Leave everything she knew—her momma, her friends, her band...

Her band.

"*Sweetheart, what's the matter?*" *he said, taken aback by her silence. He'd had many doubts about this moment, but none about her answer.* "*Don't you want to marry me? I thought you loved me,*" *he ended, releasing her hands.*

"*Elliot, honey—*" *seizing his hand again and pressing it over her breast, to forestall that edge in his voice; she hated it when he sulked* "*—of course I love you. You know I do.*"

"*So you'll do it, then?*" *All his will, his desire, his energy were focused on her. His own reservations were forgotten; the most important thing in the world was to persuade her to agree.* "*If it's the city you're nervous about, we wouldn't be living in New York at first, you know. We'd be in a small college town, in married student housing—a cute little apartment you could fix up for us. The school's in the country, just like here. Well, not exactly like,*" *he amended.* "*Greener. And colder.*"

A cute little apartment, with Elliot. It was heaven. "*It ain't New York, Elliot. I could live anywhere, with you. It's just—*"

"*Just what?*"

"*Just...what would I do there?*" *she wailed.*

He laughed. "*Do?*" *he repeated.* "*There's plenty to do, lots more than here. There're movies, and parties, and you'd make friends with the other wives—*"

"*But is there music?*"

"Music? Sure! *Chamber music concerts, a couple of times a month, and jazz concerts, and*—"

"My kind of music, I mean."

"Oh. No, not that I've heard. But, honey, you'd be my wife! You'd have your own home to decorate, and you'd be there when I got home for dinner—" he rolled on top of her "—and we could do this every night, without you having to worry. And there'd be kids—not right away, of course, but when I go on to grad school...."

Claire came back to the present with a start, amazed that her subconscious had produced this vignette while bringing her right to Stalag 17, to Yolie's house. She found, to her surprise, that she had imagined an Elliot Klein she didn't much like.

It was unfair, of course, to apply 1990s' standards of sexual parity to 1950s' relationships. Was she simply jealous, envious rather, of Jewell's Great Love?

Or was she too old and cynical to admit the possibility of a relationship in which neither party doubted their love, or calculated?

"How was Diana Dare?" asked Ramón, when she had passed into the many-gated fortress. He and Yolie were still in the office, and he looked a little weary.

"Interesting but not enlightening. I'll tell you later. And you?" she asked him. "What have you learned about C.C. Tidwell?"

He made a face Yolie couldn't see. "Quite a lot about how he got his start out here—"

"Ray means he heard way more than he wanted to," Yolie said, and Ramón grinned. "Here, let me show you," she said to Claire, opening a manila folder on her desk. "Old C.C. made his real money in oil, like everybody else in Kern County."

"I thought you said he was just a roustabout. Whatever that is."

"He was," Yolie said, "but somehow he got enough together to buy a little parcel, way over by Lost Hills where land was cheap, and sink a well. And to everyone's complete surprise, it came in big. And that was just the first of several he sank over there. They all proved out. Look, here he is, pleased as a slug on a lily." She pulled out an old newspaper clipping from the Bakersfield paper, dated September 10, 1954. WILDCAT WELL COMES IN FOR ROUSTABOUT, said the headline, and underneath was a photo of a little figure standing next to a wooden oil derrick.

"A rare image of C.C. Tidwell," Yolie noted. "Bastard doesn't like to be photographed. I'd say he's afraid the camera'll steal his soul, but there's never been any evidence that he has—"

"Wait," Claire interrupted. "Do you have a magnifying glass?"

"Sure," said Yolie, "there's one with the *OED*. Top shelf. I'm going to the can. I'll be right back."

Claire took the little magnifying glass from beside the *Oxford English Dictionary*, centered on a shelf of venerable reference books. She studied the face for a moment. It was hard to say.

"Tell me," she said presently, "C.C. Tidwell. Everybody calls him C.C. What do those *C*s stand for?"

"Cannibal?" hazarded Ramón. "Cutthroat? Charlatan?"

"Clyde Chester," answered Yolie from the door.

10

"CLYDE!" CLAIRE EXCLAIMED. "Ramón, C.C. Tidwell is Clyde!"

His face remained blank, and she realized that he hadn't heard any of Diana's story. "Elliot had a little buddy that Diana Dare just told me about. They used to double date, Diana and Clyde, with Jewell and Elliot. Diana made it sound like Clyde was Elliot's only friend, actually. Look."

She showed him Diana's photo of the four friends.

"Wait...a...minute." Yolie dragged out the syllables. Her whole face had sharpened like a slide coming into focus. Now her voice was sharper, too, crisp and businesslike. "Let me see that picture."

She stared at it for a while. "I do believe you're right," she said slowly. "But who the hell is this Elliot?"

"Didn't Ray—Ramón—" Claire began, then stopped. "Am I the only person in the world who calls you Ramón?"

"My mother does," he said, "and Miranda—"

"All your *gringas* have called you *R-r-ramón*," Yolie teased. "They theenk eet's so-o *mexicano*," rolling her inflection in a parody of a Mexican-American accent.

"All your *gringas?*" Claire echoed.

"Yeah, he goes for you Anglos. Preferably Protestant. You raised Presbyterian, perhaps?"

"Episcopalian," Claire admitted, before she could think.

"Well, there you have it," Yolie told her, smiling. She had morphed before Claire's eyes from wacko conspiracy theorist to efficient investigative reporter. "He's a self-hating Latino."

"Hey, I had a Latina girlfriend," Ramón protested mildly. "In eighth, no, ninth grade."

"I rest my case," Yolie told him. "Anyway, go on about Elliot, Claire." She grabbed a legal pad and pen and poised to make notes.

Claire did her best to present her scattershot investigation as a succinct narrative, ending with Diana Dare's story. "So he just didn't show up that night," she wound up. "Either got cold feet or…or wet feet, if he drowned."

"Or neither," Yolie said. "You mentioned a celebration over 'proving' something?"

"Right, that's what Diana said."

"Could it have been 'proving up' or 'proving out'?"

"I don't know, you'd have to ask her. What's 'proving up'?"

"That's what oilmen call it when a new well in an untried field produces. 'The sand proved out at a thousand feet,' that kind of thing."

"Oh. Oh!" Claire repeated, as certain implications occurred to her.

"Yeah," Yolie said briskly, "interesting, no?" She began ticking off items on her fingers. "Elliot the geologist finds a promising area. He needs an investor so he taps his good buddy Clyde—C.C. They buy a little parcel, sink the well. It proves up beyond their wildest dreams." She moved on to her left hand. "C.C. bashes his partner over the head, buries the body next to the Kern, and never looks back." She waggled her two leftover fingers in a gesture of farewell.

"Wow," said Claire. "It all hangs together."

Ramón had been leaning back on a navy blue futon sofa, watching the two women like a cat at a tennis match. He gave a manly *harrumph*, then said, "Yeah, so does dogshit. How do we know he didn't drown? That seems the likeliest alternative. Or just leave? Go back to his old life? Maybe he realized he was about to make a big mistake—marrying someone so different from him, just because he was attracted, and maybe intrigued by the differences."

Both women stared at him for a moment, and he shifted his weight and looked away.

"Well, it should be easy to find out if he went back to New York," said Claire. "If he didn't, surely somebody would have filed a missing person's report—his family, if not Jewell herself. The sheriff's department would have it—"

"No! Don't call the sheriff's department." Yolie sounded panicky, and Ramón opened his mouth. "No, Ray, I know you think they've changed, and maybe they have, but they still have a long way to go." She turned back to Claire. "He was a college student, right? Call his school and see if he finished."

"But I don't know where he went to college." Claire considered. CCNY? It was their heyday for smart Jewish kids.... "But—wait a minute."

She picked up Diana's picture and peered at it through the magnifying glass. "Does that look like a class ring to you—" passing the photo and glass to Yolie "—there, on Elliot's right hand?"

"Yes. It does. But I can't read it."

"I'll stick it under the scope at the lab," Claire said. "I wonder if they found a ring with the remains? That would sort of cinch it."

"*Don't* call the sheriff to find out," Yolie warned again. "They won't tell you anyway, and you don't want them to know you're interested."

At this point, "interested" seemed a tame way to describe Claire's feelings. Yolanda Covarrubias had her complete attention, this former girl reporter, current conspiracy theorist, future—well, never mind future-anything regarding the Covarrubias clan. For the moment, Claire considered Yolie the most fascinating person in Kern County.

"Is Tidwell really significant in the oil and gas history of this area?" Claire asked. "I know you said that's how he made his money, but don't lots of people make a pile that way without being directly involved?"

"Oh sure," Yolie answered. "But C.C. got his hands dirty, too. How much do you know about the history of the oil industry in Bakersfield, Claire?"

On the futon, Ramón grunted, stretched out a bit, and closed his eyes. Just as well, Claire decided swiftly.

"I know it's been a hundred years since oil was discovered, because there was just a huge hoopla about the centennial. And I know that it gives me a kind of creepy feeling to drive through the Kern River Fields north of Bakersfield." She figured Yolie would understand what she meant. This area, where the first oil well had come in at the tail end of the nineteenth century, was a bizarre hodgepodge of pipes, tanks, power lines, and endlessly pumping rocker arms.

"I need to go," Ramón said, without opening his eyes. "I'm supposed to take Sara to soccer at some ungodly hour tomorrow."

"Oh, keep your pants on," Yolie snapped, and Claire felt a flush rise on her cheeks. "Claire, let me pull together some basic research for you." Yolie frowned a moment, then moved to a bank of mismatched file cabinets in black, gray, and green. "You'll want to understand the big picture before you make any foolish moves."

It occurred to Claire that being on the prowl with a very married man might easily be construed as a foolish move.

Wordlessly she gathered up Jewell's photo album, and opened it one more time to the second, unpeopled photo on the banks of the Kern. Something kept teasing her about it. She looked at it, then closed the album.

Aha! Got it. What a coincidence.

Or was it?

While she was examining the picture, Yolie opened file drawers and pulled documents out of various folders. She squared the pages neatly, slid the papers into a manila envelope, and handed it to Claire.

"Here. It's a C.C. Tidwell primer. I have lots of other stuff from different phases of his career, but this will give you an overview. What's your e-mail address? I'll send you some more as attachments." She waved a hand at the computer, which had been rotating through a set of Impressionist-painting screensavers and was currently showing a Mary Cassatt.

Claire dug out a card and handed it over. "It's on here. My home phone—"

Yolie shook her head vigorously. "Avoid the phone whenever possible." She glared briefly at Ramón. "And watch it with the cell phone, dammit! Any idiot with a scanner can hear every word you say, and there are a staggering number of idiots out there."

Ramón was sidling toward the front of the house. "Yolie, we really do need to go."

Claire moved to join him, extending a hand to her hostess. "Good-bye, Yolie. It was good to meet you." And it had been, Claire realized, remembering her oft-unfulfilled resolutions to make more female friends.

"Same here," Yolie said, returning a businesslike handshake. "And keep in touch—seems like our interests are converging." She grinned, and her eyes flicked to Ramón. Claire wondered which interests she meant.

"God help us all," Ramón groaned, but he gave Yolie another big hug. "You take care of yourself, Yolanda. Call me if you need *anything*, okay? You still have my beeper number?"

"Number one on my speed dial. You remember our code?"

He nodded and she opened her doors one by one. "Ray, you might try looking after yourself for a change," she said. "And you—" looking straight at Claire with alert black eyes "—you watch your back."

The last door clanged shut.

What did she mean by that? Claire wondered, then realized that if Yolie wasn't entirely delusional—and there was nothing but Ramón's somewhat patronizing assertion that she actually was—well, then she, Claire, might herself be the object of some unwanted attention. That would certainly explain the car that might or might not have been following her for the last few days.

"Poor Yolie," Ramón was saying, "she needs to get out more."

They looked back at the fortress of a house and both smiled at the inadequacy of the comment. A streetlight glittered off the razor wire atop her fence. "She doesn't have to live like this."

"No?" asked Claire, sobering abruptly. "Then what's he doing there?" She pointed to the car parked across the street, lights off, a driver just barely visible in the late twilight.

"Listening to the radio. Smoking a joint. Jerking off. Hell, I don't know. But I don't think he's devoting himself to documenting Yolie's life. Her marriage was breaking up about the time this whole thing started," he said, "and my…Miranda has always thought that this retreat into paranoia was her way of not dealing with that. And of making herself out to be far more important to the world than she is."

Claire made a face, which she was glad Ramón couldn't see. Classic psychobabble. "So there's no objective evidence whatsoever that Yolie's being harassed, or threatened?"

"There were a couple of events—a car accident, a burglary, maybe—that were probably coincidences, but that Yolie interpreted as deliberate. The then-sheriff thought they were nothing."

"What kind of car accident?"

"Oh, she went off the road one night. This road, as a matter of fact." By now they were headed north on Highway 99. "She claimed she was run off, but it was dark, there was fog, so who knows?"

Claire had been nearly run off the road, very deliberately, several times, and she took this seriously. In this land of miles of deserted roads, it was an easy way to frighten, and maybe hurt, someone. And it was hard to prove.

She let the subject drop. "How does Yolie finance her... her..."

"Lifestyle?" suggested Ramón. "That's the biggest joke of all. Our great-uncle—the brother of our *abuelo*, my mother's father—actually made some money in his lifetime. He bought a couple of acres to raise watermelons, and right before he died he sold it to a developer. I got a little of his estate—paid for a year at UC Davis—but Yolie got the rest, she was his favorite. And she eventually spent it to buy that place and trick it out with top-of-the-line electronics."

"Let me guess who the developer was."

"That's right," said Ramón, his face lit by oncoming headlights. "C.C. Tidwell. He's paying for Yolie to devote her life to sending him to prison."

"There must be a lesson somewhere. But how long can she keep it up? Does she have a trust fund?"

Ramón laughed. "Nope. She actually makes quite a respectable living in another field altogether."

And what might that be? Scratch public relations. Maybe she trained attack dogs. What could you do that would make a "respectable living" without ever leaving the privacy of your own fortress?

When he didn't continue, Claire sighed. "What does she do, Ramón?"

He turned and offered one of those great grins. "She's a website designer." They both laughed.

By now they had reached the field station parking lot, where Ramón's car was waiting, and had managed to avoid touching on yesterday's conversation or their feelings about each other.

"Maybe I'll see you Monday," he said, "though I'm going to be really busy. I've been kind of letting work pile up."

Well, thought Claire, there was no reason to worry that we wouldn't be able to resume our old relationship. Seems like it's no problem at all. Old work buds, Claire and Ramón, heading into the fields and furrows of the San Joaquin Valley in search of truth, justice, and integrated pest management.

So why didn't she feel more relieved, she wondered, as she watched him walk away in the dark.

11

CLAIRE WAS AWAKENED at six-thirty on Sunday morning by the persistent ringing of a telephone. Crawling up from deep delta sleep to answer, she heard her brother's relentlessly patrician tones.

"Good morning," Charles announced. "I assume you're up?"

She resisted any number of smart-ass comments and simply answered, "Yes."

Charles went on to report that he had arrived uneventfully in Los Angeles late the previous evening and was merely "checking in." That he might have checked in at a more civilized hour on her day off didn't seem to have occurred to him. Charles was the kind of traveler who expected others to adjust to his own internal clock, a clock set rigidly to Eastern Standard Time.

"I'll be tied up with my colleagues through Tuesday afternoon," he informed her after exchanging the bare minimum of pleasantries. His patronizing tone sent a shudder through Claire, now thoroughly awake. She pictured him sitting upright at the desk in his hotel room, plaid pajamas neatly pressed, feet tucked into leather slippers. "The conference itself doesn't begin until tomorrow, of course, but you know how these things are."

Actually Claire *didn't* know how things were among members of the American Historical Association, nor did she particularly care to. "Of course," she told him, thinking again that this attempt at family peacemaking was a mistake, that perhaps the two of them would do better to reconcile themselves independently to their orphanhood. "Are you still going to come up Tuesday, or will that be too difficult?"

"Not if your directions are accurate," he told her, and rang off.

There was no hope of getting back to sleep. Claire started a pot of coffee and moved out onto her deck in sweats, watching tendrils of morning light dance through the nearby pines. Slate Mountain loomed in shadow and the rushing river below sent its soothing vapors up to calm her. Such a peaceful place this was, or (mostly) had been since she'd moved here. And now Charles was coming to disrupt it all. Arriving for his first visit to Claire in California, where no blood relative had previously come to see her, even though this seemed to have become, despite her best intentions, her home.

When she went inside to fill a mug with the freshly brewed coffee, she saw Yolie Covarrubias's neat file folders sitting where she had dumped them on the counter after giving them a quick scan the previous night. With a sigh, she carried the files and her mug out onto the deck and began working her way through them all over again. Yolie was a thorough, dogged researcher, that much was clear, and far more organized than the exterior of her house would suggest. Quite casually and in a matter of minutes, she had assembled a comprehensive information packet that someone like Charles would have dithered over for an hour.

The first Kern River oil well back in 1899, Claire read now in ONE HUNDRED YEARS OF OIL, a yellowing special supplement to the *Bakersfield Californian*, had tapped into what turned out to be a 3.8 billion–barrel reservoir of crude oil, most of it so thick that conventional drilling methods couldn't budge it. Early "jack plants" had provided steam and later gasoline power to pump the oil, which spewed from the ground along with large quantities of water and sand. The whole gooey mess was pumped into open earthen sumps, where oil and water separated while the sand settled out.

Over time, it had become harder and harder to pump the Kern Field oil, even though only about ten percent of the field's potential had been tapped. Then in the early 1960s, a dramatic change in technology moved California oil production onto a brand new plane. Steam injection arrived, with a vengeance. Pumping steam deep into existing wells warmed the crude oil sufficiently so that it then could flow easily to the surface, rather like warming refrigerated olive oil, and for twenty years, steam injection remained the norm.

Then, in the early 1980s, cogeneration plants were first developed. A cogen plant could produce both electric and steam power by burning natural gas, which created far less environmental pollution. Some of this electric power could be sold to outside utilities even as the steam warmed deep oil deposits and the rest of the electricity pumped the oil to the surface. It was a masterfully self-sufficient system.

C.C. Tidwell had been at the forefront of the steam injection movement, even as the major oil companies scrambled to adopt this new technology. His personal fortunes had taken a quantum leap around this era, even more so than usual, and reading between the lines it seemed obvious that C.C. had made himself plenty of good fortune over the years.

Reading between the lines was necessary because, in an age of far too much information, Clyde Chester Tidwell was that rarest of creatures, a genuine recluse. He did not appear at public functions of any sort, refused most interviews, was represented at various public hearings by top-level attorneys, accountants, and similar intermediaries. He was not known to have been married or to have procreated, had no known relationships with men or women, and did not indulge in anything resembling a social life.

Born outside a small Oklahoma panhandle town scoured into oblivion by a succession of brutal Depression-era dust storms, Clyde had come to California at the age of six with his mother, uncle, and two sisters, his father having died a few months earlier. Once in California, the Tidwell clan found its way from one labor camp to the next. Along the way, young Clyde developed a relentless determination. Whether it was chopping and picking cotton—activities which often earned the Tidwells their meager living—or later drilling for oil, or still later raping the landscape to establish endless suburban subdivisions, Clyde Chester Tidwell never did anything halfway.

Over time, he had become fabulously secretive, a sort of minor-league Howard Hughes, who kept adding on to a sprawling ranch house he had built overlooking one of his earliest real estate developments. He was wise enough to diversify, with current holdings and business interests scattered like tumbleweeds around every corner of the lower San Joaquin Valley. He preferred getting even to getting mad, and he made few enough business errors that when he did occasionally screw up, it was newsworthy. The only such blunder mentioned in Yolie's dossier concerned a tract of land he had missed out on purchasing back in the 1970s. That land, and a good deal more surrounding it, was part of the package Tidwell had recently acquired, at a much higher price, from the estate of Doug Collins, when Collins perished in a small-plane crash.

He was also, it seemed, sentimental. He still maintained his primary business office at Tidwell Cotton Ginning, even though he no longer had much of anything to do with the dwindling Kern County cotton industry. Tidwell Ginning was small by industry standards, and cotton gins were closing all over the place, but Tidwell had once told a reporter, in a rare interview, that he had no intention of ever shutting the place down.

Midmorning, Claire went into the lab to catch up on some of the work she was behind with, and maybe to get a head start on some of the coming week's chores. She was taking Wednesday and Thursday off to spend time with Charles, but hers was not the sort of job you could call a temp for, and the work would have to be done sometime. By Claire.

She couldn't make her field calls on a Sunday, but she had composed a mental list of projects in the lab that needed attention. Starting with Diana Dare's photo.

She stuck the photo under her dissecting scope and looked at Elliot's ring. It was hard to see, curved around his finger and shaded by the rest of his hand. "*C*," she muttered. "*O*, maybe an *R*—well, I'll be damned," she said. "Cornell." Which was *her* alma mater, or one of them. She wasn't absolutely sure, but it was worth a call in the morning.

Through the window her plot of marigolds was blazing like a grassfire. *Cempasuchl*, Ramón had once called them. The Toltecs had cultivated them, he said, calling them *cempoalsuchitl*—twenty-flowers—which the invaders had changed to *Tagetes*, formally, and marigold, after the Virgin Mary.

"Well, they're tough, beautiful little flowers," she'd said. "Your ancestors did a good job."

"Which ones?"

"Which marigolds?"

"No, which ancestors, the Indians or the conquistadores? I'm pretty much fifty-fifty."

So was she just another one of what Yolie had called Ramón's *gringas*, intrigued by his exoticness? But Ramón was about as exotic as...as a Taco Bell.

She worked until noon. A hike would be nice, she thought wistfully. In the high country, among the sequoias...but after last year's carnage, she'd been reluctant to hike alone in the mountains, and all her favorite trails, her old haunts, were, well, haunted. She needed to lay new memories over the old. Maybe she could get Ramón to hike with her sometime, as sort of an aerobic exorcism.

Anyway, even if the mountains were out, water would be just

as nice—a tumbling, rushing profusion of water. She unfolded a map of Kern County on her lab bench and put her finger on Erasmo Campos's orchard, then traced back, eastward and mountainward, to the point where the blue line that was the Kern River began to crimp and wriggle like a seismograph tracing. That was where it plunged out of the Tehachapis into the Great Central Valley. In that narrow canyon one could, supposedly, still glimpse the notorious "Rio Bravo" of old.

She squinted, sighed, and brought out a hand lens to look for dotted foot trails crossing the river. Soon she was going to have to break down and buy reading glasses. But my eyes! one part of her said plaintively. They're my only good feature! Tough, she thought; as she had told herself yesterday, there was only one way not to get old.

Along the highway south there were new scallops of sooty black carved into the stiff pale grass, where some moron had pitched a cigarette. Or maybe the grass had simply combusted spontaneously; it had, after all, been lifeless tinder for months. When she came to the oil fields north of Bakersfield it occurred to her to make a stop in town, on the off chance that Johnny's shop was open. She did still have a turntable, boxed up but accessible, but she needed one of those fat spindles, or some plastic inserts, if she wanted to play Jewell's 45s.

Treadle's Treasures said CLOSED but she knocked anyway, thinking she saw movement inside. Cars whizzed past on Edison Highway behind her, and when the wind shifted, she could smell a whiff of decay, almost like the manure-field fire the previous year. Smoke from that fire had blanketed the lower Valley with a stench that did nothing to further the cause of dairy farmers seeking to relocate to Kern County from other parts of the state.

Nobody answered. After a minute or two she gave up, got back in her car, and headed for the mountains.

Her mirror showed a lot of traffic also headed out east on Highway 178, including three or four SUVs and a black-and-white with a tiara of blinking lights. She slowed drastically and he zipped by, after other prey. Not CHP, but Kern County

Sheriff, she noted, and sped up again. She was sailing through a familiar undulant landscape of yellow hills, maybe a little shallower, a little hotter, than the Sierran foothills farther north.

This was desolate, baked land, and the new housing developments in pastel, confectionary colors, their gay flags drooping in the merciless heat, were like bizarre mirages. Standard Southern California development, tract houses that were interchangeable among subdivisions in Hemet or El Cajon or Oxnard or Simi Valley or East Bakersfield. Interspersed among them were dark citrus groves, irrigated by the river that was marked by the odd cottonwood off to the north.

Tumbleweeds lay piled in brown, airy heaps against the barbed wire fencing and low shrubs that paralleled the roadway. It was, she remembered, a permitted tumbleweed burn that had started the manure-field fire in the first place.

Then suddenly, as if pinched together by a giant thumb and forefinger, the canyon closed in, and the river tumbled out. STAY OUT—STAY ALIVE, said the sign at the mouth; 203 LIVES LOST SINCE 1968. Sobering to be sure, but she did the math quickly. Hell, that was only six or seven a year—not exactly a massacre.

Claire drove up the winding road, a steep, granite-studded hill on her right, the far side of the canyon only about fifty yards to her left. After a mile or two she pulled into a turn-out, fished her camera out of the glove compartment, and walked across the road to check out this mighty river.

She was unimpressed.

Green, rushing water churning itself into a white froth, huge boulders—oh, it was beautiful, all right, but it was very much like a hundred swift New England rivers. Only here there were no leafy green, cool riverbanks, just those precipitous yellow slopes on either side. Still, as she snapped a few pictures from the road above the steep bank, she gradually comprehended the sheer force of the water, the—what had Ramón said?—amperage: a large volume of water moving at great velocity channeled into the narrow, deep canyon the pre-dam Kern had sliced like a laser through the granite.

Okay, she conceded grudgingly, watching the water hit a jut of granite with the force of a hundred fire hoses, this was a torrent. She tossed a stick straight down into a relatively quiet pool, protected from the current by a ring of boulders. The stick floated toward the edge, hovered for a moment, then plunged down a short waterfall and disappeared under the spray at the bottom. She waited for it to reemerge a little farther downstream.

It didn't.

The roar of water rushing into itself filled the canyon, overwhelming the sound of tires on gravel from the highway, drawing her. She picked her way very carefully down to the river's edge. There was evidence of rock slides all around here: fresh scars in the rock walls, jagged boulders in the river, not yet worn to smoothness by the rushing water. This was a river that meant business. Perched on a peninsula of white granite, she was secure, but close enough so that she could have touched the water if she'd wanted to.

And she wanted to. Despite what had happened to the stick, she really wanted to step into that still pool, to immerse herself in the pure water. She wouldn't, of course, having no desire to make them repaint the warning sign—

Afterwards she really wasn't sure if she'd felt an impact between her shoulder blades or not.

Because she was immediately overwhelmed by so much sensation—shuddering shock of icy river; mouth and windpipe full of water; pain of scraping against rough granite; headlong rush downstream.

And the noise, the deep roar, all around her.

She had landed in the little pool, all right, that innocent-looking little pool, and like the stick, she had been carried over the rim of rock and slammed underwater. But the cascade was small, not powerful enough to hold her down, and in a moment she surfaced, sputtering.

The shore, she saw with incredible relief, was only a couple of yards away. But as she was whirled around and pushed downstream, she was stunned by a sudden realization: she couldn't reach shore. In fact, indignation was her dominant emotion for about twenty-five yards: That someone had pushed her, although she wasn't sure about that—everything had happened so quickly. That she'd lost her camera. That, even though her feet frequently brushed a rock and she could almost stand for a moment, she was immediately swept off-balance and back into the current.

Then she whacked up against a flat-sided boulder and stopped. Reality seemed to have returned. For a moment she truly thought this nightmare was over. But then, when she tried to scramble onto the rock, she slipped off the slick surface, and was back in the river again, moving faster than ever, her own self-propelled white-water raft.

Now she panicked.

"Help!" she yelled feebly—uninhibited screaming was beyond her, even *in extremis*, and anyway, "help" was an impossible syllable to project, and anyway, water filled her esophagus and the roar of the river covered her little peep. She concentrated, if that was the word for what was pure instinct, on keeping her head out of water and protected, cushioning herself with her poor battered arms from the black, unforgiving rocks. Maybe she could ride the current until the river was broad and shallow enough to lose power.

After about a hundred yards she managed to grasp a mushroom-shaped boulder in the middle of the river. Her feet touched a rock, and still clinging to her boulder, she felt for another, closer to shore. No good. And the current was still too powerful. So she stayed where she was, yelling and waving with one arm at the occasional car up on Highway 178. Only people driving *down* the canyon could see her; going up, the river was hidden from the road by the bank and the slope.

As vehicle after vehicle swooped past, she began to hate the self-absorbed families in their minivans and sport-utes, headed home after a few days on Lake Isabella.

Her arms were becoming numb and shaky, and after a while she was afraid to let go of the boulder to wave. She wondered with detachment what would happen when she let go entirely. The canyon had opened out a bit, but the river still seemed to have plenty of "ginger" in it. Her hold loosened momentarily and she slipped sideways a little, so that the current no longer pushed her against the rock, but around and beyond it.

And despite her frantic scrabbling to hang on, she was on her way again.

Two feet to the right and she would have been swept downstream again. But with the total arbitrariness that determines most of life's major events, she had been caught by a current that curved toward the south bank and into shallow water. For a moment she even managed to stand, but though the water stopped at her knees she lost her balance again. This time, however, she fetched up against a few flat-topped rocks and was actually able to clamber onto them.

She was safe, and only a few feet from the river's edge. She curled up, shivering and exhausted, and lay in the sun for maybe five minutes. Or an hour. Hard to know; the crystal of her thirty-dollar Timex was smashed. In fact, as she began to recover from the numbing water, it became obvious that most parts of her had been smashed, or scraped, or bruised—every part except her head. Miraculously, her eggshell skull had been spared. And she was mostly intact: she could stand, and move.

But it wasn't clear where she could move *to*. Like everything else about this river, the "shore" was abrupt and extreme—a nearly vertical ten-foot bank of loose dirt and gravel. So as a serious anticlimax to her adventure, she seemed to be stuck twelve feet from the road. About six feet downriver, however, there was a sort of gully that seemed to have been used as a path. If she could jump over to it without stepping even ankle-deep into the treacherous water...

She did, and scrabbled up the steep bank on shaky arms and legs, not without more scraping of knees and shins. Finally she was on the road, limping slowly up the canyon toward her car—

Her car! She'd stuck the keys in her pocket; they were probably in Bakersfield by now! But no, ridiculously, they were still

there. For some reason this pissed her off. Why should she have
had such major bad luck, and then such minor good luck? Although she supposed that not drowning had to count as major
good luck. *Very* major good luck. At any point the current could
have swept her under a rock—and kept her there.

After an eternity she reached her car, curled up in the back
seat, and went to sleep.

When she awoke it was late enough for the car to be in full
shadow, and every part of her felt stiff. She wondered if she
should drive herself to the emergency room at Bakersfield General, but despite the general creakiness, she still seemed to be
basically okay. She'd probably look like a Red Flame seedless
grape tomorrow, but there was not much anyone could do about
that.

But she had a tremendous desire to call *someone*; something
important had just happened to her, and someone should be informed, right?

Who? The sheriff? Her back tingled and she suddenly remembered very distinctly the feel of warm hands shoving between her shoulders. And the black-and-white that had passed
her. No, she wouldn't call the sheriff, she thought, although she
couldn't bring herself to believe that her disaster had been law
enforcement's fault, no matter what Yolie might imagine.

Who, then, could she tell? Who would be satisfyingly interested in her story? Her best friends were nowhere near, and
probably unreachable on a Sunday evening. Charles? She
laughed at the thought, noting with clinical dispassion that
laughter hurt around her rib cage.

Ramón would have met her needs, reacting with gratifying
horror and relief, but Ramón was probably out with his family,
and in any case was "inappropriate," as they said nowadays.
Yolie—now there was a real possibility. Yolie would believe without any coaxing or question that Claire had been shoved into the
river. But Yolie was not the kind of person you called up to chat
with. Hell, you could hardly call her up at all, really.

So in the end, Claire simply headed home.

By the time she reached Parkerville, her various pains had intensified enough that she thought she'd better stop at Mercy Hospital after all, just in case. Many hours, bandages, X rays, CT scans, and warnings about the Kern River later, she was handed a bottle of Tylenol with codeine, and sent on her way, thankful not to have become number 204.

12

CLAIRE WAS IN THE CENTER of a large, quiet, green lake, drowning. She couldn't seem to do anything about it: when she opened her mouth to call for help no sound emerged, and her arms and legs were too heavy to move. In fact, her whole body was unnaturally heavy. Maybe she had rocks in her pockets. Maybe she was committing suicide. A sense of inevitability, and with it a strange peacefulness, came over her. Her chin sank below the surface, she tipped her head back to take one last breath, then slipped silently into the lake. The still waters closed over her so that soon there wasn't even a ripple to show where she had been.

She woke seriously unhappy and with every part of her throbbing, including her nose. It was four A.M.—the time for bleak thoughts and more codeine. The bleak thoughts were these: If I had drowned in the Kern today, my absence would have left nary a ripple. Life would have closed right back up again like that lake. I would have been missed at work—other people would have had to take over my projects—and Charles, already conveniently on the West Coast, would have had to arrange another funeral. Ramón would probably be regretful, and a few other friends, most of whom lived elsewhere and wouldn't even get the news for a couple of weeks. But basically my death would leave a very small rip in the network of society, one which could be darned in no time.

How did this happen? she wondered groggily. How did I get to be nearly forty with so few human connections? A life as bare as a peeled twig? Did I choose this? If I'm not going to win the Nobel after all, is it worth it?

But soon the painkillers kicked in and she fell asleep again. In the morning she had a codeine hangover, a body so stiff and battered she could barely get out of bed, and a dim memory of green water.

Monday morning at seven A.M. was too early to call the Kern County Sheriff and ask about missing persons, if she were even going to do this. But it wasn't too early for the East Coast and the Cornell registrar's office, to whom she explained that she, an alumna, was trying to track down another alumnus. On the off chance that she might send them some money someday, they were extremely gracious, and promised to call her back after searching their database. She hung up, thinking that if she had the nerve to query directly about a missing person's report, all this business with Cornell would be unnecessary.

Who was right about the Kern County Sheriff? Yolie? Or Ramón, who seemed to trust the new regime?

She had a cup of coffee on the deck, then dressed, gingerly, and headed down the hill to work. But at the bottom of the mountain—or at about a thousand feet, where the road entered Riverdale—she stopped opposite Police Chief Tom Martelli's office in a nondescript cinderblock municipal services building that might have served any small town in the country.

Tom was staring out the window, but began to move papers around when she appeared at his door. He aimed a vague blue gaze in her general direction.

Seeing that vacant blue eye and soft paunch, a stranger might have concluded that the dull little retirement town of Riverdale had gotten the level of policeman it deserved. Claire knew better. Tom's mild demeanor housed a sharp, tough intelligence and a lot of nerve; Riverdale had gotten way more than it deserved. Or needed. Because Tom's only failing, if such it was, was lack of ambition. He and Marie stayed in Riverdale because it was a nice place to bring up their four kids: there were horses, dogs, summers on the river or in the high country. So the kids were ecstatic, and their parents slightly bored. Which was why Tom was a little…difficult, sometimes. At least, this was Claire's current and charitable explanation for his tendency to be uncommunicative, arrogant, and sarcastic. Not to mention downright hostile at times, and just plain insufferable.

"Do you know anybody with the Kern County Sheriff's Department?" she asked abruptly, which was Tom's preferred method of starting a conversation.

"*Kern* County? No, why? Jesus, what happened to you?"

She had dressed to cover as much of herself as possible, but even her face was scratched. "Hiking accident," she said tersely. "What do you think of them?"

"Well, Pat O'Melveny had kind of a bad rep. Not unlike our own esteemed county sheriff, except smarter. While J.T."—the Kaweah County Sheriff—"is mostly just dim-witted, Pat was rumored to be actively on the take. 'Specially from big oil, developers, cotton, and such."

"Like C.C. Tidwell?"

He nodded. "A lot like C.C. But Pat retired last year, and this new fellow Mendez is a different ball game. I hear. But it's hard to turn a whole department around," he said knowledgeably, even though his own "department" consisted of himself, one part-time deputy, and a clerk/typist/dispatcher. He looked out the window again and his eyes suddenly widened.

"Why do you want to know?" he asked, as if the question had just occurred to him.

Claire explained briefly. "So I'd like to get the coroner's report," she concluded, "and find out if a missing person's report was filed for this guy, this Elliot Klein. But without tipping off C.C. Tidwell that I'm making inquiries. Because that seems to be a bad idea. Yolie thinks so, and...and so do I." She could have bitten her tongue for mentioning Yolie. Maybe Tom wouldn't notice.

Fat chance. "Yolie?" he said immediately. "That wouldn't be Yolanda Covarrubias, would it?"

Shit, she thought, there goes my credibility. She nodded unhappily. "You know her?"

"Oh, sure. I got family down in Arvin. They all thought she was a nut, but I met her once, and she seemed like a smart little cookie to me. I see your problem." He tapped his pencil on his blotter. "Well, in any case, you can forget about the coroner's report. They ain't gonna release it to you, 'cause they'll be working the case as a homicide."

"I don't think they're 'working' the case at all, that's the problem," Claire countered. "I had the impression they'd put more energy into somebody lifting a bag of chips from the 7-Eleven."

"Whatever. I mean they're gonna consider it an open case. So the only thing you can get, as a citizen, is the missing person's report, assuming one was filed."

"Right."

"On the other hand, somebody within the department could access all that information."

"Which is what I started with," she snapped. "Tom, are you jerking me around one more time? Do you know somebody?"

"Naw, I don't. But Ricky might, seein' as how he's a *sheriff's* man now," he said sarcastically.

"Ricky" was Tom's former deputy, Enrique Santiago, who had quit last year to take a better-paying job with the Kaweah County Sheriff. "Hmm. I figure he owes me a lot of favors anyway," Claire said.

"Let's hope Ricky still thinks so. They been married for a few months now."

Claire had introduced Enrique to the most beautiful woman in the San Joaquin, whom he had married in May. Luz Perez, widowed with two young children, had revealed a softer side of Ricky that Claire found quite endearing.

"I'll give him a call. Thanks, Tom."

He grunted something and went back to staring out the window, no longer even pretending to be doing paperwork.

Just past greasy little Lake Prosperity—created, of course, by the dam just below it, on the same river that tumbled below Claire's house—and before Parkerville, she turned south along the foothills. She whizzed by the vineyards and orange groves of the eastern San Joaquin Valley and finally turned east again, into the Citrus Cove Agricultural Field Research Station. Hopefully she looked around for Ramón's truck, but knew he'd be in his office at the County Agricultural Department back up in Parkerville. Probably still returning phone calls: Han Minh with his strawberries and lemongrass, Maria Gonzalez with her watermelons, Erasmo Campos with his peaches. *Doc, I have these little white flies, Doc. I've got a bad case of thrips or scale or nematodes or verticillium—What can I spray?* By September, things would be slackening off, but in California the land never slept, and there were still the last of the table grapes and the raisins, the late stone fruits, the nut and cotton harvests coming up, and after them the citrus—not to mention planning for next year. *I was thinking about putting in a half acre of specialty vegetables; can I roadside them at a profit?* Ramón told her he loved the phone calls for the direct contact with clients they gave him, but they were relentless.

She took a couple more Tylenols, packed up for her first field call—an almond grower with a bad case of blight—and rattled north on Highway 65, and then east. This time of year the whole Valley was dust-veiled, drained of color. The sky, faintly blue overhead, faded to white at the horizon. The mountains lurked behind a curtain of hydrocarbons and particulates. Dull gray road dust coated the orchards' bright fruit and glossy leaves like powdery mildew. Just west of her client's orchard she picked up her phone and called Enrique Santiago at Kaweah County Sheriff's headquarters.

"Hey, Claire. Long time no hear."

"Hi. Yeah, I haven't talked to you two for months. How's Luz?"

"Ah, she's great. Beginning to show."

"When's she due? December?"

"December twenty-fourth. A Christmas present."

"Give her my love."

"Sure thing. You should call her." Pause. "Okay, what do you need?"

"Ricky, you're such a cynic!"

"Uh-huh." Expectant silence.

"Well, actually," she said, "I was wondering if you knew somebody with the Kern County Sheriff. Somebody reliable. I need to get a missing person's report—"

"You can get that, no problem—"

"And a coroner's report that won't have been released yet. And it's a case that might involve C.C. Tidwell."

"Oh." A pause. "Yeah, I understand. Matter of fact, I do have a buddy down there—hang on, let me get his number." Claire slowed as a truck loaded with lugs of grapes trundled onto the road in front of her. "Here it is. Name's Frank Reyna—we were in basic training together. He's a straight-up guy. Here's his number."

"Thanks a million, Ricky. I'll try to stop by and see you both soon."

She turned into the long dirt drive leading to her client's orchard, pulled off, called Bakersfield, and left a message on Deputy Reyna's voice mail. How had she ever managed without the cell phone, she wondered idly. It was one of those technological advances that had seemed absurdly elitist up until the very moment she acquired her own, when it became simply another necessity of San Joaquin life, like ample water and accurate maps.

Deputy Reyna called back just as she was peeling away an almond's velvety outer hull while waiting for the grower to show up. After she told him what she wanted, there was a long and not particularly comfortable silence.

"I'm not supposed to let that coroner's report out to the public, you know," he said finally, his tone guarded and cop-cautious.

"Right, I understand that."

"But Ricky told you to contact me."

"Yes." It was only fair to tell him the part that could land him in quicksand. "I told him there was a possible connection to C.C. Tidwell."

An even longer, less comfortable silence.

"He said you were, um, 'straight-up,'" Claire added, in a cheerful, positive tone.

"Yeah, I am. Things have changed down here, but I still can't afford to take a risk, career-wise. I got kids." More lengthy silence. "Tell you what. I could release the information to Ricky. Sort of a professional courtesy."

Sort of covering my ass, Claire translated. The grower, a middle-aged man in T-shirt and jeans, was coming down a row of trees. "Perfect! I'll just call him and get the information! Thanks so much, Deputy Rey—"

He'd hung up. Claire turned to greet her client and do her job.

At five o'clock she was back in her office, leafing through her messages. Many, many messages: from a peach grower, an extension expert up in Fresno, a plant geneticist at UC Davis, the almond grower she'd visited that morning, a friend in L.A. None from the local Small Farm Advisor. Not that she'd exactly been expecting one—after all, Ramón was a busy man, and his business didn't always bring him over to the UC field station, and she was the one who'd said, more or less, "Call me when you've left your wife." The half inch of coffee in the communal pot tasted like battery acid, but she drank it anyway. Then she went back down to her lab.

The contours of the hills outside her window made deep shadows. The days were shorter, the fall equinox only a couple of days away—no! What was she thinking? It had been a week ago! She'd lost track; she still did that here every year—looked out at the baking hills and thought, It's high summer. And then felt completely disoriented on realizing that it was actually October, or even November, if the rains started late. Travelers to the Southern Hemisphere who looked up at a whole different sky must feel that same queasiness, that sense of dislocation. She'd felt it when she saw the first pictures from Mars, too: This is unnatural. Along with excitement, of course. Once upon a time she'd taken freshman biology instead of introductory astronomy, because it fit better with her schedule. She'd never looked back, but from time to time she still looked up.

But come to think of it, Mars had proved to look a lot like Kern County.

It was now six, and she'd wasted a hell of a lot of time on thoughts she'd had before. Time for some new ideas.

She settled herself in front of her six "ant farms," opened her lab notebook, and with a certain excitement peeled back the aluminum foil on the first. The roots looked perfectly healthy, and when she looked at them through the light, there was no autofluorescence; she pressed a clear grid against the glass to measure root growth and jotted down the numbers on a pad. Only then did she peel the tape off the ID number: 7250. It was one of the grasses, as she had already known. She transcribed the numbers into her notebook, and moved on to the next. The roots were beginning to brown off, and autofluoresced like crazy under the blue filter. Not only had the roots not grown, some had died back, and one she remembered that had earlier shown some mycorrhizal activity had disappeared entirely. She made a note, and peeled off the foil to read the label. It was 7257, a tumbleweed.

And so on, through the other ant farms. Without exception, the grasses showed the vesicles of mycorrhizal infection, and were thriving; the tumbleweeds were browning off.

Just as she came to the fourth and last sample (the fifth and sixth were controls: she wouldn't disturb the foil on them, in case that had an effect), her phone rang. She grabbed it, but instead of Ramón's resonant baritone a lightly accented tenor said, "Man, don't you ever go home?"

"Oh, Ricky. Hi. Yeah, don't ever say the taxpayers of California don't get their money's worth. Did you hear from your friend?"

"Yep."

She suppressed a sigh. He had learned from Tom the trick of never answering more than exactly what you asked, or maybe that was something drummed into them all at the Police Academy. "And he said…?"

"The coroner's report is still pending. Should be available by the end of the week. But Frank checked out the missing person's reports on microfiche."

"And?" she prompted, anticipating a withholding of further information.

"Hold on, I'm gettin' there…. There was one for Elliot Klein in 1954. Filed by an Isaac and Sophie Klein of Brooklyn, New York."

Claire drew in a long breath. So whatever had happened, Elliot hadn't simply returned and picked up his old life. She wished she could tell Jewell.

But then, maybe Jewell had known.

"Okay," she said, "that's what I was waiting to—"

"Hang on, there's more. You always this impatient, or just had a bad day?"

"More? More about Elliot?"

"More, like a second missing person's report."

"Oh. Filed by Jewell Scoggins, same year, by any chance?"

"Nope. Wanna keep guessin', or want me to tell you?" Not waiting for an answer, he said, "This one was filed much later, um, let me look—in 1977, in fact."

"Twenty-three years later?" How could this be? She felt bewildered.

"Yep. Frankie thought it was weird, too. Filed by a dude name of David Klein—and yes, it's for the same person, Elliot Klein of Brooklyn, New York, who disappeared in 1954."

A pause. "Huh," she said. "Could I have this David's New York address?"

"I've got an address and phone, but it ain't in New York. It's local. In Bakersfield, I mean."

"Really? A motel or something?" Maybe he'd been passing through.

"Nope. Regular old street address, on Oak. 'Course, it's over twenty years old now, but here it is if you want it."

She called the phone number and got Valley Nails 'n' Curls. They'd been there for five years. Just for kicks, she tried Bakersfield information for David Klein, and to her surprise a number came back. Just one; most bigger cities would have many David or D Kleins, but Bakersfield was still pretty undersupplied with Jews, if he was.

Whatever he was.

Whoever he was.

Illegitimate son of Elliot and Jewell given up for adoption? Let's see, born in 1955, in 1977 he would have been…

She dialed the number.

13

WHILE THE PHONE RANG and rang, she composed a message for an answering machine, but finally a male voice answered curtly. "Yeah?"

Well, she thought, he sounds like a New Yorker anyway. "Um, hi, my name is Claire Sharples, and I'm calling...that is...I'm trying to find out...are you by any chance the David Klein who filed a missing person's report on Elliot Klein about twenty years ago?" she finally blurted out.

There was a silence so absolute she thought she must have missed the click of the phone hanging up on this crank caller.

But eventually she heard a cautious, "Why?"

Bingo.

So then she explained that she was interested in the disappearance of a man named Elliot Klein because she'd been good friends with someone who'd known him quite well, "when he worked out here in the oil fields. In the early fifties. If it's the same person," she ended, and waited.

"Sounds like it."

"Are you a...a relation?"

Another long silence, broken by strange honking in the background. Pet geese? "Brother," he finally answered. "Elliot was my big brother. Look," he said after a moment, "I can't talk now, I'm just finishing up a lesson here. Are you in town?"

"Not too far." God help her, that forty-minute drive to Bakersfield was starting to feel like a short hop.

"Why don't you stop by tonight? Or meet me for coffee? I'd like to hear what this is all about."

They arranged to meet at an old coffee shop called Pete's at eight o'clock. This gave Claire time to finish her last ant farm and to answer her e-mail.

Pete's was the kind of funkily decrepit place that had inexplicably survived recessions, neighborhood changes, the advent of chain coffee shops, the rise of Starbucks, and the ravages of time. Actually, the ravages of time seemed to be getting the upper hand. The red vinyl booths were patched with black electrical tape, the Formica tables were chipped and dented, the linoleum flooring so worn through in places that the original pattern was completely gone. The waitresses seemed original as well.

Claire arrived five minutes early and found an empty booth in the back, near a door labeled RESTROOMS that she fervently hoped she wouldn't need to use. The waitress, identified as "Lil" by a little plastic badge perched on her ample bosom, pulled a pencil from her epoxied beehive and seemed genuinely surprised that Claire wanted only coffee. "We got some great pie," Lil confided, nodding toward the counter at the front where Claire had noticed an assortment of dispirited pastries quietly breeding bacteria beneath glass covers. "The peach is fresh."

Claire politely demurred, wondering how "fresh" was defined here and hoping that David Klein wasn't going to stand her up. She ached everywhere, and the realization that Charles would be arriving in less than twenty-four hours suffused her with dread. She had no business being in this or any other dive tonight; where she really belonged was home in bed, covers pulled over her head, stockpiling sleep for the coming familial ordeal.

When David Klein walked through the door, she recognized him instantly, even as she registered that he looked far too young to be Elliot's brother. He seemed older than her, but must have been very young when his big brother disappeared. And Elliot certainly got the looks in the family. David was small and narrow-shouldered, with a thin, deeply lined face and a sort of ugly-appealing Frank Sinatra charm. The primary family resemblance was in the wire-rimmed eyeglasses, which were dead ringers, so to speak, for the ones Claire had disinterred.

He was carrying an intriguing manila envelope, dog-eared and stained. He set it on the table beside a brown triangle that appeared to have been made by an iron, though it was difficult to imagine anyone pressing linens under this roof. As he carefully shook her hand, she noticed that his fingers were slender and gentle, which for some reason surprised her.

"So," he said, niceties out of the way, "who are you and what do you know about my brother?" He jingled the change in his pocket, then slid into the booth opposite her.

"First let's figure out if we're really talking about the same person," Claire suggested. She was making a real effort to like this guy, and he wasn't doing anything to help. She opened Jewell's album to the photo on the bank of the Kern, and laid Diana's picture of the four friends at the Lucky Spot next to it. "Is that your brother?"

He studied the pictures intensely, drumming his fingers on the table. "Oh, my God," he muttered, "oh, my God." He closed his eyes a moment, then opened them and peered again at the pictures. "It sure looks like him. I was only seven when he disappeared, but he looks the way I remember him. And like the family pictures."

He fished out a photo from the battered manila envelope and snapped it down like a playing card beside the other two. It was a high school graduation photo, complete with mortarboard and tassel. The subject seemed impossibly young, his face plump with youth, but there were the symmetrical features, the high-bridged nose, and the pale eyes. "This is the last one my parents had of him."

They both stared.

"Looks like three of a kind, doesn't it?" David said after a minute. He was fidgeting like a two-year-old, and Claire realized that he had not stopped moving for more than a few consecutive seconds since his arrival. Was he always this agitated, or was it the stress of finally finding his long-lost brother?

"That's what I was thinking."

"So where is he?" David demanded, suddenly hostile. "What happened to him?"

"I'm not absolutely sure," Claire answered slowly, "but I think he...died. About the time he disappeared. I'm sorry."

David had slumped back in his seat, and for a moment was actually motionless. "No, that's what I assumed. Why else would he not have called?" He sat up straight again, leaned forward, and began scratching behind his ear. "Elliot was the good son. *I* was the mistake, right from the start. Right from conception, I think. Anyway, how did it happen?"

"Again, I'm not sure, but we think he drowned. In the Kern River. Some remains were found last week.... The police are looking at them now, and they may never be identified for certain, but I have some reason to believe that they—that it, was your brother."

"You 'have some reason to believe'.... You're not the police, then—" He turned his watch round and round and round on his wrist. Lil came by with the coffeepot and Claire resisted the impulse to snatch the mug she brought right off the table. She wasn't sure she could take a caffeinated David Klein. What he needed, in her opinion, was warm milk. Or Ritalin.

"No. I'm a farm advisor, actually," she said. "I was on a field call when I found the...things."

"Bones?"

She nodded. "And eyeglasses."

He winced. Or anyway, she thought he winced. His face fidgeted like the rest of him, so that it was hard to distinguish between a passing tic and an actual expression. "Elliot's one imperfection. He got the family eyes—" motioning to his own glasses. "Or, the eyesight, not the eyes. Everybody else has—had—brown eyes, but his were green, I think. That's what Mom and Pop told me, anyway." He took off his glasses and rubbed the bridge of his nose; Claire could see now that his own eyes were really wonderful, too, in their own way—warm and expressive.

"He was a lot older than you, I guess," she said.

"Fourteen years. There was a sister in between, but she died of polio when she was twelve. So you can imagine how my folks felt when their son disappeared. And not just any son—their golden boy, their first-born."

It would have been better, David said, to know that Elliot was dead, because then his parents could have sat shiva or whatever and gone on. But as it was, their lives were in a sort of suspended animation. They just kept waiting for something. "Death, I guess," he said, "because that's what showed up."

It was Sophie's final illness, in fact, that had sent David out here in 1977 to try once more to locate his lost brother. "It was for myself as much as for Mom or Elliot. I don't know, I always thought that if I hadn't had this…this mythical big brother, my life might have turned out… Well, at the time I came out here, I was pretty aimless, doing a lot of drugs and so on—"

"That was the times," Claire reminded him.

"Yeah, but I embraced the times, I ran to meet them with arms open wide and tongue hanging out, let me tell you."

She laughed. She was beginning to like him.

"And I come out to this god-awful place—sorry, don't mean to be rude, but to an easterner—"

"I know. I'm from back east myself."

"Oh, yeah? Might have guessed. Not New York, though."

"New England."

"Ah. Well, then, you know what I mean. Bakersfield can seem like a bad joke. But the point is, I *liked* it! I liked the space, and the sense of possibility—big frog in small pond." Here his eyelids drooped, his cheeks puffed out, and for a moment he looked exactly like a bullfrog. "And I'd always liked the music. I'm a musician myself, you know, and there was a lot happening right then. I could get studio work, and produce a little—things I couldn't have done in a bigger town. I know, because I went down to L.A. for a while and went broke. I'm still not exactly raking it in, but between music lessons—"

"Clarinet?" she guessed, remembering the honking.

"And saxophone. And I still get a little session work and do some songwriting, so I just about make my mortgage and child support."

"Child support... So you met a woman out here, too?"

"Yeah. I got a nine-year-old and a twelve-year-old. What do you mean, 'too'? Oh, the girl in the picture?"

"Yes. I met her as an old woman, but she'd been a country singer back in the fifties, when she knew Elliot—what?"

David had made a strangled noise. "My wife—she was a country singer, too. Pretty weird." He drained his coffee. "Guess I'd better stay away from the Kern, huh?"

"Sound idea," she agreed, feeling her elbow, which seemed to have taken the brunt of the river. "Though nobody knows for sure that's what happened to your brother." He looked very alert—or his facial muscles contracted, anyway—and she said quickly, "That is, the remains haven't been identified. They probably can't be. This is all *my* speculation, based on what Jewell told me." She explained briefly, without going into some of her other speculations, and he seemed to relax.

"So he and this girl were an item," David said.

"They were going to get married."

"Oh, man, my parents would have loved *that*. Elliot marrying a hillbilly singer. Probably better he should disappear." He picked up the photograph. "What was her name?"

"Jewell Scoggins."

"Jewell Scoggins?" he echoed, astonished. "The Cherokee Rose? *She* was my brother's girlfriend?"

"You've heard of her?" Claire felt both surprised and pleased. Proprietary, almost.

"Yeah, I mean, I'm sort of a connoisseur of that era of the Bakersfield Sound. And her name always comes up. God, I'd love to meet her. For a couple of reasons, now."

Bad timing, David. "She's dead," Claire said gently. "Died last Thursday."

He sat bolt upright, quivering. "Last *week?*" He sounded outraged. "All this time we could have known each other, and she died a few days ago? No, that just can't be."

"It is."

"Life," he said, with an exaggerated shrug that seemed to be truly that, rather than a twitch. "And I've got another lesson in a half hour," he said, looking at his watch. "But listen, I'd love to talk to you some more. I don't think I've really processed all this yet, and I need to think about it all. I just can't believe that after all these years I've finally made some connection with Elliot. And that Elliot—my brother, the golden boy—that Elliot was engaged to the Cherokee Rose. It's all too weird."

He shook his head in wonder, then thought for a moment. "Would you have any interest in hearing a band I've been producing? They're playing in town this Thursday. Bring your husband—" he glanced at her left hand "—or a friend. Hell, bring an army. Thursday night isn't exactly prime time; seats will be very available. I'll put you on the guest list and they'll waive the cover."

"No, I don't think I can," she replied automatically. On Thursday night she'd be enmeshed in ego-to-ego combat with Charles.

"They're pretty good. And Trout's is a neat little club. A lot like the ones Jewell would have sung in," he coaxed.

"Well…" Claire suddenly found herself entertaining a wicked thought. Charles was a historian, was he not? One who had studied and written and lectured extensively on very specific events and movements around the United States. Charles had written his dissertation in Gary, Indiana, for God's sake, on patterns of immigrant assimilation in the steel mills. The history of the Bakersfield music scene was downright cheerful and antiseptic by comparison and might prove just the ticket for filling those awkward familial hours.

Also, it sounded as if David Klein knew plenty about the subject, and he was sharp enough and articulate enough to field the kind of inquisition Charles was likely to put forth, in the name of Research.

"My brother's coming to town," she told him. "He's a history professor. Would it be all right to bring him?"

David Klein smiled. "There's a lot of brothers floating around all of a sudden, you know? Sure, why not bring him. The more the—et cetera."

"Thanks." It occurred to her suddenly that she hadn't heard any live music in—well hell, it had been *years*. She began embroidering the guest list; perhaps Ramón would be interested in joining them, too, and they could ask Yolie, and maybe Sam and Linda would like to come, Sam being such a country music aficionado.

She administered a sharp mental slap to her right cheek at the very notion. For a few moments, she realized now, she had entirely forgotten the creaky joints and bruised muscles tucked away out of sight beneath her long-sleeved cotton shirt and khakis.

"Eight o'clock," he said. "It's on Union, down by the circle."

14

CLAIRE WAITED FOR CHARLES on her deck, wineglass in hand, watching light fade throughout the canyon. He'd called not long ago, as they'd arranged, to let her know he had exited Highway 99 and was heading up into the mountains. Unless he got lost or waylaid—neither prospect, regrettably, likely to occur—he would be at her door in a matter of minutes.

And then what? Claire had labored over mental lists of entertainment possibilities, assuming that he wanted to be entertained and not merely accommodated. Mindful of the genuine pain that David Klein seemed to be suffering in having lost his own brother—a brother he had barely known and hadn't seen for decades—she had decided to make a particular effort to get along with Charles.

It would not, she knew, be easy.

They had been bound, through years with no meaningful

communication whatsoever, by separate and nearly invisible tethers to their mother. With her gone, and—perhaps even more important to someone as grounded in *place* as Charles—with her house, the family home, sold to strangers, they would have to find some new common ground. Seeing where Claire lived, and how, would allow Charles to classify her in much the same way as she had him mentally catalogued: *magister historiae superbus.*

She had never mentioned this to Charles, unsure how good his Latin really was. He had no facility for foreign languages and had suffered through German and French only to the extent necessary for his various degrees. But Charles was not a stupid man, and he might well realize that this Latin designation, which appeared on its surface to be laudatory, actually meant "arrogant history professor."

Which he was, make no mistake—the kind of self-important bozo that Claire had never been able to stand.

Charles Manchester Sharples had never been a Charlie, or God forbid, a Chuck.

He had always carried an aura of formality, even as a slight lad on the boyhood schoolyard, where he was beaten up with some regularity as he waited patiently for his day to come, that glorious and inevitable time when peer recognition would accrue from intellectual accomplishment rather than athletic achievement. Claire, following him through school at three years' distance, had both benefited and suffered from the shared surname; benefiting in classrooms where Charles had paved the road of academic respect for her, and suffering in the unavoidable association with his geekiness.

That she herself possessed much the same kind of geekiness was a realization she did not come to until years later, when she caught her reflection in the Saturday-night window of a Cambridge laboratory and thought, Why, that's Charles!

He had plowed a stellar ivy path through Amherst (B.A. in history, *summa cum laude*, tennis team captain, Rhodes Scholar finalist) and Yale (M.A. and Ph.D in American history, with a nearly published dissertation). Charles had never really left New England for any longer than it took to complete his steel mill dissertation research in Gary—where he had been, so far as Claire could determine, thoroughly appalled and repelled by the town and everything within it. At the first opportunity, he had fled back to the safe harbor of New England when he landed a tenure-track position in the history department at Dartmouth. And there he'd been ever since.

Charles had a C.P.A. wife and two predictably overachieving children, now nine and eleven, and he rarely ventured beyond the New Hampshire border, or maybe Boston for something really important. For him to be attending the AHA Conference at UCLA was somewhat unusual, although not unheard of; for him to be extending his trip to visit Claire in the outback was unprecedented.

She poured herself more wine as she considered what could be regarded as the significance of the occasion. Not one blood relative—all right, an admittedly limited field, even when you extended into first cousins once removed and second cousins, but still—had ever come to visit Claire in California. This was okay; she had, after all, deliberately distanced herself from her kinfolk. Still, in a culture so cluttered with various extended families—modern Latino farm workers, Dust Bowl immigrants, even the Chinese descendants of Leong Yen Ming, the Potato King of Kern County—it was impossible not to occasionally notice that she herself was unencumbered by family engagements.

So what had motivated Charles to make this trip, anyway? He was relentless in his scorn of California. His youthful liberalism had calcified into a crotchety conservatism best evidenced in his most recent scholarly publication, a treatise justifying the underpayment of Carnegie steel workers as a necessity to ensure sufficient funds to build all those libraries. Claire had not even attempted to argue that one, had merely choked and nodded when he mentioned the paper not long after their mother's funeral.

Why *was* Charles coming now?

A sense of duty, Claire suspected, a motivation that had less to do with any desire to cultivate sibling quality time than with a sense of awkward familial obligation. *We who remain must bond.*

She heard his car then, cautiously traversing the switchbacks to her house, and she turned on the burner to warm up the dinner, a family standard that she made on occasion from the recipe card written in her mother's cramped and joyless hand. Chicken and dumplings. With a ridiculously expensive and very fine Napa Valley chardonnay, which she had just been subjecting to quality control. The perfect meal for a woman with one foot mired in each culture.

She heard the car door slam and went to meet her fate.

Three hours later she was quite loaded and Charles, who had brought along a bottle of his favorite pretentious Scotch, a single malt variety with a name loaded with improbable consonant combinations, was proving to be exceptionally loquacious.

"Are you ready for the ephemera?" he asked now, sitting with one leg crossed primly over the other. He was dressed down for the occasion in jeans and a heavy, cable-knit fawn-colored cotton sweater, with rugged suede hiking boots just worn enough to be believable.

Ah yes. The ephemera. Like Jewell's photo album, and Diana's scrapbook, only related to the Sharples family. Charles had been vague about exactly what he had brought, but he had carried in a small leather suitcase that Claire recognized immediately from the attic of their mother's home. Their childhood home.

A home now occupied by a family with three children under the age of ten, a family that Claire liked to picture laughing, on those rare occasions when she thought of them or the house at all. She had snatched out a few objects before returning to California after the funeral, taking things almost at random and automatically investing them with value. A small, badly framed painting of a waterfall that had hung in her childhood bedroom.

The nearly antique Oster blender. A weathered pewter pitcher used to hold daylilies in the summer and chrysanthemums in the fall. The button bag. The lamp she had made in seventh-grade home mechanics. Her parents' wedding portrait.

These items had now been so fully integrated into Claire's home that she no longer noticed them other than as part of her personal landscape. Except for the wedding portrait, which she had tucked into a drawer for reasons she could not articulate. On arrival, Charles had cast a curator's eye about the place, identifying each item from their past instantly, and with a certain measure of pleasure. It had given her, she saw now, a sort of buffer zone of time and sentiment, before they had to actually start relating.

And at the moment, she realized, she had related as much as she was capable of in a single evening. "Tomorrow," she told Charles. "Let's hold the ephemera for tomorrow." And then, determining that he had all the necessary bedding and required no further attention, she stumbled off to more painkillers and a deep, dreamless sleep.

By the time Claire opened a cautious eye in the morning, Charles—still on New Hampshire time—had been up for hours. She followed a not particularly appealing aroma of coffee and burnt toast to find Charles ensconced in the same chair he'd occupied the previous evening, working his way through a pile of scholarly journals.

She watched from the doorway for a moment before announcing herself. He was, she realized with an odd and uncharacteristic pride, quite a distinguished-looking man, unmistakably an intellectual, but not of the variety that proved hopelessly effete when removed from library or classroom. Here, with the mountainside just outside the window, clad in a hearty plaid flannel shirt and suspiciously smooth jeans—did he press them? did his *wife?*—he might actually have been the homeowner instead of the out-of-town guest. Now he looked up over his glasses and nodded. "I took the liberty of making coffee."

"*Mi casa es su casa,*" she replied, in her most polished accent. "Did you find everything all right?"

He nodded, then frowned. Claire realized too late that the baggy T-shirt in which she slept had left her arms and legs revealed in all their hideously hematomaed glory. Her appendages resembled tie-dyed efforts by a rookie who just couldn't quit, had kept dipping till everything had a murky, purply-green, streaky quality.

"I fell in the river," she announced. Better to hit this one head-on and get it over with. She'd been crazy to think she could hide it, and why bother? She went through the story as concisely as possible, leaving no openings for questions. When she finished, she rewarded herself with a cup of coffee and used it to wash down the morning's Advil, which were more necessary at this point for her throbbing head than her aching muscles.

"So what would you like to do?" she asked, nibbling on a muffin. The previous night she had outlined a menu of possibilities beginning with what she considered the obligatory visit to her workplace. It had been, she noticed at the time, a fairly short list.

"Your laboratory, of course," Charles dutifully began. "And then perhaps that historical village you mentioned?" His tone held doubt that this desolate wasteland possessed any sort of history that he, a trained professional, would find worthy of his attention.

"I haven't been there," Claire confessed, backpedaling reflexively. "So I can't speak to anything but its existence." If she didn't visit a local attraction within two weeks of her arrival in a location, she had discovered, she never went there at all until something or someone, usually an out-of-town guest, forced her hand. You could put together a very respectable guidebook listing all the museums and historical sites she had failed to visit while living in Boston.

The Ag Station visit went smoothly enough, everyone polite and adequately respectful of Charles. She took him around to meet the others first, introducing her boss, Ray Copeland, and co-workers Mac Healy and Bob Higgenlooper. Kate Dolmovic was out somewhere, as was Sam, and there was no sign of any recent visitation from Ramón. They then adjourned to her own lab, where time seemed to stretch like Silly Putty. She had decided it was foolish, while she was there, not to try to tie up some miscellaneous loose ends that would only become looser if neglected further. Charles perched dutifully on a stool and feigned interest in various technical publications, his relief palpable when they left to drive down to Bakersfield.

"The town was named pretty literally," she told him now, assuming a knowledgeable air. Claire's local history was mostly anecdotal; she knew no dates, but could tell you, for instance, all manner of detail about Fanny Tracy, the Bird Lady of Buttonwillow, who raised a herd of ostriches and made a pretty penny with her feather factory back in the early twentieth century. "Colonel Baker earned his rank at nineteen in the Ohio State Militia, before Ohio was even a state, so I don't think he was really much of a military man. This Central Valley was partially a vast wetland full of tules. Colonel Baker made his money draining swampland, and he made it late in life. But he's remembered because he planted an alfalfa field on his property and let travelers camp there. Baker's Field, they called it."

"Hmph," Charles said, clearly unimpressed. "Place names tend to be related to the original settlers. Shafter was another one I noticed yesterday, and I keep thinking I ought to know who that was."

Yes, maybe you should, *magister*. "Pecos Bill Shafter, the fattest general of the U.S. Cavalry, Spanish-American War." Occasionally it was an advantage to have a mind that catalogued random bits of useless information. "The one I think you'd enjoy even more is Rosedale. That was a colony of Brits who came out in the late nineteenth century and set up a *rancho* where they planted rose gardens in which to serve tea. They were big on concerts and Shakespeare festivals, but they didn't know shit about farming and most of them eventually went back to England or moved on to South America."

Charles nodded wisely. "Remittance men."

Claire decided not to give him the satisfaction of asking exactly what that meant; most likely an earlier version of the trust-funders she'd encountered occasionally in Boston, writing unpublished autobiographical novels or producing their own little films starring their friends.

"To be honest, the town names that I most enjoyed driving up from L.A. yesterday were Pumpkin Center and Weed Patch. I trust they weren't named for Messrs. Pumpkin and Weed."

Claire laughed. "How could anybody *not* love a town that dares to call itself Pumpkin Center? And Weed Patch was a slough, and apparently the natural vegetation could be seen at quite a distance. There was a work camp there during the Depression that Steinbeck wrote about in *The Grapes of Wrath*. It's where the Joads stayed."

"Hmph," Charles said. Migrant workers of any era seemed to hold little appeal. He waved a hand at a field they were passing, where dozens of cotton modules sat in neat rows like so many overgrown loaves of Wonder Bread. "I assume that's cotton, but what's the point of leaving it sitting out like that?"

Aha! Something that actually played into Claire's area of expertise.

"Those are cotton modules," she told him, "and if you form your own in the field, then the gin will transport them for you. The technology's only about thirty years old, actually, and the idea came out of haystacks in Texas, but it works better with cotton because seed cotton sticks to itself. See over there on the left?"

She indicated a cluster of agricultural equipment in the middle of a newly stripped field. A huge cage of freshly picked cotton was pouring a waterfall of fluffy white bolls into what looked like a boxcar. "Once the cotton's picked, it gets stuffed into the module maker and tamped down hydraulically. They pull the framework away once it's formed and cover it. After that, it can sit right there in the field for a pretty long time without any danger of significant damage because it's so dry here. Even if you have a flash flood, only the bottom six inches or so will be affected."

Charles craned his neck as they passed—a good sign; his interest in the San Joaquin Valley had not, thus far, elevated above rock-bottom civility. "Then how do you move it? Those things are enormous."

"They weigh tons," she agreed. "You use a module-mover. Back a flatbed truck up to the module and tilt it back. Then moving chains pull the whole thing up onto the flatbed and haul it to the gin. Which leaves your equipment free to make the next module, instead of having to wait around for your truck while your cotton's being ginned."

They were coming into Bakersfield now, and Charles summarily nixed Claire's suggestion of Mexican food for lunch, explaining tersely that it did not agree with him. Chicken McNuggets, however, apparently did, and he dipped each one methodically into the faux-barbecue sauce, nibbling delicately, apparently comforted and reassured by the familiarity. Claire self-righteously ate this month's offering for noncarnivores, a dispirited salad, then headed for the Kern County Pioneer Village.

The Kern County Pioneer Village turned out to be a hodge-podge of relocated and/or reproduced historical buildings from around the county, scattered on fourteen acres north of town, acreage that had once housed winter labor camps. Though Jewell Scoggins had perhaps lived in this very camp as a girl, it was difficult to think of this space in that fashion, at least in the flat white heat of the early October afternoon.

"Colonial Williamsburg it's not," Charles announced, after ten minutes.

The grounds were uncrowded, though the Sharples siblings had dodged several well-behaved groups of Latino schoolchildren and the occasional silver-haired retired tourist couple; mostly, however, they had the place to themselves. Now they stood outside the Undertaking Parlor, peering through the windows of the small frame building at yet another slice-of-life representation, a technique that varied dramatically in effectiveness from one building to the next. Here the effect was downright creepy: wicker and wooden sample caskets were displayed in a public area at the left; behind a screen to the right, a sinister male mannequin hovered above a sheeted figure on a marble table, wielding a nasty-looking primitive trocar that resembled nothing so much as Lucifer's trident.

"A bit hokey," Claire conceded cheerfully. Perhaps they could hustle through the rest of the place and go back home. She needed more ibuprofen and a nap. Fortunately Charles had reacted with horror when she halfheartedly suggested a visit to the scene of Sunday's Kern River adventure. "But I bet the kids like it just fine. Nice and gruesome, you know?"

Charles shuddered and moved on, finding fault with the various exhibits—this one too poor a reproduction, this other too common a Victorian home, still another a pathetic... Claire was tuning him out, until he suddenly sprang to life when they reached the back of the museum grounds, looking like a hunting dog who'd just scented prey.

It was an elephant's graveyard of abandoned machinery lying behind some minimal wire fencing that had caught and held Professor Charles Sharples's attention. Interesting, since this was the one area that did have a feel of previous habitation to it, where it was possible to imagine the hardship of those labor camp winters. There were ghosts in that jumble of antique wood and iron, ghosts of the men and women who had lived and worked and died here.

Claire recognized most of the farm implements—a melange of hay balers and combines and other primitive agricultural equipment—mostly because she knew their upscale modern-day descendants; she took a certain perverse pride in being able to identify them for Charles. And then, mercifully, it was time to head for home, for charcoal-broiled cowflesh and ephemera.

Which proved less daunting than Claire had feared.

Charles had brought several old family photo albums, most of which she remembered, and the feelings that rose from their pages were largely pleasurable ones. A collection of mimeographed playbills for amateur theatrical productions revealed a genuine surprise: her parents had both, in their courting days, been budding thespians.

"What happened?" Claire wondered, turning over a faded mint-green program from, predictably enough, *Our Town.* Neither parent had played lead roles, but both names were there, and Mom was also listed under costume production.

"I think *we* did," Charles answered. "These were in a box in the attic, along with a lot of old *National Geographic* maps. The latest date I could find for any production was four months before I was born."

"And then it just ended?" There was something so very unsettling about his sudden revelation, as if getting a glimpse into her mother's carefree youth, into her emotional life before Claire. Even at this safe remove it wasn't easy, though certainly safer than it would have been when she was actually alive.

Charles peered over the top of his glasses at her. Imperious didn't begin to describe it. "If you had children, Claire, you'd understand."

Oh, swell. She did not feel inclined to wrestle with that particular alligator, so picked up a cooking scrapbook that had sat on the top shelf of her mother's pantry for as long as she could remember and began carefully turning the crumbling pages. It was filled with brown-edged recipes clipped from newspapers, and the dishes were not ones that she remembered ever gracing the Sharples table. Who had put this together, she wondered for the first time, and why? Was it a sort of culinary trousseau, perhaps, for her mother or some other female relative? There were no dates on any of the neatly trimmed recipes, no way to guess their age, beyond *old.*

She found the candy section particularly fascinating: fudge recipes calling for "butter the size of a walnut," page after page of Divinity, actual recipes for marshmallows. Many of the recipes were absolutely identical.

"You know, the original marshmallows were chewy because they were made with a gelatinous extract from the roots of mallows that grew in marshes." Even as she made the statement, Claire realized that she had blown both her botanical and culinary wads here; if Charles asked a single follow-up question, she would have to confess that she knew nothing more about marshmallows other than that they went well with Hershey bars and graham crackers.

"Huh," he grunted, flipping through their father's high school yearbook. He looked up, frowning. "You know," he confessed, "I had an idea that going through this with you would be somehow synergistic, but it doesn't seem to be working that way."

"If I recall correctly, that's characteristic of most things related to this family," Claire told him. "They don't work according to plan. I think maybe we're trying too hard, Charles. And I think I'm going to start the coals."

15

IN THE MORNING, inspired by her brother's apparently genuine interest in the cotton modules they had seen the previous day, Claire offered to arrange a cotton gin tour for him, and much to her surprise, he accepted. It being the height of ginning season, finding a place in operation was simple enough, but there seemed no reason not to go for broke. After ten minutes in the shower, arguing the pros and cons with herself and relieved to see that her various bruises were finally healing, she called a friend for the number of the manager of Tidwell Ginning. Introducing herself with an emphasis on her state position, she had no trouble getting his agreement to show her and her out-of-town guest through the place. They could stop by any time after ten, he told her. And oh yeah, his name was Walsh, Frank Walsh.

Walsh was in a small, freshly painted building several hundred yards from the gin when they arrived at high noon. Modules of cotton were lined up between the gin and the road and from this perspective they seemed gargantuan. A half-full trailer of cotton hauled by a no-nonsense woman with an awesome beehive was backing into the uptake area outside the gin.

Walsh was a friendly enough fellow in his late forties, with a head of sandy-silver hair, a protruding gut, and a missing chunk on the end of his right ring finger. He caught Claire's quick appraisal when they shook hands and offered a deprecating laugh. "All us old-timers are missing a joint or two," he explained with a joviality that didn't even seem forced. "That equipment can be wicked. Our head ginner's called Stumpy."

Beside her, Claire was aware of Charles clenching and unclenching his fists. This was a little more reality than he'd bargained for; in his line of work, mutilation was far more subtle and revolved around the psyche.

Claire smiled appreciatively. "You worked here long?" There was a secretary's desk, unoccupied, just inside the door and a closed door in the back. Tidwell's office? Was he here? There were various dusty pickups and vehicles scattered outside, most presumably belonging to gin employees. No red SUVs.

"Ten, fifteen years. Mr. Tidwell's had the place since 'fifty-nine, but I worked at Kern Delta a long time before I come here."

"Mr. Tidwell here today?" She hoped the question seemed nonchalant. Certainly it was irrelevant.

Walsh shook his head. "He's in and out during the season, but haven't seen him today."

Claire was disappointed, although she had no idea what she would have said to the reclusive developer/wildcatter/ginner/maybe-murderer had he walked through the door. Heard from Elliot Klein lately, Clyde?

"So," Walsh went on, "you got us at the height of our season here. Let me give you a little fast overview, 'cause once we get inside that gin, ain't no way to talk. It's *loud.*"

"I know," Claire said. "The professor brought earplugs." Might as well bond a little with the guy, two Joaquinos against the Yankee, although Frank Walsh didn't seem too terribly perceptive. "You have a Lummis gin?" It was one of three possible gin manufacturers, a popular Valley choice, and a safe enough guess.

Walsh nodded. "We're a lot smaller than some of the big guys, but it's the same operation. We preclean to get the trash out of the cotton, then we warm it up in the tower drier and send it into the feeder. That's pretty much it."

Claire picked up a fluffy, fairly pristine boll off his desk and showed it to Charles. "This is how it looks when it's just picked, only it's likely to have a lot of dirt or plant debris in it. The precleaning removes that, and the heat in the driers softens the fiber so it can be broken down into single locks, with one seed per piece. Then when it gets into the gin itself, rotating saw blades pull the fibers off the seeds. Those blades are the source of the accidents he was telling us about." Charles still had his fists clenched; he hadn't forgotten.

"And then what happens to the seeds?" Charles asked, looking a trifle queasy. "Do they get made into cottonseed oil?"

Claire raised a surprised eyebrow. This was more than she'd expected him to know.

Frank Walsh laughed. "Useta have to go to a lot of trouble with the seed, but no more. We sell it as cattle feed these days and the cows eat it like it was popcorn."

Charles frowned and seemed to be running down a mental checklist. "From what Claire's been telling me, this is basically the same process that Eli Whitney used. Is that correct?"

Walsh looked momentarily puzzled. History around here mostly had to do with last week's bale totals.

"More or less," Claire told him. "Frank, we don't want to hold you up. How about we take a look inside the gin now?"

"You betcha," he answered, and she could tell he'd bitten off the "little lady" that would have automatically followed.

As they headed outside, Charles inserted his earplugs. Inside the gin it was every bit as loud as promised, and then some. Deafening, if you wanted to be honest about it, which Claire didn't really. She watched with moderate interest as Frank Walsh pointed out the tower driers and the whirring saw blades of the gin. But she was fascinated by the bale press at the end of the process. The cleaned and ginned cotton, in the final step on its journey, was sent down a chute where it accumulated, under repeated hydraulic pressure, until sufficient was present for a bale. Then the finished bale popped up at floor level again, ready to be automatically wrapped, tied, and sent to market.

"Had us a fellow got crushed in one of them years ago," Walsh said when they were back outside. Claire could feel her fillings vibrating from the residual racket. "Not here, another place I was working. He went down to unjam something and the guys up top didn't know he was down there and turned on the baler. Couldn't hear a thing, 'course, even if he'da yelled for help. Guy on the baler passed out cold when he saw what come out."

A grisly image, indeed. Charles, who had once lost his teenage composure when the dog pulled a used tampon from the bathroom trash, paled visibly.

There was ample time for an early dinner before meeting Ramón and Yolie to hear David Klein's band at Trout's, an event that Charles was making an obvious effort to be a good sport about. Dinner was Charles's treat and he wanted what he called American food; they found it at the Sheraton, a locale and meal that reassured Charles much as McDonald's had the previous day. As the visit moved into its final hours—Charles would depart before first light in the morning to head down to L.A. and his passage homeward—Claire had the sense they were both relieved to have it nearly over.

Ramón and Yolie met them in the hotel lobby, Yolie swiveling her head like a lawn sprinkler as she surveyed unsuspecting businessmen for signs of God-knows-what. Ramón had required no coaxing to invite Yolie on the outing—great minds—and it turned out that Trout's had once been her favorite hangout.

The men sized each other up in that butt-sniffing, ground-pawing manner that males of the species so often exhibit, and she could feel their impressions: pompous ass; immigrant rube. Claire ignored them both. But as they climbed into Charles's rental car, the mood changed perceptibly and they all seemed giddy as teens on the town: Charles, to be nearly through his passage in purgatory; Claire, to be going on a pseudo-date with Ramón; Ramón, for maybe the same reason; Yolie, to be going anywhere at all.

On the way, Yolie pointed to a franchise fast-food restaurant and said, "That's where the Blackboard was, up until a few years ago. Where Merle and Buck and every other important Bakersfield musician played. I can't believe they let it be torn down. Well, of course I can. Greedy bastards." Claire thought of Jewell.

Just beyond the erased Blackboard, they turned into a parking lot in a neighborhood of auto part suppliers, repair shops, smoggers, tire stores, and car washes—an area designed to offer maximum care for your pickup. Trout's itself was in the same block as a tattoo parlor and a storefront ministry.

Above the door of the club a neon trout leaped and glittered, fell back, arched again; its incessant motion reminded Claire of David Klein, who was already sitting at the bar racking up empties when they entered. They found a table near the dance floor, and David joined them. Tonight he just sat, motionless; the beer had evidently depressed his central nervous system to normal.

The club was dim and loud with the roar of the already-drunk and the music of a country band. David's band, she supposed. They were not bad, although none of them could sing—they could have used a Jewell Scoggins, or even a lesser female singer—but they were tight, and the fiddle player was good. A tall, skinny guy, very dark, with a piratical goatee, he would have looked more convincing in a turban than in his white felt cowboy hat. Charles crossed his arms in the manner of an anthropologist in the bush, Yolie and David immediately fell into animated conversation about Trout's, Ramón went off to get them all drinks, and Claire settled back to study the dancers, moving three feet away from her.

It always surprised her that the local Anglo-macho-cowboy culture did not consider dancing unmanly. The men were more than proficient, they were into it—as a demonstration of athleticism and as a declaration of personal style. They steered their little two-person cruisers around the parquet dance floor, defining the coupling technique—traditional hand-on-back, modified tango straight-arm, possessive neck-clutch, and the mood—exuberant, insouciant, flamboyant, or smoldering. Only when the band played an occasional straight rock 'n' roll number—"Proud Mary," say—that defeated coupled dancing, did the women come into their own, bumping and grinding with abandon while the men moved around them, waving feeble arms like overturned beetles. And the women also dominated the fiendishly intricate line dances.

"Sorry that took so long." Ramón, breathless, slid in with a tray full of beers and tumblers of Scotch. Hardly looking up, Yolie and David grabbed beers. Charles carefully lifted his Scotch and took a tentative sip.

"I've been observing," Claire said. "The sociodynamics of dancing are just as revealing as they were during Jane Austen's day."

Charles raised an eyebrow; Jane Austen was not a name he'd expected to hear in this setting.

"And what do you conclude?" Ramón asked.

"That men need couples more than women."

Ramón opened his mouth to retort, but just then the band took a break, scattering to various ripe-looking blondes sitting along the edge of the dance floor. The fiddle player looked a little lost for a moment, then joined their table.

"Hey, Garo," David said, and made introductions.

Garo looked at Yolie, decided she was with David, looked at Charles, decided he was with the Census Bureau, and asked Claire to dance to the taped music now playing. She made excuses. She had once learned to do an inept two-step, but basically she didn't dance. He shrugged and made a beeline for a fluffy blonde who had just walked in.

"Do you really not dance?" asked Ramón.

"Yes, I really don't. Do you?"

"All Latinos can dance. It's part of our genotype." He held out his hand and motioned toward the dance floor.

"Well, it's not part of mine," she said, reluctantly grasping his hand and letting him haul her up, acutely aware of Charles watching. "And I really can't follow, so don't try anything fancy."

But once on the floor, she forgot all about Charles. Ramón was a traditional hand-on-backer, and with a good deal of embarrassment, and a few more pleasant emotions, she slid her arm around his shoulder.

"Don't worry," he said. "For a big man I'm light on my feet."

"Big man?" she repeated as they shuffled along in a staid two-step. "You think you're fat?"

"Well," he said mournfully, "at fifty I started to thicken. Like all the Covarrubias men."

"I would have said, substantial." Though he was an armful, after Sam's skinny frame. Not that Sam would dance.

"Substantial." He tried out the word. "I'll take that. You, on the other hand—" gathering her in a little "—are as lissome as a teenager."

She snorted. "Is that on the same chromosome as the dancing gene? Heavy-handed flattery?"

He grinned and tried to direct her through a turn; she stepped on her own feet and nearly fell.

"Don't *do* that!" she snapped as she found the rhythm again.

"It's easy. You just have to relax and trust me."

"Trust you, huh?" It was uncomfortable to have his face looming so close; she found herself staring at the line of lighter skin around his upper lip, like the rim left by a sculptor's chisel. She was very aware of the not-quite-healed scratches on her nose and cheekbone, and that she had yet to discuss her river adventure with him. Over his shoulder she said, "How about if you just describe what I'm supposed to do?"

There was a pause. "Always got to be in control."

"I just like to know what I'm getting into."

"Hmmm. Okay. Let me think. Um…as my arm comes up and across, you're going to step back with your right, no, left, foot, and pivot—"

She listened carefully and after a couple of beats they tried again. This time she ended up balanced and facing him, flushed and triumphant.

They continued dancing even after the band came back, and eventually Claire began to enjoy the socially sanctioned embrace, and stop worrying about her feet, and about pulling her sleeves down to hide her bruises. Almost.

And then there was a slow song with a lyric that mirrored her own confusion. She moved in rhythm with Ramón as she listened. *The faster that I go, the farther that I get behind, and I think there's a part of me that's still on mountain time.* In silent agreement that the moment had gone far enough, they returned to the table, carefully avoiding each other's eyes.

"The saxophone!" Yolie was in animated conversation with David when they sat back down. "That's one of my favorite instruments. How long have you been teaching?"

Claire smiled. Yolie obviously had also gotten the flirting gene.

Ramón looked at his watch. "Oh, Jesus, it's almost eleven. I have to be at work tomorrow at six."

Charles, on his fourth Scotch, looked up hopefully. He wasn't going to be the one to break up this little gathering, oh no, but he wouldn't argue departure. They all stood up, including Yolie.

"I can run you home later," David said quickly. There was definitely something going on here, something Claire found herself cheering from the wings. Yolie was too interesting, too special, too irrepressible to stay locked in her crack-house dungeon forever.

Yolie looked uncertain, twirled her braid. "No, I'd better go on with the others. But here." She pulled a card out of her pocket. "If you get the machine, keep talking. I screen my calls."

"Me, too," David said. "Fucking telemarketers."

On the way back to the hotel where Ramón had left his truck,

Yolie interrogated Claire about David Klein, until she finally seemed reassured that he was what he appeared to be, and not part of a nefarious scheme of C.C. Tidwell's to catch Yolanda Covarrubias off-guard. This was not the time, Claire decided, to tell her whose cotton gin they'd visited that day, or to see if the story of a man crushed to death in a baler was actually true. The more time passed, the more she sensed that Frank Walsh had known exactly who she was and had been deliberately trying to scare her. Which was, of course, the first thing that Yolie would tell her.

After dropping off the cousins, Claire settled back into the passenger seat of Charles's rental car, weary of conversation and even more weary of her brother's visit, which seemed to have lasted at least a month. Dancing with Ramón had created the illusion of intimacy and a hunger for more, and Claire found herself beset with the familiar doubts and anxieties that accompany courting rituals. What *did* she want?

Simple. She wanted what she had not, and could not, get.

16

ON THE FOLLOWING Tuesday, Cornell called back. Claire had forgotten about them, since the Kern County missing person's report had rendered their information moot, and they were apologetic about having taken so long. Her request had been mislaid, somebody'd been out sick, they normally responded much more quickly. Alumni contributions must be way down.

Their information matched her own. Elliot Klein had been a Cornell student, class of 1955—but he hadn't graduated, and they didn't know why not; it would be difficult to ascertain after all this time. The last address they had for him was his parents' in Brooklyn, and that was in '54.

Immediately after Claire hung up, Yolie called to say she was about to send a fax. She had done this once before, fax being the method of communication Yolie deemed least likely to be suborned, and while Claire respected the paranoia, it was still a pain in the ass. So in a few minutes, she went upstairs to the office fax machine and waited for the note with its distinctive *shred this—shred this—shred this—shred this* sender line to come through. What would it be? Hot new revelations about Kern County land mismanagement? Clyde Tidwell's medical records? The latest skinny on corruption in the Sheriff's Department?

When the fax arrived and she read it, Claire laughed out loud. It was purely social. David had invited Yolie to see his band record; would Claire like to come, and could she provide a ride? Yolie didn't want David to see where she lived, which could be either embarrassment or paranoia. Still smiling, Claire scrawled a response and sent it back, agreeing to play duenna. She added, "Yolie, if you're going to be dating, you have to let your date see where you live sooner or later." As she was leaving the room, the machine whirred again.

"I'm not going to be dating," Yolie had written beneath Claire's comment, in what was likely to be the most disingenuous comment of the week.

"Let's try another take on that vocal, Jimbo." David spoke into a microphone in the control booth of the Music Barn, an old house on A Street in Bakersfield. "Try and do a growl on that first phrase."

"*I don't know why, but I never knew, the sky was exactly that color of blue,*" came experimentally through the speakers, ending in a sort of gargle.

David rolled his eyes at Yolie and Claire and flipped on the mike again. "Okay, maybe no growl. Just sing it straight. From the top."

In a moment the guitar player's voice came through the speakers. He could hear the entire track through his headphones, but in the booth all they heard was his naked voice, uncertain and unadorned. It was a good song, and she found herself wondering how Jewell would have sung it.

Claire had finally made her peace with country music,

dropping her resentment for what it lacked—rhythmic and me-
lodic originality, for example—and appreciating what it had.
Country music was about voice. Not *singing*, exactly, the singing
had its own limitations; but *voice*, the timbre of yearning. Sometimes the lyrics were clever and well-wrought, too, but that
hardly mattered: in the right mood, Claire could choke up at
Vince Gill singing the sappiest, simplest declaration of undying
love, with some sweet, tight harmony behind him.

She especially liked the subgenre of "Baby, I know you've
been burned, but don't give up on love; let me kiss away those
scars and teach you how to love again," sung by a male voice. She
found herself wondering now if Ramón could sing. He could
definitely growl.

Jimbo wasn't much on either, but he did make it to the end
without screwing up really badly, and he actually improved during the chorus:

> *'Cause you, you are a miracle worker,*
> *Oh you, you do your sorcery.*
> *I don't know how, but baby, you bring*
> *Some kind of magic to everything.*

"Okay, Jim, that's a keeper," David said reassuringly to the
singer, then switched off his mike and muttered to the engineer.
"What do you think? Maybe the verse and chorus from this one
plus the bridge from two?"

"Sure!" the engineer agreed with fake heartiness, as if this
were the most exciting band ever to record in the Music Barn.
Earlier, when Claire and Yolie had been the only people in the
booth, he had been regaling them with stories of the absurd
hopefuls who had trooped through his studio during the years:
Faith, Hope, and Charity, atonal triplets; a barbershop quartet
of Shriners in Al Marakail jewelled fezzes; the lipsticked seven-
year-old whose mother had one eye on Broadway and the
other on Hollywood; an endless parade of Elvis imitators. His
favorite of this last group had come complete with cape and

mini-entourage, who had listened intently to each playback, pronouncing it "just like the King" when he was satisfied. All that had been missing was banana-and-peanut butter sandwiches.

While Jimbo labored through his part, the rest of the band had been lounging in a corner of the recording studio; now they meandered into the control booth, perhaps seeking the sorcery that the song had promised. Claire looked for the cute fiddle player, Garo, and realized she wasn't the only one window-shopping when Yolie leaned over and whispered, "Don't you think Ray would look sharp with a goatee?"

"Hard to imagine. But—yes. Sort of rakish. He wouldn't do it, would he?"

"Nah. He's not vain enough."

David played the partially mixed song now and it was surprising to hear the vocal with the track around it and harmonies stacked above it. It was no longer embarrassing; not that different, in fact, from run-of-the-mill radio fare. The band was happy, anyway, fizzing with post-performance euphoria.

"Nice fiddle part," Claire told Garo, and meant it.

"You guys take a break," David said, "and I'll lay down that sax part on 'Miracle Worker.' Be right back," he told Yolie—he addressed both women, but was obviously talking to Yolie.

When he disappeared into the recording studio, it was suddenly like watching him on TV, in pantomime: David picked up his saxophone, ran through a couple of silent scales, settled the headphones, leaving one ear free so he could hear himself.

"Let me try one," came his voice from the speaker.

Once again they couldn't hear the track in the booth, just the sax solo. But this time that was a blessing, because David was considerably better than his protégés, with the possible exception of the fiddle player. The sax filled the booth and left Claire humming.

He finished a take that satisfied him and came back into the booth. "So what do you think of the band?" he asked Yolie and Claire.

"They're okay," Yolie said with a smile that on anybody else would have been described as coquettish. "You're better."

He looked pleased. "Yeah. I think I blow some pretty good horn. But a guy's gotta make a living."

"And so does a gal," Claire said. "I've got to get up in the morning, Yolie."

Once again David offered to run Yolie home, and once again she refused. Claire drifted tactfully out into the hall, where the boys in the band were smoking and drinking vending-machine coffee. After a short time Yolie joined her.

"Let's go."

"You're sure you don't want to let David take you home?"

"Positive."

But in the car on the way home Yolie said, "He did ask me if I wanted to go out to dinner some time, and I said I'd think about it. Would you and Ray come, too? As sort of a double date?"

Double date. Claire winced. "He's going to think you need chaperons."

"I don't care what he thinks. Look, when he learns anything about me he's going to think I'm weird and delusional, probably, like everybody else, and that'll be the end of that. But I wouldn't mind going out to dinner first. Would you go? Oh yeah, and give me a ride?"

"You start sleeping with this guy, am I going to have to rent you a motel room?"

Yolie laughed. "Watching you and Ray at Trout's, I'd say I'm not the one who'll be needing a motel room."

Claire wasn't going to touch this one; it felt too close to the surface and too close to the truth. "If you're really adamant about this, all right. I'll give you a ride. And if Ramón wants to come along, too, that's fine. But Yolie, if you like David…"

Yolie seemed to hesitate. How long had it been since she'd been on a date? Spoken to somebody who didn't need a website designed? Gotten laid? "David's not a bad guy. I'm glad I met him."

"He's interested," Claire assured her. All but pawing the ground, actually.

"Yeah," Yolie conceded, "although I think he's mostly just lonely, and generally available."

"'He had an affectionate heart; he must love somebody,'" Claire quoted. *"Persuasion,"* she added when Yolie looked blank. And when the blank stare remained, she further added, "Jane Austen."

"Ah, Jane Austen. Never could read her." Yolie stretched her legs out straight and raised her hands above her head, flexing the fingers, giving every muscle a sort of isometric workout. "Too boring. But you and Ray—" She shook her head. "You're two of a kind."

Claire started to protest and Yolie held up a hand. "You really are, you know. Ray's totally smitten."

"He is? Has he said anything?" Claire had a strong sense of absurdity as she uttered the words. It was a conversation for a tenth-grade slumber party, not one to be conducted as they approached Yolie's boarded windows and triple-locked doors, where a slavering Rottweiler patrolled the yard under floodlights.

"No, but I can tell. I...I've known Ray all my life."

Ah, and maybe had a little crush on cousin Ray, Claire thought.

"Anyway," Yolie was saying, "it's you two who should be dating. For real."

"There's a slight problem with that," Claire reminded.

"I know. I wish he and Marilyn would just call it off. We all thought it was going to happen last year, but no such luck."

"Marilyn?" Who the hell was Marilyn? Oh, God, did Ramón already have a...a mistress?

"Miranda, I mean," Yolie corrected as they parked in front of her house. "Hi, asshole!" she called to the car parked across the street, giving him the finger. "You got a minute to come in?"

"Sure." This was too good to cut off now and it wasn't really that late anyway. With Charles back on the East Coast, Claire had felt a tremendous burden lift from her. She was better rested, less agitated, more inclined to spontaneity.

Yolie opened a padlock that would stop bullets, then signaled Claire to stand still. Moments later a silent blur came around the corner and Claire had no trouble remaining frozen. What was giving her difficulty was breathing.

"Rover, chill!" Yolie ordered the huge creature who braced in front of them, fangs bared. Awesome fangs at that. Rottweilers were not a breed Claire found appealing; too big, too authoritarian, too Germanic. But they were handy to have around when your life felt threatened, and the name was a nice touch. Rover, indeed.

"Good girl," Yolie praised, scratching the creature's ears, and moving toward the door. "Now, where were we?"

Trying not to piss our pants, Claire thought. "Marilyn?"

Yolie chuckled. "Ah yes. The ersatz *gringa*. Marilyn was her name when she came out here. She changed it to Miranda about five years ago, but I still call her Marilyn to piss her off. Of course, it's never been much of a challenge to piss that woman off. She may be the least tolerant therapist in the entire state of California. And by extension, the world."

Trashing Ramón's wife. Claire decided she was going to like this. While Rover wagged her tail, Yolie began the rigamarole of entry, a procedure that would give the CIA pause. Assuming, of course, that it wasn't the CIA sitting outside in that Chevy down the block. One, two, three doors and then they were inside, Yolie carefully relocking each one, Rover at their side, breathing heavily. The dog had quite an engine.

"When Ray met her back east, she'd already changed her maiden name from Wojcik to Winston," Yolie explained. "Her father was a butcher in Bridgeport. She seems to be constantly reinventing herself. Got lots of energy, I'll say that for the woman. But surely you know all this."

They were inside now, in the office-cum-living area where they'd gathered that first night. Rover moved to a blanket in the corner and curled up contentedly. Yolie left for a moment and returned with a pair of chilled beer bottles which she uncapped with her shirt-tail.

"Actually," Claire admitted, "I don't know much at all. And I'm not sure I want to. Married men…it's not something I'm comfortable with."

Yolie flopped into a chair. "Marriage or married men?"

"Both, I guess."

"Hmmm." Yolie had worn makeup tonight, and when she rubbed her eyes now, her mascara smeared. "I can't say that I really think of Ray as a married man anymore, but technically…" Technical marriage seemed akin to technical virginity, a rationalization to circumvent the primary issue. "Hasn't Ray told you anything about them?"

"Uh-uh."

"Ah, he's such an honorable son of a bitch. Well, I have no such compunctions. I really, really don't like Mar—Miranda. I wanted to. I mean, I usually feel an upwelling of sisterly solidarity for the women who marry into this family. But Marilyn—" losing the name battle "—made it very clear that she didn't want to be here in the Valley, or have anything to do with any of the subhumans who lived here, and far as I can tell that's still her position."

"She wasn't exactly cordial to me the one time I met her. But I can certainly understand her not wanting to live out here." Though not as much anymore. Claire realized that Charles's visit and his perceptions had somehow cemented her own relationship to what was, apparently, her new homeland.

"Yeah, so can I, so can Ray. So can anybody. But Christ, that was the deal! She agreed to it when it became obvious he couldn't get a job in comp lit *anywhere*, anytime soon—much less Yale, which I think is what she had set her ignorant little heart on—and that if he didn't want to be a substitute teacher for the rest of his life, he was going to have to try something else!" Yolie snorted in disgust. "If she hates it so much here, I figure, why doesn't she just leave?"

"The girls?" Claire suggested.

"Well, of course the girls. She could take them with her, but that would break Ray's heart and theirs, too—and frankly, I don't think Marilyn wants 'em, though maybe that's unfair. But in any case, she knew what she was getting into when Ray came out. The deal was, she'd stay back east with the kids while he got his ag degree, then they would join him and he would support her while she got her master's in family counseling. Marilyn, a counselor—what a joke! Though I gather that she's tired of that now. God only knows what she'll decide to do next. This family isn't big on practical career moves."

"Not much she decides on could be less practical than comparative lit," Claire said.

"True," Yolie conceded. "But that was a strange situation, a deal between Ray and his dad made before Ray really knew what he wanted—"

"Ramón's very big on deals, isn't he?"

"Yeah. You know the Spanish expression, *cumplir con sus deberes?*"

"Um, sort of 'fulfill your obligations'?"

"Right, that's Ray. *Cumpliendo con sus deberes*, all the fucking time. I mean, he *went* to business school; he's *staying* with Miranda until the kids get out of school—despite whatever other desires he may have."

Claire flushed but said, "That's the new deal?"

"That's the new deal, and frankly I think it's ridiculous." This from a woman who needed ten minutes and half a dozen keys to get into her own house. "John is graduating from Berkeley this year, so he's a big boy. Alice is in eleventh grade and Sara's just started seventh," laying out the timetable. "It's all very civilized, him and Marilyn. But they don't sleep together, and frankly, even if *I* have to live like a nun, I'd like to see Ray get laid, if nothing else."

So would I, thought Claire. In fact, I'd like to be there when it happens. But what she said was, "Do you? Have to live like a nun, I mean."

"For now."

"How long is 'now'?"

Yolie shrugged. "Till C.C. gets put away, I guess. Or the *fatwah* is lifted. Thing is, Rushdie got all this sympathy. No one even believes me." Her relentless feistiness slipped for a moment. "I think even Ray suspects this is all in my head." She looked hopefully at Claire.

"I don't know what he thinks," Claire had to say. "If there were any physical evidence that you were in danger..."

"The physical evidence is likely to be my lifeless body, retrieved from some utterly convincing accident. Like Doug Collins in that Piper Cub crash. Or Elliot Klein, found forty-five years later buried in a riverbank. I almost died a year ago, when somebody ran me off the road on Highway 99. 'Fog,' everybody says. 'It was dark.' Shit, I've been driving that road all my life!"

Yolie slumped and Claire felt a sudden urge to put an arm around her shoulders, to offer whatever limited succor she could. "I believe you, Yolie."

"I know, and it fascinates me. Why? You barely even know me. Whereas the folks who *do* know me think I'm just a wacko crackpot."

"I don't know. So much weirdness has happened to me since I've moved out here, all of which would have been incredible to me in my former life, or to any of my old friends. And—" Claire hesitated. "Since Jewell died, I think somebody's been following me. The other day, I fell into the Kern—only I don't think I fell, I think somebody pushed me. That's how I got so scratched up."

Yolie's eyes got big. "You told me you slipped while you were hiking!"

Claire shook her head. "A lie; I went into the Kern. Up the canyon a ways. I was a mess: bruised, concussed, scared shitless. But I can't swear I was pushed, and I don't want a fatherly reprimand from your cousin."

"What *do* you want from him?"

"Um..." Wait a minute. Just who was pumping whom for information here, anyway?

Yolie grinned. "You work on that answer while I go pee. Be right back."

She had barely left the room when the phone rang. The machine picked up on the second ring, and Claire heard Yolie's terse message followed by silence at the other end. But not absolute silence; Claire heard the soft bellows of someone's breath. And then the voice started: a low, affectless, cyborg monotone, reciting a litany of bloody retribution and sexual torture. The details were horrific and sadistic—and someone had had a good time inventing them.

Then Yolie was back, punching buttons on the machine, cutting off the ugly words. "Sorry you had to hear that," she said. "For a while I was blowing an air horn in his ear, but it didn't seem to make any difference. I'm not even sure it's a live human. Sounds computerized. Do you think Stephen Hawking could be making obscene phone calls to me?"

"Did you report the calls to the phone company?" Or did Yolie's notion of the conspiracy extend to Pacific Bell? "What about Caller ID?"

Yolie shrugged. "Blocked. And the phone company said they couldn't trace it. I didn't really believe them—I even hacked into the Pac Bell database once and checked out the calls from C.C.'s various phones: from his ranch up in the hills, and his office in the ginning company. That's where he hangs, mostly—likes to watch those fluffy dollar bills pile up in the yard."

Claire felt herself flush. Yolie would be furious when Claire told her about the Tidwell Ginning visit, but that wasn't going to happen tonight.

"Anyway, no calls to me," Yolie went on. "They're either calling from a pay phone, or somebody else's cell phone, I guess."

Claire sat silent for a while. "How long has this been going on?" she said finally.

"The calls?"

"No, the whole—" She motioned around the room. "The whole gestalt."

"Oh. Well, I wrote my first, and as it turned out, only article on C.C. Tidwell three and a half years ago, shortly before I got reorganized out of a job, a reorganization that also killed the piece but good. But I only started to protect myself seriously—" mimicking Claire's gesture "—about two years ago."

Two years! "Oh, Yolie," Claire said helplessly. "Do you want me to stay?"

"Stay? Why? I'm used to this, Claire. This is my life. But thanks for the offer."

At the front doors, Claire gave Yolie a hug, knowing she couldn't offer Ramón's big, comforting presence. "Be careful," she urged.

"You, too."

When she slipped through the gate, the Chevy on the far side of the street turned its lights on, then off, to see her—or for her to see him. She wasn't sure which was worse.

17

THE NEXT WEEK WENT BY in fairly normal fashion, that is, in a blur of miles and orchards ticking by, of sick fruit, tedious meetings, and half-written papers, and of balmy mountain nights, with stars like salt spilled across the sky.

On Tuesday, Claire found herself on the road from Pixley to Tulare, attempting to twirl from Valley Public Radio to *Radio Bilingüe* without hearing a syllable of either a Bible-thumper or a country-western song. Dammit, would she ever become resigned to the airwaves of Kaweah County, so severely depauperate by the standards of Cambridge, Massachusetts? In Boston, from the comfort of your cockpit, you could hear the best of Bach or jazz or Irish folk music or R&B or Chicago Blues, or hell, even country if you really wanted to, which of course she never had.

Today she miscalculated and got Merle Haggard after all,

Merle of the legendary born-in-a-boxcar Oildale background, Merle known only by his first name in these parts, though had he not existed in all his roughened glory, the kind of folks who so adored him would've told you that Merle was no name for a man, not unless he wanted to spend his life getting beat up.

Merle was singing about "Tulare Dust" and she had to admit he'd got that right. If the Valley's airwaves were too thin, its air was too thick. San Francisco's rush-hour crap blew east through the Carquinez Straits, leaving the Bay Area smug and smog-free and the Valley pickled in ozone. Not that the San Joaquin was blameless, of course: chaff burned in the fields, poisons spewed from crop dusters and oil refineries, bone-dry soil stirred into trailing wakes behind tractors. When she got back to the lab, she wrote her name in the dust on her fender, resisting the impulse to add "+ Ramón" with a heart around the whole thing.

Ramón stopped by the lab now and then, in between visits to check on Pablo and his beans or Han Minh and her strawberries or other of his desperate clients. She realized that their comfort zone had tightened—they needed to stand about twelve inches apart, as opposed to two or three feet, and every now and then one of them would touch the other in a friendly way. Just friends. Cautious, tentative. Nothing really offered, nothing really taken. Claire felt the presence of MarilynMiranda somehow hovering over him, and yet she simply couldn't maintain her previous distance.

On Wednesday, she checked her ant farms again. There seemed to be no doubt now. The mycorrhizae was definitely killing the roots of the *Salsola*, the tumbleweed. It seemed tumbleweed didn't grow in disturbed areas simply because it could and other species couldn't—but because it *had to*. It couldn't survive well in an area with the mycorrhizal fungi characteristic of rich, undisturbed soil. It was an opportunist, a sort of botanical blockbuster.

This made Claire happy for a couple of reasons. One, it gave her a rationale for doing this research at all, on company time. She couldn't claim mycorrhizae increased yield, since so much water, phosphorus, nitrogen, et cetera were added to food crops that any incremental increase in uptake of nutrients bestowed by MR was irrelevant. But if it was pathogenic to invasive weeds, well, that was of interest to the agricultural establishment.

And she had another reason for being pleased at the results.

That afternoon Ricky Santiago called. His friend Frank had faxed him the preliminary coroner's/archaeologist's report on the remains by the river.

" 'Fully articulated skeleton of young adult male, eighteen to twenty-five years of age, Caucasian,' " Ricky read. " 'Condition of bones indicates burial from twenty to sixty years buried.' Frank said they can't narrow it more for such a long time ago—"

"Do they think he...it...was buried that whole time?" Claire interrupted. "Not in water and then deposited?"

"Um...doesn't say. Only that it was buried for that long."

"Oh." So no matter how convinced she was that Elliot Klein had not died accidentally, this part of the report at least wasn't going to say whether the river had taken the young adult male and then coughed him up onto its shore—or if he had simply been buried to begin with. "Can you find out?"

"Jeez, you're demanding, for somebody who's getting a big favor in the first place!"

"I know, I'm sorry. But there's a reason." She explained.

"Yeah, okay, I can see that might be important in establishing cause of death. And you know, there's something else here that might shed a little light on that, too. Says the skull had a severe fracture."

"Right. I saw it. But if he had been in the river—"

"It might have happened there. Got your point. Except that it also says, 'Mixing of soil horizons—' "

" 'Soil horizons'?"

" 'Soil horizons,' " he repeated firmly, " 'suggests pit. No gravel or other flood debris present.' "

"Ah," she breathed.

" 'Pro-*vee*-nience,' " he continued, sounding it out. "What the hell is that?"

"I don't know. Maybe it's like 'provenance' in art. Which is the documented history of who's owned a piece of art, going back forever. Go on."

"Okay. 'Provenience. Curled posture of skeleton typical of burial. Remains found in context with: Number one, eyeglasses, World War Two GI issue—'"

"Wait!" she said. Elliot Klein was in grade school during World War II. "Are they sure about that? Because the person I think this might be—"

"The guy all those missing person's reports were for, right?"

"Right. He would have been way too young to have served in World War Two."

"I can't tell you if they're sure about it. I can only tell you what it says here: 'World War Two GI issue.' But you know, that only sets the earliest limit for date of death. I mean, people use army surplus for years. I had a sleeping bag when I was a kid that was made for Korea, I think."

"Oh, of course," she said, sheepish and grateful for Ricky's intelligence. "Go on."

"Okay. 'Number two, three metal rivets, possibly from jeans. Number three, four metal eyelets. Number four, two fragments of rubber soles. Numbers three and four possibly from boots. Number five, two strips of leather, also possibly from boots.'" He was silent for a moment. "That's about it."

"That's *it?* That's all they found?" Rivets and bones. Not much to show for a life, or a death.

"Yep."

"No class ring?" she couldn't help adding.

"Um...no. Nope, don't see it here."

"Oh." Could they have missed it? Not likely if they were finding things as small as rivets.... "Okay, Ricky. Many thanks."

"Sure. Think he's your man?"

"Could be. There's nothing in what you told me that disproves it." Except the absence of the ring, she thought. But maybe he didn't always wear it.

"Because this sure sounds like an old homicide to me. Burial, caved-in skull, the whole…situation. Surprised they aren't working it as a homicide, though I guess it'd be a pretty cold case. That guy you told me about, the brother, you think he'd want to do DNA?"

"Shouldn't the county be responsible for that?"

"Hard to justify for something this old and stale. DNA testing's expensive. And it might not work anyway. DNA degrades over time."

"They find DNA in zillion-year-old insects in amber," Claire protested.

"Oh, it's probably there. But they might have to run a bunch more samples to find it. Expensive samples. And for a case that's just as easily cleared by saying some unknown dude fell in the Kern. 'Course if the brother wants to spring for it…"

Claire doubted that David Klein could afford to spring for lunch. "Don't know that that's an option, Ricky, but I'll suggest it to him. How's Luz?"

"Wondering why you never come see her. I told her you called me, she says I should tell you to stop by. She's getting pretty big, you know." The pride in his tone was palpable, that rather baffling gloating so common to many men when their women are heavy with child.

"Tell her I'll do that, I promise." Claire hung up and held the phone a moment, mumbling, "Provenience."

But on the very next day, she found herself with a dual opportunity. Ramón asked her to come along and visit one of his small farmers who had a vexing nectarine problem, and the orchard in question was not too far from the little farm the newlywed Santiagos had moved to. She called Luz, who squealed with delight and offered lunch.

Ramón drove and they found Rogelio's place with little difficulty, pulling off the narrow gravel road and parking in a bare-dirt yard. As she slid down from the truck, Claire surveyed the landscape, visually bewildered by the piles of indecipherable stuff. She mentally sorted the piles. One was, indeed, stuff—broken machines, empty fuel cans, the rusty carcass of a tractor—all of which merged seamlessly into the next pile, which was actually the ramshackle farmhouse. A third pile, apparently crumpled polyethylene, was in fact a sort of greenhouse, homemade, sheets of plastic stretched across an armature of curved branches.

It was a structure that showed a certain ingenuity, and she focused with interest on the slight young man with a timeless *indio* face who was stooping over a bean plant with Ramón.

Then Ramón called her over and asked her opinion on Rogelio's nectarines. She eyed the wall of trees behind them. A multi-generational orchard: a few acres of mature trees, and then some rows of two- or three-year-olds. Many of the youngsters drooped dispiritedly.

"I put them in three years before," Rogelio told her in commendably good English; Ramón had told her he was not a native and was, in fact, probably illegal. "They was fine at first. Last year they start to wilt like this, in the spring. Then they was okay by harvest. But this year they stay sick."

With her fruit knife she half severed a branch and bent it backward. The fresh-cut fibers that sprang free were streaked with brown and black. Verticillium.

"Black heart," she said. "It blocks water uptake early in the season and your trees never get a chance to recover."

"What can I spray?" Rogelio answered. Ramón claimed this was the first English sentence most of his farmers learned.

"Nothing," she answered. "Ramón tells me this land was planted to cotton before the nectarines, and the cotton that was here before is a host for verticillium. It's still in the soil, Rogelio. You're going to lose some of these trees no matter what you do. But some will recover on their own." The tough ones, but wasn't it always that way?

Certain that the authorities were holding out on him, Rogelio hardened his expression into stubborn, martyred lines as he slapped an ant that was running up his arm. Claire and Ramón exchanged glances, Ramón shaking his head slightly as if to say, Don't bring this up now.

But Claire launched into her speech anyway. "You know, those ants are your friends," she said, sounding distressingly like a kindergarten teacher. "Those gray field ants. Crazy ants, they call them. Here, I'll show you. Ramón, do you have an aspiration tube?"

"Nope. But hold on." He patted his pockets and came up with a big red plastic fast-food straw. "I usually keep one of these on me. Works in a pinch."

While Rogelio watched in bewilderment and Ramón in amusement, Claire knelt in the dirt, straw poised.

"There's one," she said, and followed a busy worker with her tube. When she had a bead on him she darted in like a raptor and sucked him up, then tapped him out into her palm. None the worse for this experience, he scrambled over the hillocks of her palm toward her fingers.

"See?" she asked, rotating her hand when the ant approached the rim of his new world. "He's gray. With a red thorax—the middle part, right here. He'll keep your peach tree borers under control. You want to be good to these ants."

"They talked about that on the local farm radio show last week," Ramón told him. "You ever listen to that show?"

"*Solamente escucho a los programas cristianos,*" Rogelio replied sullenly. "*Son más puros.*" Then, very slowly, he ground an ant under his foot, not bothering to check whether it was gray.

"Well, fuck you, too," Ramón muttered as he and Claire climbed back into the truck. It surprised her to see him thus angered. Surely by now he was used to being ignored.

"I guess you're insufficiently pure," Claire responded lightly, but thinking about dancing, about Ramón's strong arm around her back.

"Rogelio may be spiritually pure, but he's chemically promiscuous. Seriously, I don't think he's ever taken a single piece of advice I've given him. I get the feeling he can't wait to fail so he can suffer like the saints. But enough of my professional failures. Tell me how to get to your friend's house."

5

An otherworldly sky of an intense magenta framed the Aztec warrior queen. As befit a warrior, she was tall, lithe, mocha-colored, her hair a thick cloud of black, her face strong with the bones of a new world as yet unviolated by the blood of the old....

Claire blinked and the queen was Luz smiling with welcome, the magenta sky a funky farmhouse painted Pepto-Bismol pink, just like the home of Erasmo Campos across the Valley on the bank of the Kern.

By now Claire was used to the fact that the first sight of Luz would have the quality of an optical illusion. Extraordinary beauty seemed to overload her mental circuits, so that her brain had to scramble to make some sense, however fantastical, out of the data. And incredibly, pregnancy had made Luz even more magnificent. Her fine-grained skin stretched poreless over high Indian cheekbones, like a smoothly polished stone. Onyx, perhaps.

Luz Perez had been a migrant worker when Claire first met her: dirt-poor, recently widowed, two little kids, no prospects. And then one person's bad luck—the worst luck, a violent, untimely death—had sent other people's luck spurting in unpredictable directions. Like Luz, who met Deputy Enrique Santiago, a dashing, decent young man with a good salary. And Enrique, who had been flattened by Luz like a penny on the tracks. It was his great good fortune that Luz was not only amazingly beautiful but also smart, tough, lovable, and loving.

Ricky himself was only one generation removed from the fields and wanted to stay that way. But Luz had a plan, and to nobody's surprise but Ricky's, the newlyweds now owned a tiny farm with a couple of acres of peaches. His capital, her labor, that was the deal. Claire was not sure how this arrangement would work on their other collaboration. The labor on that one seemed pretty specifically allocated.

The two women embraced, and Claire introduced Ramón.

"It's been too long!" Luz cried. "Come, see my house and my trees! The kids are with my *suegra*, my mother-in-law. They will be sad not to see you."

They walked toward the pink house, which had the random look of many of the farmhouses out here: begun as a single-celled organism that budded into further rooms as needed.

"Nice color," Claire said, meaning it, and Luz laughed.

"Enrique hates it," she confessed. "He call—calls it 'wetback pink.'" Living with a native speaker had perfected her English verbs and accent.

Claire raised an arm and pointed at a seventies Oldsmobile Cutlass—one of Ricky's classics, undoubtedly, but brush-painted schoolbus-yellow. Against the magenta house it was gorgeous. "I hate to tell him, but his tropical roots are showing, too."

18

DOUBLE DATE. That had been the title of a book Claire read in junior high school, by an author whose name she no longer remembered, the story of a pair of twins and their search for romance. How much simpler life had been then, both for the girls in the book and for Claire herself, whose biggest worry at the time was that others would learn what Charles had discovered about the Sharples family phone number: 729-3825 could more easily be be remembered as RAW-FUCK.

Now here she was, closing in on forty, going on a double date of sorts in a motley configuration that the earlier author might have blanched at: one WASP, one Jew, two Mexican Americans. A San Joaquin salad bowl special.

She made every effort to treat the night casually, but it somehow felt important to make this work for Yolie's sake, to get the poor girl out of her dungeon and on a legitimate date with this reasonably eligible guy who seemed definitely interested. Claire could have told her—in fact *had* told her—that such specimens were not always readily available on today's market, and Yolie hadn't always been a recluse, so she knew that much on her own. Even so.

Claire even managed to mask her horror when David insisted that they eat at one of Bakersfield's famous Basque restaurants. A small but sentimentally important group of Basque sheepherders had roamed the foothills of the Tehachapis with their flocks, beginning in the 1800s, and they'd left a few legacies: a cross in the middle of nowhere that hikers still came upon, and a handful of restaurants in the old downtown.

Claire had been to one of these restaurants early on and found it wonderfully atmospheric, with a terrific neon sign and long, family-style tables. The food, however, was pretty awful. Either the cuisine had been corrupted by years of exposure to Bakersfield, or maybe it hadn't been that good to begin with, and at this point it hardly mattered which. She charitably recalled it as hearty, with all-you-could-eat floury white bread, bad salads, Southern-style pinto beans, the whole business capped by a tough, garlicky lamb chop.

But tonight's meal, surprisingly, turned out to be much better, a reminder—as if the exit of Charles hadn't sufficiently reinforced this notion—that while most prejudices arose out of specific situations, they weren't necessarily universal truths. There was no communal dining here, for starters. They had their own table, and while it wasn't a meal to remember, nor was it one that she wanted only to forget. In fact, the lamb chops here were rare, tender and delicious. She thought, as she slowly chewed, what a pity she hadn't known to offer this option to Charles. If he ever came back—but no, she was fairly sure that wouldn't be happening any time soon.

It was fun seeing Yolie out in public again. Her nervous surveillance of the area quickly dwindled to the mere curiosity of a normal restaurant-goer checking out the other patrons, commenting on the shepherdess on the ladies' room door, noting the ubiquity of sheep in the restaurant decor. Ramón also seemed to be enjoying himself, and Claire forced herself not to think about the kind of restaurants that Miranda might favor, although if what Yolie said was true, it was probably time for Miranda to re-invent herself yet again and like something altogether new. Had she been through a Basque period yet, Claire wondered.

Actually, the only real problem with the evening was the guy who'd put it all together: David Klein. He had called in to the Kern County Sheriff's Department and he wasn't happy about the results.

"So I fill out this ream and a half of paperwork," he said now, "and I answer a million fucking questions, and when it's all done, they kind of nod and say, 'We'll be in touch, Mr. Klein' in this way that you just damn well know means nobody's ever gonna talk to me again. I ask them what about DNA testing, don't they even want to know if it's Elliot, and I get this runaround that pisses me off so much I can hardly see straight by the time I leave."

"I don't know why you're surprised," Yolie told him, launch-ing into a lengthy recitation of grievances against the depart-ment. She was careful not to be too personal or specific here, al-though Claire knew she could have cited chapter and verse from her own experiences. Instead she focused on the public record, which was admittedly pretty deplorable.

David paid some attention, but not, to Claire's way of think-ing, nearly enough. He wasn't really conversing, as much as waiting out what other people said until he had a chance to talk some more. Maybe Yolie was right, and he was less interested in her specifically than in generalized female attention. Of course, he might also have finally been discouraged by Yolie's continuing reluctance to be alone with him.

Or maybe he was just a jerk.

In any case, Claire was disappointed to note that he didn't even protest when Ramón and Claire took Yolie with them around nine P.M., when everyone had finished two cups of coffee and there was no reason to stick around the restaurant one minute longer. It didn't look like David was going to rescue the princess from her thorn-girdled tower; Rapunzel was going to have to climb down by herself.

But what if her tower was the only place Rapunzel felt safe?

"Don't look now," Yolie said as Ramón drove them home, "but there's a car following us."

Claire glanced at the truck's side mirror and saw one, two, three cars behind them. "Which one? How do you know?"

"Silver Chevy," Yolie said. She was angling a large makeup mirror in her hand to look behind her, a sort of portable rear-view. "He's the guy who sits across the street sometimes. He pulled out of that mini-mart just as we left the rest—*ow!*" She fell roughly against Claire as Ramón made an unexpected sharp left turn. They were nowhere near the turnoff for Yolie's street.

"Let me know," Ramón said, and Yolie nodded. There was a nice level of cooperation and teamwork here, the kind of family sensibility Claire herself had not experienced once during Charles's visit. She felt a sudden twinge of envy, until she realized with a guilty start just what they were doing here.

"Still there," Yolie reported in a couple of minutes.

"I see him," Ramón said. "Let's have a little fun here, okay?"

Yolie laughed. "Your idea of fun, Ray, not mine."

"So let's see if he follows us to your house." He took a circuitous route through the suburban maze that surrounded Yolie's compound, and by the time they had actually reached the house—approaching from the side—the silver car had disappeared and Claire had no idea whatsoever where they had been.

"He'll show in a few minutes," Yolie said with resignation. They watched her until she was safely inside her fortress, then Ramón pulled around the corner and parked with the lights off.

"Why are we here?" Claire asked eventually. She sat beside the passenger door, thinking about the concept of double dates, feeling the absence of Yolie between them almost more than she had felt her presence.

"One, I'm curious to see if this car actually shows up, or if he's just Yolie's paranoid fantasy. Two, I don't really feel like going home yet. You in a hurry?"

"No."

They talked quietly for a while, mostly about Yolie; at one point Ramón picked up Claire's hand in an absentminded way. But then he suddenly seemed to realize what he had done and hurriedly released it, looked at his watch, said, "It's been forty minutes," and started the truck.

"Well, he could probably see us waiting there," Claire pointed out. "So he wouldn't come while we're here."

"Maybe." After a block or two he said, "You know what? I *still* don't want to go home. Let's find the Lucky Spot."

Claire was stunned. She could think of five hundred things he might have said, and fifty places he might have suggested, and this would not have been on either of those lists. "The Lucky Spot?"

"You know, the bar where Jewell and Elliot—"

"I know what the Lucky Spot is, Ramón. But I thought it was gone. Didn't somebody say it had burned down?"

"I think the facade's still there. And I just want to see it—it should be right down the street from Johnny's shop."

So they drove to East Bakersfield, crossing the railroad tracks, then following them. Edison Highway was dark and completely deserted, seeming far more desolate at night than it did in daylight.

"Here it is." Ramón braked suddenly in front of an old storefront. Claire climbed down and walked slowly toward the door. The storefront building to the immediate right showed much more obvious signs of the fire that had apparently passed through the structure. The Lucky Spot itself just looked abandoned. By moonlight she could read the dead neon script saying *Lucky Spot*, and *Dancing*. But the door itself was boarded and nailed, and there was no evidence that anyone had danced here for a good long while.

"The café would have been right down there." Ramón had come up behind her. "And the whorehouse, if that's what it was—"

"The Sad Sack," she said, tracing the outline of a darkened splotch on the building facade with her forefinger. Incredible to think that this was it, the place where so much had started, where Jewell had sung and Diana Dare had flirted with pumpkin-headed Clyde Tidwell and Elliot Klein had romanced his Okie sweetheart, the Cherokee Rose.

"And that there's the Ridge Route, whur the Joads come over." Ramón broke her train of thought with a terrible Okie accent, and she was just as glad to let it go.

They both turned to face the dark line of the mountains beyond the rail yard, standing with shoulders just touching. They stood that way for several minutes, smelling the diesel from the yard, feeling the heat still rising from the sidewalk and the cool air rolling down from the high country. They were waiting for some outside agency—a thunderous train, a rainstorm, a mild earthquake—to release them, but nothing came; they were on their own.

So finally Claire slipped her arm around Ramón's waist as if they were about to dance, Ramón bent and kissed Claire on the mouth, and then it *was* like a train wreck; no tender cupping of each other's faces, but knowing hands reaching for exactly what they wanted: breast, thigh, buttock. Claire ran her fingers along Ramón's crotch, feeling his erection through the stiff armor of denim, and he gasped.

"Ah, God," he moaned, "let's go somewhere. I'm dying."

"Go somewhere," she said in a muffled voice. Her mouth was pressed against his neck, the back of her head against the deserted stucco wall. "Like 1954?"

"I was thinking more of a motel."

She flashed on the conversation with Yolie last week. "A cheap motel in Bakersfield. I guess it was bound to happen."

"It doesn't have to be cheap," Ramón said defensively, and they both started to laugh—then froze like guilty kids as headlights swept by and a car passed slowly down Edison Highway.

It stopped at the curb maybe a hundred feet beyond them. Claire first assumed that it was the car that had followed them earlier, but it was too big. Its headlights cut off, and a smaller light shone briefly as a door opened and a man stepped out, stooping to clear the doorway. Ramón expelled his breath and she wondered if he'd been expecting Miranda.

But whoever it was wasn't interested in them, maybe hadn't even seen them. He headed not back in their direction but straight across the sidewalk, and Claire heard the faint jangle of keys. She realized with a jolt that the big man was Johnny Treadle, and that the building was Treadle's Treasures.

"Must have forgotten to lock the cash register," Ramón was saying, having identified the figure, too. "About that motel—"

But Claire was distracted, and suddenly chilled with an inchoate fright. Another car had passed, revealing the parked car in its headlights.

"Ramón," she hissed. "Johnny's car!"

"What?"

"It's a sport utility vehicle—a red one! Like the one that went to visit Jewell before she died!" And the one that's followed me from time to time ever since, she thought but didn't say, because she hadn't mentioned it before, and because it was too easily dismissed, like Yolie's fears.

"Like the thousands of other such vehicles in Bakersfield," he answered. "Claire, are you suggesting Johnny Treadle visited Jewell the day she died? 'Cause while I did kind of have the impression he had a crush on her, it seems to me he said he hadn't seen her in years."

"He did." She struggled upright, slipped sideways away from him against the wall.

"Okay, what's happening here?" he asked, stepping backward, moving away. "If it's just that you want me to back off, all you have to do is tell me."

"No, I'm seriously puzzled about the car." Which was true, because if it were Johnny who had visited Jewell, then he would have been the last person to see her alive. And might have taken the photo. She'd almost forgotten that strange missing photo. But *why?* Why any of this?

"And what I want," she continued, "is to fuck ourselves into little puddles on the floor—" Ramón leaned toward her again and she held up a hand "—*after* you've left Marilyn. Miranda. Which I gather won't be for years and years, until after the girls have all left home."

"I see," he said slowly. "Yolie's been spilling the family beans." He shook his head and amusement seemed to dance across his moonlit features. "Frankly, I wouldn't have taken you for such a rigid moralist. But okay." He began rebuttoning his shirt.

"Morality has nothing to do with it," she responded angrily, tucking in her own shirt. "Or not in the way you mean, anyway. I mean, I'm lonely and horny, too, and I'm not a saint, and if you want to break your solemn vows to your wife, that's *your* lookout. It's the deceit I don't like, having been on the other side of it. But mostly I'm only trying to protect myself, to avoid entanglement with someone who's not available."

"And just how available do you want me to be? *You* were the one who liked to keep things separate. Take your DNA with you, et cetera."

Is that my appeal? she wondered. The absolutely independent woman, the zipless fuck?

"That's all I know how to do. But I don't want to rule out..." she didn't know how to finish the sentence "...anything," she finally said, "by beginning badly."

Now, would that scare him off?

It seemed to; he was silent. But presently he said, "I don't see it. Maybe this is just my dick talking, but frankly, I'm already 'involved.' I don't see how a roll in the hay would make much difference. Other than being sweaty and sweet and really, really swell, I mean." He reached for her hips.

"Mmmm." He was making sense; at least, at the moment he was. This wasn't 1954, they weren't teenagers, and sex wasn't such a big deal, was it? What was the moral distinction between having intercourse and thinking about it all the time? The military made the distinction, and the Catholic Church—and she wouldn't be surprised if Ramón's wife did—but did Claire?

"This feels like more of your Jesuitical reasoning," she said slowly. "But let me think about it."

His own response was instantaneous. "*Think* about it?"

"Yes, think about it!" Suddenly she felt herself getting mad. "This requires some thought, some analysis. You're not exactly unencumbered, you know. You'd feel compelled to lie about it, and so would I, and I wouldn't like that and I'm not very good at it. So you should probably think pretty hard, too. I mean, *you're* the one breaking a promise."

He let his hands drop to his sides, leaving big spaces of interstellar cold around her waist. "More of a business contract."

"Whatever. It's supposed to be binding. You're *cumpliendo con tus deberes*, right?"

"We both meant it at the time, yes. But it wasn't very realistic. I don't know what Yolie told you, but I know for damn sure that *I* haven't told you any of this. I'm not sleeping with Miranda, and as for looking down the road at six years without sex…I'm not *that* old yet." He backed away. "But okay. If this is what you want…"

No, she wanted to scream, *this is not what I want! This is what I can have!*

But she took a long, shaky breath and said, "Anyway, how would you explain an all-night absence?"

He offered a brief laugh. "Simple. I'd say Yolie was freaked out, and she wanted me to stay. Perfectly plausible."

"You had that one ready," Claire said, opening the door to the truck and climbing in.

"For a couple of weeks." He climbed in the driver's side, started the engine, and pulled a wide U-turn to head back to Highway 99 and what was certain to be a very long ride back.

Claire leaned back and closed her eyes, considering. Ramón clearly didn't have any trouble with lying, she thought first, and then, with a quickening of her pulse, *I wonder if he's done this before?*

And would he do it again, somewhere down the line, with her? That thought cooled her down considerably.

She began to think instead about the red SUV and Johnny Treadle. Johnny had seemed genuinely shocked and distraught about Jewell's death. What exactly had he said that morning? She replayed the conversation in her head, and then took a mental survey of what she'd seen at Treadle's Treasures. Junk, pure and simple.

"Ramón," she said eventually, "those SUVs are pretty expensive cars, right? I mean, like thirty thousand a pop?"

"Something like that." He seemed quite content to pick up the conversation as if they'd never gone to the Lucky Spot at all, which was a comfort of sorts. "Depending on the make, of course. I was just thinking about a used Isuzu Rodeo I saw on the bulletin b—"

"How do you think Johnny could afford a car like that?" she broke in. "On the income of a junk store, I mean?"

He gave it some thought. "How do we know that's his only income? Maybe he bought Microsoft in 'eighty six, and the store is a tax dodge. He might hold the mortgage on Buck Owens's Crystal Palace for all we know. But why would you care what kind of car Johnny Treadle drives?"

She didn't answer.

19

AT THE FIELD STATION, where Claire had left her car, Ramón parked and said, "So just how long is it that you need to think about this?"

"I don't know. But I see a lot of cold showers in the near future, for both of us."

"Cold showers! I'm not even going to make it home tonight, without a little...rest stop."

"Fine. Just don't tell me about it." After a moment she said, "I've always found work or some other intellectual endeavor to be effective sublimation."

"*Libido sciendis,*" Ramón said.

Claire riffled through memory banks, dredging up rusty Latin. "'The lust for knowledge'?" she asked.

"Right. Hobbes claimed it was more powerful than any mere physical spasm—and just as sinful, by the way."

"Hmmm. Well, I guess I'm doomed to live in sin, then. Let me show you something dirty. C'mon inside."

She unlocked the door, unset the alarm, and led the way down to the lab. "Meet my ant farms."

He regarded her with patient tolerance while she dragged out the glass boxes and unwrapped the foil.

"Go on, look at the roots," she said, and showed him the browned-off *Salsola* roots. "See? The mycorrhizae seem to actually kill the tumbleweed."

"Very interesting. Not as compelling as what was happening an hour ago, but interesting in its own way. Thank you for sharing that." He started for the door.

"Wait—that was just the introduction!" She set Jewell's album on the lab bench and opened it to the second river photo. "What do you see?"

"I don't have my glasses," he said plaintively.

"Hold on." She rummaged in a drawer for her hand lens.

"It's awfully small." He pinched the little disk between thumb and forefinger.

"Yeah, yeah, but what do you see?"

"A riverbank," he began gamely. "A ridge in the background. Trees—two trees, sycamores. Greenery—"

"What do you mean, greenery?" she interrupted.

"Well, I guess technically it's 'grayery,' since this is a black-and-white photo—but there's some tall grass over here—" pointing with a blunt finger "—and a sort of mounding shrub, right in the middle."

"Okay. Now look at the first photo. At the 'greenery.'"

He flipped back several pages. "Well…there're the trees, and here's the tall grass, next to Jewell. And here's…oh. No shrub. It would be right in front of Elliot."

"Any idea what the shrub is?"

He squinted at it. "God, it could be anything. Saltbush, maybe."

"Actually, I think it's a tumbleweed." She waited for a reaction.

"Uh, could be," he said politely. Then, "Oh. *Oh!* It wasn't there two months earlier."

"Exactly. And since tumbleweed can't coexist with mycorrhizae, we conclude...?"

"That the mycorrhizae—"

"Which ordinarily would be abundant in that rich riparian soil—" she interjected.

"Right. That the mycorrhizae in that spot were somehow stripped between—" he squinted some more and read the dates "—between August and October of 1954." His expression changed. "An excavation?"

"A grave," Claire corrected. "Which is essentially what the archaologist suggested, too, but this date-stamps it."

She read him the archaeologist's report.

"So what we have here," he said slowly, "are three separate phenomena. Exhibit A, a body—evidently buried in a shallow grave from twenty to sixty years ago—"

"Postwar, because of the glasses."

"Right. Okay, Exhibit B, a man who disappeared sometime in the fall of 1954; and Exhibit C, evidence of an excavation during the fall of 1954, exactly where Exhibit A was found."

"Which was an area frequented by the missing man."

" 'Frequented,' " he repeated. "That's a nice touch."

"Thanks. Anyway, wouldn't you say that adds up to Exhibit A equaling Exhibit B?"

"It's pretty suggestive," he agreed. "Why don't you call the Kern County Sheriff? Or I'll call him. I know some people in the department. But you know, this isn't anything that a cop is going to consider *evidence*. Hell, Claire, I'm a soil scientist and I have a little trouble making the leaps."

He was absolutely right on the evidence. A picture in a book that somebody had labeled that might show a certain location— it was less than nothing, really. Except that she *knew* it meant what she thought it did.

"Actually, I quite agree that there's no real point in reporting it. I just wish there were something we could do with the information. Face it, there were only three people who really cared what happened to Elliot Klein—and that's down to two, now that Jewell's dead. Me, and his brother. I'll call David, of course, and I'll show him the pictures, but both of us are already pretty convinced that the bones were Elliot's. And no matter what you may think about Yolie and her various conspiracy theories, I agree with her on this one. I think there's a real good chance that C.C. Tidwell, in his former humble incarnation as Clyde, the geeky buddy, *is* implicated in this."

"Jesus, I wish you and Yolie had never met," he said as they walked back upstairs. "I can't believe I was stupid enough to introduce you. I've created a monster."

She followed him out to the lot, shoved him in his truck before there could be any clinches, and waved good-bye.

Was she really going to do this for six years? Wave him off to his allegedly chaste marital bed? Emphasis on the allegedly; every married man who'd ever had an affair had put forth the same tired old lines about a loveless, sexless marriage. But even in the event that Ramón's claims were true, six years was a very long time. Either Ramón would reconcile with Miranda, or Claire would cave in—or one of them would find somebody else.

But I don't really *want* somebody else, she realized.

Bone-weary but buzzing, she drove home, and sat on her deck for a long time, watching the southern sky. Every few minutes the stars would wink, as the black shadow of a bat flitted across them.

Over the weekend Claire's nervous energy overrode her anxiety about hiking in her mountains.

She had tried unsuccessfully to interest Charles in hiking; his hiking boots had turned out to be only for show. Naomi Weissberg was much more receptive. She and Naomi took a long walk through the Freeman Sequoia Grove, following the creek as far as "Big Mama"—Claire's name—a huge tree, maybe twenty feet in diameter, close to a hundred feet tall. Not the grove's largest tree, but its most graceful, its presiding presence.

The tree clasped the ground with roots like an enormous hand, and Claire and Naomi rested comfortably between the knuckles of that hand.

"Wow," said Naomi, as a shaft of late afternoon sun slanted down, lighting up ferns along the stream—and her own halo of red curls, if she had known it. "I don't get up here enough. Not since…"

"I know. Me neither." She remembered the previous summer.

Claire was perfectly happy. It was astonishing how secure she felt with a little company. Astonishing and irrational: Naomi could do very little in a real crisis, not that there was any reason to expect one, not anymore. But in the case of any normal mishap—sprained ankle, snakebite—at least one of them could go for help.

That was important, thought Claire, settling back against the sequoia's fibrous trunk and trying hard not to think about Ramón, which was rather like telling a child not to think about elephants, or ice cream. Yet another advantage of being partnered: simple, diverting conversation.

At eight thousand feet, the hike was hard enough work so that she felt relaxed and purged of pesky desires by the end of the afternoon. Still, she found herself wondering at intervals just what Ramón was doing, home with his family. With its leafy streets of Victorian houses, Visalia was the most charming and hip city in that part of the Valley—this was all relative, of course—and the only place, according to Yolie, that Miranda considered sufficiently civilized in which to live. Would Ramón be taking a five-mile run? Clearing out brush? Building a deck?

Something exhausting, she hoped.

On Monday she faxed Yolie. She wanted to stay in contact, no matter how difficult her situation with Ramón became, and she had also considered something Yolie had told her before, about hacking into the phone system for information.

She began, however, with trivial pleasantries, or maybe not so trivial. "Hi, Yolie. How's David?" she wrote.

In a few minutes *shred this* replied. "Haven't heard from him since dinner the other night. I told you he wouldn't stick around, once he knew anything about me."

Shit, thought Claire. Why on earth couldn't this work out? People fell in love with prisoners all the time; why shouldn't that happen for Yolie? Why shouldn't her situation make her romantic?

Because it was *women* who fell in love with prisoners, she answered herself; men generally weren't masochistic enough. And because there was a strong chance that Yolie's sentence was self-imposed.

Now she faxed the sheet she'd prepared earlier. "Jewell's neighbor said she heard her phone ring the day she died, right before it happened. Any chance you can find out about calls in and out of her place?" Jewell's phone number followed, as well as the numbers for Tidwell Ginning, Tidwell Land Development, Tidwell Enterprises, and Treadle's Treasures.

The turnaround was almost instantaneous.

"Piece of cake," Yolie scrawled.

Claire checked her calendar. She was meeting a colleague from UC Davis for dinner, but the afternoon was flexible. Wide open, actually; two appointments had cancelled on her at the last minute. She had a mountain of paperwork she had slighted due to Charles's visit, but nothing that couldn't keep a few days longer.

All of which provided sufficient rationalization for paying Johnny Treadle a little visit. After guessing that his car was the one that had visited Jewell, Claire had begun to formulate various theories on how this had occurred, and the one she liked best was nearly watertight. On the day of her death, Jewell had heard her long-standing suspicions about Elliot Klein's disappearance confirmed by Claire: Elliot had not simply left her, which she had always known, nor had he drowned in the Kern. Someone had hit him over the head.

So, reeling from the news, Jewell had picked up her precious picture, and then called Johnny, good old reliable Johnny, who had always been sweet on her, and who was the only person around who remembered the old days. And Johnny had promptly come over to comfort Jewell, as she had known he would.

Very nice, Claire thought smugly. A few small leaks in her craft—like why had Johnny taken the picture? Had Jewell dropped it somehow, and he'd offered to have it repaired? That was possible. Actually, Claire hadn't figured out this part of the story. Nor had she explained why Johnny had said—no, it was his wife who had said—that he hadn't seen Jewell for years. Could he have forgotten the visit? But these were small gaps, and no doubt could and would be caulked by a little elaboration, and by a visit to the Treadles.

She set out for Bakersfield.

Johnny and his wife—what was her name? "Honey" was all Claire could recall—were nowhere to be seen when Claire entered Treadle's Treasures, and for a moment she was alone with the inmates: the vege-form salt and pepper shakers, the tattered paperbacks, the bins of glossy records, the purple player piano, the kitsch of generations.

Then suddenly she heard stirring from the back of the store, and there was—Peg, that was it! Peg, doing whatever it was she did, and looking mighty snappy about it. Her hair was once again perfectly flipped in that 1962 cheerleader 'do, and today she wore a navy and white sailor-girl outfit, complete to gabardine bell-bottoms and nicely polished red pumps. She wore an expression of mild surprise, much like Johnny's the other day; Treadle's Treasures didn't seem to have a lot of drop-in trade.

"Hi," Claire said, offering her most congenial smile.

Peg's eyes widened slightly in recognition and then she suddenly rushed forward, beaming with welcome. "Why, hello there!" Her tone was cordial and she offered a light, ladylike little handshake, catching Claire off-guard. "You were in here to tell us the sad news about poor Jewell Bonebrake passing on. I remember *you!* You were planning to put together some kind of a memorial service, which I thought was just terribly sweet of you." She frowned slightly and cocked her head like a perky little finch. "But I'm so embarrassed, I'm afraid I absolutely *cannot* remember your name, and..."

"Claire Sharples. I don't think I ever introduced myself, actually."

Peg's makeup, Claire noticed now, had the flawless execution of a country-club matron's, lots of it—way too much, really—but tastefully applied and nothing that garish. Her lipstick exactly matched her shoes and fingernails. She was actually quite a good-looking woman, in her own fashion, and the body in that sailor suit was trim.

"Oh yes, of course," Peg exclaimed. "Claire! And I'm Peg, Peg Treadle. But my husband isn't here, I'm afraid, if that's who you're looking for." She emphasized *my husband* in the way some women do, particularly when they think they're talking to somebody who might not have one. "I know he'll be sorry to have missed you."

"When do you expect him back?"

Peg laughed conspiratorially, girl-to-girl. "You know those men. He was off to see a fellow about some fishing tackle and he's likely to be gone clear through supper." She waved toward a shabby wine velvet Victorian settee with some suspicious little holes in the upholstery. Beside it was a two-and-a-half-foot tower of *Architectural Digest*s. "You're welcome to wait for him, if you'd like. Can I offer you a Coca-Cola?"

Treadle's Treasures began to feel even more oppressively claustrophobic, and the thought of plowing through those magazines on that mouse-nibbled settee made Claire quite frankly queasy. She rummaged in her bag for a card and offered a rueful smile, continuing Peg's us-against-them theme. "Doesn't sound like he'll be back any time soon, but I really would love to talk to him. Here's my card, with my cell phone number on the back. If you could just ask him to give me a call..." Too late, she realized that the last thing she wanted was a phone call from Johnny Treadle, who could barely communicate when you were right there in his face. But Peg had already taken the card, glanced at it, registered mild surprise—at the UC connection or the occupation?—and tucked it into a pocket of her sailor suit.

"Absolutely!" Peg's smile dissolved into an inquisitive little frown. She had almost certainly once been named Cutest Girl at some high school. "I don't suppose it's anything that *I* could help you with?"

Claire took a deep breath; she was about to embark on a series of small lies, something she was not very good at. One more reason why she'd make a lousy adulterer. "Like you remembered, Peg, I'm putting together a memorial for Jewell, though it's actually more of an album than a service. I was just wondering if Johnny had picked up a snapshot from Jewell's trailer when he saw her. You know, the afternoon she died."

This time the frown wasn't quite so pretty. "Johnny didn't see her the day she died," Peg said sharply. "We hadn't seen the poor dear for months."

Months? Last time she'd said years. Claire had finally managed to reconstruct nearly the entire previous conversation in her mind, and that part of it was quite clear. Peg had said it was three years since they'd seen Jewell and she was "pretty much of an old wreck."

"Oh, really?" Claire let herself sound perplexed; it wasn't difficult. "Somebody told me they'd seen a red Explorer out at her trailer. Even got the license plate." She recited the number she'd written down the other night after leaving the Lucky Spot, when she needed something to do with her hands. "Isn't that your car?"

"We do have a red Explorer," Peg admitted, looking really confused now. "But I have to say I've got no idea whatsoever what the number is. You know, I really think you must be thinking of somebody else's car."

"Maybe so," Claire agreed pleasantly. "I just figured it made sense that if she was feeling poorly, she might have called him."

Silence. Claire decided to try the Big Bluff, which she had learned from Tom Martelli. "I mean, he always went when she called him, didn't he? Ever since the old days? She calls, and he jumps?"

Peg turned away, picked up a little dust rag, and gave the bowl of a commemorative spoon a vicious twist. "I can't imagine what you're talking about," she told the spoon.

Claire waited for a moment, then turned to leave. It had been worth a try. "Well, thanks anyway."

No answer. Claire left, giving the door an extra shake just to hear the bells jingle.

Claire walked slowly back to her car. When she passed the gutted Lucky Spot, which now held sentimental value for another couple, she realized she had come too far, but she kept walking. And walking. And walking some more.

By now she was a mile or so from where she'd started, and in a completely unknown neighborhood of East Bakersfield. She crossed the street and began walking back along the far side, returning beside the railroad tracks, not seeing either them or the occasional car, or even the Lucky Spot when she passed it on the other side of the street.

Seeing only Jewell, stumbling in the dark along the river, forty-five years ago. And then that recent afternoon, hearing from Claire herself what she must have come to suspect: that she *had* heard Elliot and his "good buddy" Clyde that night when Elliot failed to meet her as he'd promised, and that Elliot *hadn't* simply fallen in the river and been swept away. Not with a caved-in skull and his glasses resting neatly beside him.

So what happened then? After Claire had left her, Jewell must have called C.C. in a fury and spilled her accusations. Not a smart thing to do, given what she suspected about him—and the more recent rumors about his current incarnation, though she might not even have known about them. And then C.C. had dispatched their old friend Johnny to cool her down.

And...then what? Had she had a heart attack while Johnny was there, flinging her photo against the wall in a paroxysm?

Okay, but then why had Johnny lied about when he'd last

seen Jewell? Of course, he might genuinely have forgotten, given the pathetic state of his memory.

But what had happened to the picture?

She turned on her heel, walked back up Edison, and crossed the street to her car. Maybe another clear thinker could help her with this—not an antagonist, like Ramón, who was so wary of paranoia that he missed genuine conspiracies, but someone who could enter into the spirit of historical reconstruction.

Yolie.

But not today. Today she had to drive back up Highway 99, to meet Anita Barker for dinner.

Anita worked at UC Davis, and they'd gotten together like this several times in the past, using Visalia as a middle point, and also, since dinner was usually on the University of California, as the place with the best restaurants.

Claire arrived early and asked for a table near the door, ostensibly so Anita could easily spot her, but really so that she could survey the room. The Valley's high society was not a group she saw very often: doctors, lawyers, empire-builders, and spouses of same. There, for instance, was a big, rough-looking man she recognized as a successful vineyard owner. A slim blonde in mauve who might be a realtor; another—*whoa!* Claire looked again, and then one more time.

Yes...she was almost sure...and then she *was* sure. It was Miranda. Marilyn-Miranda Wojcik-Winston-Covarrubias. She was tiny and blond and perfect, and Claire felt a sudden wave of nausea.

Miranda was looking right back at her with a fixed expression, and Claire wondered in stunned horror if she'd been recognized. Her mind raced. They'd only met the one time, but it was possible, she supposed, particularly if Ramón talked about her occasionally, reminding Miranda offhandedly of Claire's existence. That was possible, even plausible. She began a tentative smile, wondering how in the hell she could manage to be civil, could conceal the welter of emotions suddenly coursing through her system, turning her limbs to jelly and her mind to mush.

Then Miranda's hand shot up like a rocket and her face broke into a welcoming smile. Suddenly Claire realized that she wasn't looking at her at all, but at the door. And that whoever she'd been waiting for—dear God, was it going to be Ramón?—had just entered.

Very slowly Claire turned her head, expecting the worst, preparing to tell them what a lovely surprise, and wasn't it a shame that her friend had stood her up so she'd have to be running along.

But it wasn't Ramón. Nor was it one of Miranda's friends meeting her for a girls'-night-out dinner parallel to Claire's own.

It was a man.

A younger man than Ramón by at least a dozen years, and one considerably more European than Señor Covarrubias. He wore a tailored gray suit with a hint of a chalk-stripe, a crisp white shirt, and a tastefully muted rep tie in burgundy and navy. He had the look of Boston or San Francisco, not the Valley, and she thought *doctor-lawyer-accountant*, it must be some professional relationship—just as Miranda raised her face for a lingering kiss on the lips and slid over in the booth to make room beside her. She turned her vivacious little face up toward his and they laughed together with a shared intimacy that excluded everyone else in the room.

Claire was still staring, dumbfounded, when Anita plopped into the chair opposite her.

20

RAMÓN WAS MERCIFULLY not in the office during the next few days.

Claire didn't know what she would say to him, or how. Did he know about Miranda's infidelity? If, indeed, what she had witnessed was infidelity and not something else, something far more innocuous and mundane. A Connecticut cousin, for instance, out on business in San Francisco. That would explain the clothing, though not that kiss, or the hurried departure suggestive of heated need.

Miranda and her mystery man had spoken briefly and then abruptly departed, only a few minutes after Anita's arrival. Claire did not believe they had decided on the spur of the moment to try another restaurant, unless it delivered to hotel rooms.

That it was Miranda she had no doubt, and in a sick sort of

sociological sense, it fascinated her that Miranda would meet a lover in a fine restaurant in her own hometown—a fairly brazen move under any circumstances. But of course Ramón was an oblivious sort in many ways, and not likely to interact with the sort of muckety-mucks who'd been in that restaurant, unless their kids were on the same athletic teams.

The question, then, was did Ramón know? Certainly Claire was not prepared to tell him, even if she'd been able to think of an approach that would be effective, yet kind. "Did you know your wife is fucking a guy who looks like the cover boy for Brooks Brothers?" did not really seem to be the best approach. "I happened to be in Visalia…" sounded lame and contrived. Nobody happened to be in Visalia. Perhaps a straightforward, "I met Anita Barker—remember her? from Davis?—for dinner the other night, and…"

Or maybe she should just let it go for a while.

Ramón called her at home that night, just after nine.

"Yolie got busted," he announced, "late this afternoon." There was a hint of I-hope-you're-satisfied in his tone that made her nervous. And more than a hint of anger.

Oh, hell. "What happened?"

"I haven't seen or talked to her yet; I'm about to drive down and bail her out. Anyway, this is all from her lawyer, some guy she pulled out of the Legal Aid pool. He says she was caught red-handed, or hot-wired, or whatever the correct term would be, hacking into records at Pacific Bell."

Double hell. Hacking into records at Pac Bell at Claire's specific—no, Claire's *faxed*—request. Did Ramón know this? And she thought with a shudder, Had Yolie followed her own rules and shredded Claire's incriminating fax? The one that had the—oh shit!—the phone numbers she wanted Yolie to check on. Not to mention the sending number of the Citrus Cove Agricultural Field Research Station.

"Can I do something?" she asked, beset with guilt, realizing as soon as the words were out that of course there probably wasn't a damned thing she could do. Except perhaps consult a criminal attorney herself.

"Nah. I'd send you to get the dog, which they've also got locked up somewhere, but I think that'll have to wait till tomorrow morning." Claire had forgotten all about the dog; at least they hadn't shot poor Rover. Whoever *they* were. Who *did* make arrests on behalf of the phone company, anyway?

Out of nowhere she recalled a line from an old "National Lampoon Radio Hour," a line about Chilean copper mining that Yolie would appreciate, one Claire would have to tell her when she got out of the slammer: "El Allende is dead...so that your phone won't be."

Ramón reported back after midnight. "I'm at a pay phone at a truck stop and Yolie's with me. I'm taking her to my house for the night, and then in the morning I told her we'd go bail out Rover. I can't decide which of you to strangle first."

Either Yolie's lawyer had learned enough specifics on the charges for Ramón to fill in the blanks on whose request Yolie'd been filling, or else she had told him the details, which seemed far less likely. Neither scenario was good, however.

"I'm sorry," Claire said, hoping that an all-purpose apology might buy her a little time. What she really wanted was to talk to Yolie, but she wasn't going to ask. And having just been busted by Pac Bell, Yolie probably wouldn't want to chat on their lines any time soon.

"It wasn't your fault," Ramón said, "at least it doesn't sound like it. They apparently allege that she'd done this before and that they'd figured out how she did it. So they had a trap in place to catch her if she tried again. *When* she tried again; I gather these hackers tend to be serious recidivists. I'm a little fuzzy on the electronics here, but they claim to have her cold."

He was silent for a moment, but Claire couldn't think of anything to say.

"Between you and me," he continued, "I think she's a little

disappointed they set her bail so low. You know, showing that she isn't really dangerous."

"Or a flight risk," Claire put in. "Where would she go?"

"She *could*—" with great gravity, an air of paterfamilial pontification "—go almost anywhere in the world and continue to do the work that supports her. She designs websites, remember? She's self-employed and she works on a computer. All she needs is a phone line. Though as a matter of fact, I understand that Pac Bell is talking about cutting off her service altogether, which might up the ante, and encourage her to hit the road."

"A valid point."

"Anyway, she wanted me to ask you to meet us at your lab in the morning. Then we can go down and see about bailing out Rover and installing eight hundred new locks."

In the morning, with sun streaming down on the Citrus Cove parking lot, Yolanda Covarrubias was not in the least contrite. Her clothes were rumpled and she looked a bit the worse for wear, but her hair was freshly washed and hung sleek and thick down her back. Her eyes glittered and she all but glowed with a sense of accomplishment.

She jumped down from the cab of Ramón's truck and gave Claire a big hug.

"You were right," Yolie told her exuberantly. "You were absolutely right. Before they cut me off and busted down the gate, I was able to check on the numbers you asked me about."

"I knew it," Ramón muttered darkly, turning away.

Yolie ignored him. "On the afternoon that Jewell Bonebrake died, a call was placed from her trailer to Tidwell Ginning, on C.C.'s inside line. And a subsequent call from that same private line went to Treadle's Treasures. Three minutes later, from there to Jewell." She smiled pleasantly but impersonally, in the manner of a flight attendant. "Does that provide any assistance?"

Did it ever.

Johnny Treadle, retired mechanic, had opened a store that seemed to do no business shortly after the small-plane accident in which Doug Collins was killed, a crash that paved the way for Tidwell Land Development to itself pave much of the southwestern Valley.

"There's more," Yolie went on, climbing back into the truck. Claire climbed up after her and Ramón pulled out of the lot. "I was planning to give this to you in a neat little presentation, maybe put something together with PowerPoint, just to be cute, but the goddamned phone company kind of interrupted me. I did some other checking on Johnny Treadle, Claire, and what I found out was pretty interesting. Johnny and his wife, Peg, have been married since 1957 and they lived in a little house in Oildale forever, at least until right around the time of that plane crash a few years ago. Johnny worked in a machinery rental yard out on Stockdale Highway."

Claire knew the type of place she meant, a huge lot filled with miscellaneous agricultural and petroleum-related equipment and machinery, looking like a toddler's sandbox under a huge magnifying lens.

"And then—*then*—at just about the very same time that poor Doug Collins flew into the side of the mountain, Johnny and the missus moved into a four-bedroom house in one of the nicer Tidwell Homes subdivisions. A home that's *owned* by a Tidwell subsidiary, one about four corporations removed from anything that actually has the Tidwell name on it. I really had to work at tracing that one."

"You are awesome," Claire told her, with sincerity. "You got all that just futzing around in cyberspace?"

"I'm not done yet. Johnny Treadle has Alzheimer's, diagnosed three years ago."

My, my, my. Not a surprise, though, not really. And it explained a lot, starting with the vagueness, and with Peg keeping such an eagle eye on him. How long before Johnny started wandering out onto Edison Highway?

"So whatever he did," Claire thought out loud, "he might not even remember? Is that what you're saying here? How odd."

Ramón grunted and they both ignored him.

"Wait a minute!" Claire turned to Yolie, frowning. "How'd you find out about the Alzheimer's?"

"His medical insurance records," she replied blithely.

On Sunday morning, Claire was feeling particularly disconnected.

She had not heard from Charles since his departure, which was fine, really, though she was starting to think of herself as utterly alone in her world, perhaps not an indication that the visit had been terribly successful.

On the plus side, Yolie *had* apparently shredded all of Claire's incriminating faxes prior to her arrest, so for the moment, Claire was home free. Legally, anyway.

What was vexing, however, was that when she was away from the lab—at home, for instance, on an exceptionally clear and beautiful fall morning when the leaves were finally starting to shimmer gold across the canyon—there was no communication channel to Yolie. She was now willing to "speak" only by fax, though Claire knew she was still operating her emergency cell phone, because it rang when Claire called it. It also seemed to take her voice mail messages after Yolie's cryptic *Click-click* message. Yolie claimed to have connected it to an amplifier that could be heard without picking up the phone, so that she could screen calls as the messages were recorded.

But Yolie never called back.

And of course she was probably a bit distracted anyway. Her newly hired hotshot criminal attorney was trying to keep Pac Bell from cutting off all Yolie's phone service, and by extension, her website design business. The attorney's argument, as Claire understood it, was quite simple: if the phone company did not automatically cut service to people accused of murder, rape, pedophilia, or treason, then it was patently discriminatory to cut service to somebody merely accused of breaching the phone company's own security. So far the lawyer was winning; Yolie still had working phone lines, but since she refused to use them, the victory was Pyrrhic.

As for Ramón, he wasn't available either.

After devoting the better part of a day to the various chores involved with restoring Fortress Yolanda, he had pronounced himself disgusted with paranoia and conspiracy theories and anything whatsoever having to do with one Clyde Chester Tidwell. Claire had not heard from him since. She had not mentioned Miranda and neither had Ramón.

Stalemate.

She was seriously considering a trip down into town just to have something to do when the chirp of her cell phone from its charger on the kitchen counter surprised her. Nobody ever called on that line when she wasn't out in the field somewhere.

"Miss Sharples?" The voice was vaguely familiar and then Claire had a sudden flash of flipped-up hair and terminal perkiness. "This is Peg Treadle calling. I'm so very sorry to bother you on a Sunday." She emphasized the *Sunday* as if she just knew she was keeping Claire from the worship service of her choice.

"No bother, Peg. What can I do for you?"

"I just don't...I suppose it's nothing, but...have you heard from my husband? Johnny Treadle," she added helpfully, in case Claire had forgotten. Her voice started fading; transmission was always problematic up here in the mountains.

"No, I haven't, Peg." Claire carried the phone outside, but the call started really breaking up then, so she went back into the kitchen where it was much clearer. Go figure.

"I don't know what to do," Peg moaned. "He went out last night and hasn't come back, and he'd been talking about getting in touch with you after I told him you'd come by. I couldn't get him to tell me why, though. Are you *sure* he hasn't called?"

Like Claire might have forgotten. "If he did, he didn't leave a message. I know I haven't spoken with him. Did you give him my number?"

"Oh, yes." She was silent for a moment. "It's just that he left behind some notes here in the store that I can't figure out, and I'm kind of concerned. His handwriting's gone really bad these last couple years, but he's written the name *Jewell* over and over, with a bunch of question marks and then there's a list, or anyway I think it's a list, of names. I thought if you could just look at those names, maybe you could figure out where he's gone. I don't want to call the sheriff."

Claire sighed and looked at her watch. It was almost forty-eight hours since her last trip to Bakersfield. "Did you say you're at the store? I'll meet you there, but it will take me a while."

It took a little bit over an hour and a half, counting getting dressed and stopping to pick up a doughnut. She stopped at the Ag Station to fax Yolie, but when *shred this* didn't answer in five minutes, she left and continued south. As she turned onto Edison Highway, she made one final attempt to reach Yolie on the cell phone and hung up in disgust when Yolie's voice mail went *Click-click*. She stuffed the phone into her jacket pocket and got out of the car.

The sign on the glass door of Treadle's Treasures was turned to CLOSED. When Claire knocked, Peg emerged from the rear of the store and trotted to the door.

"Thank heavens you're here!" Peg exclaimed, offering her fingertips for another of her cute little handshakes. She was in mauve today, one of those one-piece jumpsuits that women of a certain age are so inexplicably fond of. Hers had a matching mauve leather belt and pumps, and did not seem to be a statement that *When I am old, I shall wear purple*. More like, *When I am old, I shall dress like a toddler*. "I just don't know what on earth I'm going to do, and I'm absolutely beside myself worrying. It isn't like Johnny to wander off this way."

But it would be soon, Claire thought. As the Alzheimer's progressed, Johnny would be more and more likely to disappear without warning; Peg might as well get used to the idea. Of course, Claire wasn't supposed to know about the Alzheimer's. "I'm sure he's fine," she soothed. "You know how men are."

Peg stepped behind the counter, reaching down for something. "If you could just take a look at this…"

She straightened up, and *this* turned out to be a gun. A fairly small, very shiny gun, with a great big barrel pointed right at Claire's heart, which immediately began pounding like a pack of racehorses on the final turn.

"What are you—" Claire began shakily.

"Oh, knock it off," Peg snapped. There was nothing coy or perky about her tone; it was all business now. "You and I need to take a little trip."

Claire laughed unsteadily. "If this is supposed to be some kind of a joke, Peg, I don't think I get it."

"No joke, missy." *Missy?* Peg lifted the phone from its cradle with her left hand and punched in some numbers. The gun never wavered. "It's me," Peg said into the receiver a moment later. "I'm bringing you something. Stay put." She hung up without waiting for a reply, then waved at the front door with the gun. "We'll take your car."

Edison Highway was even more deserted than usual and there was nobody to see as they crossed the sidewalk and got into Claire's car. As Peg belted herself in, Claire fumbled with her own seat belt and groped in her left jacket pocket for the cell phone. She hit REDIAL and what she hoped was MUTE. Meanwhile, Peg settled in and aimed the gun at Claire's midsection. "Turn the car around," she instructed, "and don't try anything stupid like running a red light."

But I've *already* done something stupid, Claire thought. I came when you called. What she said, however, was, "I don't have any intention of breaking any traffic laws, Peg, not with that gun pointing at me."

Peg gave directions and deflected any attempts at conversation with a curt, "Shut up." Claire drove automatically and carefully. At first she had no idea where they were heading, half expecting Peg to direct her southwest, toward Taft and Jewell's trailer park. Instead they headed north, and when Peg announced their exit off Highway 99, Claire knew exactly where they were going.

"Tidwell Ginning," Claire announced. "I should have known."

Two minutes later they were there. The giant loaves of cotton remained sprinkled around the yard, but there were no employees' cars and trucks spread haphazardly around the lot today. No vehicles at all, for that matter, at least none that didn't have TIDWELL GINNING painted on them somewhere. The place seemed utterly deserted.

Peg had Claire park in the back of the little detached office building where she and Charles had so recently met the plant manager, Frank Walsh. "No funny business getting out of the car," Peg warned.

"Believe me, I'm not trying to be amusing," Claire told her. With the gin not running, it was strangely silent here today. "I really think this is all pretty silly, Peg."

"I don't believe anybody's asked for your opinion, missy." Peg waved Claire toward the door. "Open that door and head on inside. And don't try to run."

"I'm not going to run," Claire answered irritably. "I'm not dumb enough to try to outrun a gun." Peg was right behind her now, the gun jammed into Claire's ribs.

The overhead fluorescents were off in the front office, making it surprisingly dark after the bright sunlight. The outer office was as empty as the gin yard, but off to the right, the door to C.C. Tidwell's private office stood open just a crack, a stream of light coming from inside. Peg pushed Claire toward the inner sanctum and used her left hand to swing the door open wide.

And there he was.

C.C. Tidwell, scourge of Kern County.

Claire's first thought was, *Why, he's an old man!* and then she saw the anger glittering in his small dark eyes and amended that to *He's a very dangerous old man.* But he wasn't a large one; even seated behind the desk, that much was clear. He'd lost a lot of hair since those old pictures, but his head was still disproportionately big for his body. He wore a red plaid shirt and jeans.

He totally ignored Claire, turning his full attention to Peg Treadle. "And just what in the goddamned hell do you think you're doin' here?" After all these years, there was still plenty of Oklahoma in his voice, which came across low and slow and mean.

"I didn't have a choice, Clyde. She knows about Johnny and the Explorer."

For a moment, doubt crossed Tidwell's grim features. "The Explorer?"

"The *car*," Peg snapped. "She got my tag number."

"So?"

"So she said somebody saw it out at that trailer park."

"*You* killed Jewell!" Claire blurted out to Peg. "It wasn't Johnny at all, running to help her. It was you, running to stop her from telling anybody whose body it was we found out there by the riverbank."

"I didn't kill her," Peg replied indignantly. "She had a heart attack."

"When you started waving that gun at her?" Claire asked. It was interesting how bold adrenaline could make one. This had to be why men kept fighting wars. "Or was it when you tried to take that picture of Elliot she had sitting by her bed?"

"She had a heart attack," Peg repeated.

Red Explorer. The red SUV that she'd seen on the Sunday afternoon she went up Kern Canyon and nearly came home in a body bag. "And it was you who shoved me into the river, too, I suppose?"

Peg smirked.

And then, with no warning whatsoever, a gunshot exploded in the room. Peg's little body jerked backward and fell, a huge red stain spreading on the mauve jumpsuit.

Frozen in terror, terror of a magnitude that made the possibility of any kind of heroic action purely academic, Claire moved only her eyes: first to Peg's body, lying five feet away with blank eyes staring up at the ceiling; then to the little man behind the desk, holding a handgun so huge it appeared to be a toy.

The handgun was now pointing right at Claire.

"She was a good little gal," C.C. said, with what seemed to be a twinge of regret. "Just didn't know when to keep her mouth shut. Or how to mind her own business." He turned up the corners of his mouth ever so slightly. "You seem to have a lot of difficulty with that one yourself."

Claire noticed that the room was beginning to tilt: first to the left, then to the right. "I think I'm going to pass out," she said.

He waved the gun at a chair. "Then sit down." He looked over at Peg's body, something Claire was trying to avoid doing again at all costs. If she passed out, she was afraid C.C. would shoot her for making a fast move. Carefully, she lowered herself into a chair.

"You came to visit my gin," C.C. Tidwell said. "You thought maybe I wouldn't hear about that?"

"I figured you probably would," she said. "But so what? I'm an agricultural employee of the state of California. There's no big deal about my going to a gin."

"Don't insult me, Dr. Sharples."

And why not? He was obviously going to kill her anyway. "I thought it was Johnny," she said slowly, "that he did...things for you, as a mechanic—"

"He did indeed, and what of it? I employ a lot of mechanics."

"Not to sabotage airplanes."

He raised an eyebrow. "That tired old story again?"

"Not so tired to Doug Collins's widow," Claire told him, "or his kids. And I'm not the only one who knows these things, either, about Johnny working on that plane and the payoff, getting his store and car and a big new house."

"If you mean that little Mexican gal, nobody's gonna pay attention to her." He shook his head slightly and offered a broader smile. "You know, I never could understand what Johnny wanted with that store. I went in there once and it was the consarnedest collection of crap I ever did see." He glanced at the body on the floor. "Peg hated it."

"You and Peg...?" She made it a question, but a very mild, nonchalant one.

He nodded and smiled, lechery flashing momentarily in his eyes. "Oh my, yes. Fine little lady, she was."

"But not so fine that you married her," Claire noted.

"She was already married," he said, as if that explained everything. Or anything. "You know that story about the Achilles' heel? I reckon Peg was mine."

"So you killed her? I don't get it."

He shook his head regretfully. "She was getting to be a problem."

It occurred to Claire that she still was a big problem, albeit a dead one. "You can't just leave her there."

"Oh, I won't. You neither. 'Member when Walsh showed you 'round the gin, that tale he told you about the fellow getting mashed in the baler?" He shook his head. "That Walsh is one morbid old boy, I must say."

A fresh wave of nausea passed over Claire. "You can't—"

"Oh, probably not," he said agreeably. "Too hard to explain why you're there."

Now was the moment, she realized suddenly, when he'd shoot her, too, now that she was off guard. Just like Peg—

Yolanda Covarrubias and her Rottweiler burst into the office. Claire screamed and dove out of the way as gunfire exploded again and again in the tiny space. The first shot dropped the dog in its tracks and the second one smashed into the wall as Yolie leapt sideways with the grace of a prima ballerina.

Number three, fired by Yolie herself, blew the gun right out of C.C. Tidwell's suddenly ruined hand.

As the wiry little man howled in pain, Claire slowly and carefully rose to her feet. Yolie was screeching at Tidwell. "You killed my dog, you motherfucking asshole!"

Claire picked up the phone and dialed 911.

"Try not to kill him," she told Yolie over her shoulder.

"Then those cops had damn well better hurry. This little Mexican gal's got a twitchy trigger finger."

21

IT TOOK A LONG TIME for the Kern County Sheriff's Department to sort things out, and none of the various law enforcement officers who came to Tidwell Ginning seemed the least bit happy about any part of the affair, starting with having to arrest one of the wealthiest and most prominent men in the lower San Joaquin.

Fortunately, the need actually to read Mr. Tidwell his rights was forestalled by paramedics, who declared him in imminent danger of exsanguination and rushed him away by ambulance. And nobody had to cuff him either, his dominant hand being rather dramatically out of commission.

The bodies of Peg Treadwell and Rover remained on the floor of Tidwell's inner office, as the living participants were removed one at a time from the scene. Yolie—out on bail from her skirmish with Pac Bell and literally holding a smoking gun—was immediately arrested, while Claire was driven in the vomit-stained rear seat of a different county patrol car back to a grim little room for questioning.

Claire knew that the answers she gave would satisfy no one, and insisted on being allowed to call Ramón before she talked to anybody. She told him where she was, said that she would only tell her story once, then gave a brief but lurid recital of the afternoon's events. She explained that she had dialed Yolie's cell phone from her own, hoping that his cousin would hear what was happening and keep the connection open as she and Peg drove to the gin, and that her desperate plan had worked.

She thought she heard a long, deep sigh. Then Ramón said, "I'll get Yolie's lawyer over there right away. It'll take me at least an hour to get down there."

"No rush," Claire told him. "I don't think anybody's going anywhere for a while."

In the weeks that followed, C.C. Tidwell underwent reconstructive surgery on the ruins of his right hand and was charged with first degree murder in the death of Peg Treadle and the attempted murders of Claire Sharples and Yolanda Covarrubias. No charges were filed in the death of the dog.

Yolie's bail was reinstated and she was released. She sold the full story of C.C. Tidwell's corruption to *The New Yorker*, was interviewed by a flotilla of broadcast journalists, then peddled a book proposal of her own adventures to Time-Warner. A Rottweiler breeder horrified by the death of Rover offered her the pick of a new litter, and she and David chose a puppy that even Claire found charming.

Perhaps the most gratifying fallout from what Claire began to think of as the Shoot-out at the Cotton Corral was that David Klein rallied to Yolie's side even before she was released from custody and had stayed there ever since. It was David who insisted that the plywood come off the windows of Fortress Yolanda, David who arranged to have the razor wire removed from the fencing, and David who lobbied to get the place whipped into shape and sell it. Throughout all of this, Yolie was uncharacteristically compliant.

Kern County scrounged enough money to run DNA testing on the bones from the riverbank, compared the data to similar tests on David Klein, and subsequently identified the decedent as Elliot Klein, reported missing in 1954. No charges were filed in this death.

Throughout all of this, Ramón was scrupulously polite and excessively formal. Claire found herself making excuses to avoid him, and noticed that he wasn't around enough to require much avoidance. When he *was* there, the silence thundered.

Then, the Saturday before Thanksgiving, he called and asked to see her.

"I don't know that that's such a good idea," Claire told him carefully.

"I do," he answered. "It is. Give me directions." He had never been to her house.

In the hour it took for him to arrive, she found herself roaming restlessly from one room to another, moving indoors and out, trying one CD and then abruptly shifting to another, lifting and setting down random objects around the house. The third time she found herself fondling a snowflake obsidian paperweight, she conceded defeat and hiked briskly for half a mile up the road. Then she pivoted and hiked back home.

She had just gotten back when Ramón's truck pulled up at the house, so she didn't even need to come outside to meet him. She had already decided that she wasn't going to let him inside.

He stepped out of the truck holding a bouquet of marigolds, tall varieties in citrus shades of orange and gold.

"Help me celebrate," he said. "I filed for divorce yesterday."

She felt suddenly weak, opened her mouth, and closed it again. "But Miranda—" she began weakly.

He smiled, that big wide open grin that split his face and sliced into Claire's heart as it did. She realized in that moment just how much she had missed seeing his smile.

"Miranda's in love with a lobbyist," he said. "She announced on Thursday that she's moving to Sacramento."

Claire's mind reeled. "But—the girls. What about the girls, Ramón?"

"The girls are staying with me, at least for now." He carefully laid the flowers on the hood of the truck. As he moved toward her, Claire felt the air between them crackle. He put his hands gently on her shoulders.

"And speaking of 'for now,'" he went on, his voice deep and rich, "I have this recollection of some extremely unfinished business from that night out at the Lucky Spot."

From inside the house she could just hear the clear soprano on the CD she'd left playing when she went for her impromptu hike.

The past is written on the wall,
Choices made, the shadows fall.
Till just one road is left at all,
Still you hear the river call.
Say that time was like a river,
Flowing to the sea....

She looked him right in the eye and reached up to touch his cheek. "I hate unfinished business. Let's step inside and discuss it."

<hr/>

Tommy Dodson

Rebecca Rothenberg was the author of three previous novels in the Claire Sharples Botanical Mystery series. She received nominations for both the Agatha and the Anthony awards for Best First Mystery for *The Bulrush Murders*, which was also named as one of the *Los Angeles Times*'s Ten Top Mysteries of 1992.

Rothenberg was a graduate of Swarthmore College and UCLA, and worked at Harvard, MIT, Vanderbilt, USC School of Medicine, and Caltech, in epidemiology programming, public health data analysis, economic research, and public relations. An amateur botanist who lived in Pasadena, she was president of the San Gabriel Mountains chapter of the California Native Plant Society. She began her eclectic career as an aspiring songwriter in Nashville, and used her knowlege of the history of country-western music in her unfinished manuscript of *The Tumbleweed Murders*.

Rebecca Rothenberg died on April 14, 1998.

Taffy Cannon is the author of *Guns and Roses*, an Irish Eyes Travel Mystery; a mainstream and a young adult novel; an Academy Award-nominated short film; and three books in the Nan Robinson mystery series. One of the latter, *Tangled Roots*, is set in the Southern California floriculture industry.

Bill Kamenjarin

Cannon holds undergraduate and graduate degrees from Duke University. A friend and colleague of the late Rebecca Rothenberg, she lives in the San Diego area with her husband and daughter. Her website may be visited at www.taffycannon.com.

MORE MYSTERIES FROM
PERSEVERANCE PRESS

Available now—

Keepers, A Port Silva Mystery
by Janet LaPierre
Patience and Verity Mackellar, a mother-and-daughter private investigative team, unravel a baffling missing persons case and find a reclusive religious community hidden on northern California's Lost Coast.

Blind Side, A Connor Westphal Mystery
by Penny Warner
The deaf journalist's new Gold Country case involves the celebrated Calaveras County Jumping Frog Jubilee. Connor and a blind friend must make their disabilities work for them to figure out why frogs—and people—are dying.

The Kidnapping of Rosie Dawn, A Joe Barley Mystery
by Eric Wright
Edgar and Ellis Award nominee, Best Paperback Original
A Toronto academic sleuth goes on an odd odyssey, to rescue student/exotic dancer Rosie Dawn, and find out who wants her out of the way, and why. One part caper, one part satire, and one part love story compose this new series entry.

Guns and Roses, An Irish Eyes Travel Mystery
by Taffy Cannon
Agatha Award nominee, Best Novel
Ex-cop Roxanne Prescott turns to a more genteel occupation, leading a History and Gardens of Virginia tour. But by the time the group reaches Colonial Williamsburg, odd misadventures and annoying pranks have escalated into murder.

Royal Flush, A Jake Samson & Rosie Vicente Mystery
by Shelley Singer
Jake and Rosie infiltrate a dangerous far-right group, to save a good kid who's in over his head. The laid-back California private eyes will need a scorecard to tell the ringers in the gang from the real racist megalomaniacs.

Baby Mine, A Port Silva Mystery
by Janet LaPierre
The web of small-town relationships in the coastal California village is fraying, stressed by current economic and political forces. Police chief Vince Gutierrez and his schoolteacher wife, Meg Halloran, must help their town recover.

MORE MYSTERIES FROM
PERSEVERANCE PRESS

Forthcoming in 2002—

Open Season on Lawyers **by Taffy Cannon**
Somebody is killing the sleazy lawyers of Los Angeles. LAPD Robbery-Homicide Detective Joanna Davis matches wits with a killer who tailors each murder to a specific legal abuse.

Another Fine Mess **by Lora Roberts**
Bridget Montrose wrote a surprise bestseller, but now her publisher wants another one. A writers' retreat seems the perfect opportunity to work in the rarefied company of other authors…except one of them has a different ending in mind.

**Available from your local bookstore
or from the publishers at (800) 662-8351
or www.danielpublishing.com/perseverance**